Iowa's New Corn Goddess

Mark Wekander

Iowa's New Corn Goddess

Text by Mark Wekander

ISBN 978-0-9849447-8-1

Published by Rubber Tree Books
111 Calle Washington 4
San Juan, Puerto Rico 00907

Cover Design by Beatriz Rodríguez Torres

Iowa's New Corn Goddess

The notebooks began after that day. She had the sense that she was being pulled into the landscape and wouldn't know how she got there or what was going on unless she kept track. She had fooled around with various titles - *Map of My Soul, The Bread-Crumb Trail in the Woods, If You Can Get There You Can Get Back, The Forest is Alive, You Change the Trail by Walking It.* This was all she wrote the first day.

It hadn't occurred to her that she was supposed to give him lunch. He came and asked for a glass of water at noon, but she had already eaten and hadn't thought of him any more than she thought of the roar of the lawnmower going by the kitchen window. The smell of cut grass unsettled her, like a face she recognized but couldn't place. She was smelling it through the sediment of thirty-seven summers, each with that first-of-the-summer recognition of cut grass.

She left the sink where she was unpacking and washing china and stood by the window next to the kitchen table where she could see the lawn up to the row of lilac bushes on the knoll.

The boy had his shirt off and his back muscles tensed as he pushed the mower up the small ridge -- up and back, up and back. The sunlight was silver on his wet pink skin. She had a vague sense of watching herself look out the window at the boy, of herself behind glass, of sound reaching her without a source, as if it were produced by her ears.

At that moment he was pulling back the lawn mower from the hill and instead of pushing it up again, he turned and faced the window. Irene lowered her head and rubbed her hand against the table as if she were polishing it. Her eyes drifted up again. He was now shoving and pulling the mower in and out of the lilacs. Old leaves whizzed from the sides of the mower and a cloud of heavy dust circled his waist. Small twigs and shards of leaf stuck to his sweaty torso. The machine jolted as it ran over a stump that was a few inches above the ground. He stopped to let the engine charge back to life. A few minutes later a plastic grocery bag shot from the mower with a slap. It sputtered and he pulled it back and pushed down on the handles to lift the motor off the ground and it roared back.

The dishes were wedding presents that she and Tom hadn't had room for in the Seventh Avenue apartment in Brooklyn. Her father had stored them in his house in Morristown. When Tom first suggested moving to this little town in Iowa, he had mentioned, as if it were a dream of hers, that she would finally be able to get her china. It had put her on the floor laughing. But it wasn't funny after a few weeks, and when she stopped laughing at the comment, she had let it stand as a kind of uncomfortable truth.

Tom had wanted the wedding. Irene had been happy living together. Neither of them believed in getting married, but Tom needed a wife. His new firm was conservative, at least the senior partners, and that was the check that paid the rent. Tom told their friends that he was getting married to get his gold card, instead of a green card. Irene recognized it as her joke. She took it as a compliment when he appropriated her words.

Tom had said that if they were going to do the wedding, they should do the real thing. His parents would be crushed if their only child got married and they weren't even invited. She'd done a cartoon of his parents under Godzilla's foot and taped it to the refrigerator door. His mother's head stuck out between two toes and she was saying, "If he'd only invited us to the wedding, we wouldn't be here."

Her own father told her that he was used to her not being married and would have rather come some other time just for a visit. She'd written back that it didn't matter to her either. Then she got a call from her father. Tom's mother had sent him a letter explaining how important this moment was in Irene's life.

Her mother-in-law, Doris Marston, had chosen a blue delft fruit basket pattern, an imitation of a Victorian china pattern. But the cupboards, such a luxury of space after that Brooklyn apartment, were filling up with these foreign coffee cups, saucers, serving bowls; everything that had been stored from the wedding. Because of some mess up in shipping, the china came first. Her own plates, either made by herself in a period when she shared a kiln with an earlier lover, purchased at junk stores, or inherited from friends, had gotten lost in shipping. She had a lot of the inherited ones from gay friends who had died from AIDS in the mid-eighties and early nineties. Ed had started it when he broke up a set of Bavarian china before he died, giving almost forty people a piece. At the time she thought of it as shared memory, the china being a part of a set that could have gone on growing, but was now always finite and separate. And being china, it could break and even the pieces would have to be imagined as part of a whole.

In her own wool gathering she imagined her death and considered whether the plate's history, the cup's design, the saucer's resale value would go into who got what. Today as she looked at the cupboards that she had duly filled, it struck her that her will would stipulate that an ad be placed in the *National Inquirer* offering a piece to the first fifty people who sent in a postcard. Later there would be a lurid story about how she tried to humiliate her mother-in-law from the grave.

Whenever she had been feeling most antagonistic towards Doris Marston, who insisted that she call her mom, she phoned her up as a type of penance, or to be sure that she hadn't through extra-sensory perception felt the hostility.

"Hello, Doris, oh yes of course I can. Mom, we have this

boy here mowing the lawn and he started at about eleven and has about another hour to go. What I was wondering, should I give him lunch? Maybe a sandwich or something. I don't want people saying I'm cheap or stingy. Not yet." She laughed at her own joke, but there was silence on the other end.

"Well, should I?"

"I usually do. Not if he gets there at noon, but if he comes a little before. It's Joey, isn't it?"

"It's someone Tom got."

"A tall good looking kid. Kind of has a sneer all the time and doesn't smile much. His front teeth are crooked. Irene, I'm sure it's Joey."

"I didn't get a good look at him. He came for water at about noon and I didn't think a thing about it." Irene sensed her attempt to please was making her sound ridiculous. "Well, if he goes without lunch, maybe he'll show up earlier next time."

There was another silence. "Well, thanks. I'll give him lunch. Bye."

Irene cupped her hands around her mouth and yelled but couldn't hear herself over the roar. She was afraid of getting too close and walked in a wide circle around the mower, waving her hands over her head. He looked up. She noticed one incisor crossed over another tooth as he raised his upper lip and squinted to show he didn't understand. She shouted again. He listened, arching his head higher as if he could stretch above the din. Then he turned off the mower.

"What did you say?"

She stood back. The silence created an embarrassing intimacy.

“I just wanted to know if you’d like some lunch. I called my mother-in-law Mrs. Marston. I guess you do her lawn, too, don’t you? And well she said I should. It’s not much, but you must be hungry.”

“I’m more thirsty than hungry, lady.”

“My name’s Irene, Mrs. Marston, Irene Marston. Tom Marston’s wife. You’re Joey, right?”

“Yeah. I’m sure all of that’s right. Your husband was some kind of baseball hero or something here, wasn’t he?”

He didn’t look at her when he talked. “I’ll finish this part and be in in ten minutes. That okay?”

She waved her hand to get his attention and protest about that being too soon but he turned his back to her and pulled the string starter.

The sandwich had been sitting on the kitchen table for ten minutes when he tapped on the aluminum door. He made a face and pushed his nose and lips into the screen. Behind him was the bright June light. From the dark kitchen his body and face were dark like a photograph of a person taken against the sun.

“You don’t have to eat the screen. I’ve got a sandwich for you. Come in.”

He smirked.

“You cut a lot of lawns?”

“Yup.”

“What do you want to drink?”

“Coke?”

“Pepsi okay?”

"Guess so."

She sat across from him. He pulled the lettuce off the sandwich and dropped it onto the plate. He ate with his mouth open and looked off.

"Well, I'd better get to work." It sounded as if they had been having a conversation.

She slapped a wet rag at the cobwebs in a cupboard and then poured a cleanser on the rust stains left by old cans. Of course, she should have gotten the stool. Instead she stretched as far back as she could. Joey's presence was exaggerated by the silence. He slurped the last of the Pepsi and burped loudly.

"Thanks."

When she finished one cupboard, she put on shorts, a summer blouse with lapels and a straw hat she had bought for a Sunday at Jones Beach. She went to the side of the house where Joey wasn't working. Crab grass wove into the beds of peonies and she sat down to weed. Later when Joey mowed the lawn around the peonies, she stood up and walked to the shed next to the garage.

The motor died. She could hear herself breathing.

Joey cleared his throat. "There's not enough gas to finish. I'll do what I can. You could get some."

As she got up, she took off her garden hat and put it in front of her breasts. "Can't you go?"

"That's not what I'm paid for."

She now saw the sneer. The sweat had formed beads over his shoulders and chest. "But you could be paid, couldn't you?"

"Yeah, sure, but I've got other lawns to do."

"How much?"

"Five bucks for the gas and trip, mostly because I don't want to do it."

"Okay. Next time I'll remember."

While he was gone, Irene sat down and stretched out against a maple tree and fell asleep. She felt the sunlight moving across her face as the wind moved the branches.

Then there was a constant shade, perhaps a white billowing cumulus cloud passing across the sun. She opened her eyes. Joey was standing beside her.

"Too busy to get gas, huh?"

"Money needs no excuse." She tried not to act startled, not to adjust her position, but she realized that two buttons on her blouse had come undone. When he bent over to put the red plastic gas can down, the sunlight flashed on her face. She picked her hat up and laid it across her chest.

"What's that about money supposed to mean? You got so much?"

"Enough to pay you to mow my lawn and get gas." She tried to say this without an edge.

"Is it your money or your husband's?"

"If I'm giving it to you, it must be mine. But I'm giving it to you when you finish." The bark of the tree scraped her back as she got up. Joey was gone before she could get away. The house had an almost cave-like coolness. She counted out the money and sat at the kitchen table with it in front of her. She jotted down a few things on her grocery list.

The doorbell rang and she yelled for Joey to come in. He met her in the hall where it was darker and she held the money out to him. "Here. It's mine and now it's yours."

"Thanks." His back was already towards her. "Tell your husband to fix the back tires of the mower or the things are going to fall off."

"I'll see you in a couple of weeks if it rains." Irene sighed as if she were bored.

"What does the rain have to do with it?"

"It makes the grass grow, didn't you know?"

"I heard that. It makes it grow as green as money, huh? You left your hat outside. I think I might have accidentally clipped it with the mower."

After he left she went upstairs and opened a box of books. She hadn't cleaned the books when she packed and they had a film of city dust and grime. The air went dead. Afternoon sun heated up the room. She brushed sweaty strands of hair from her forehead and hung them behind her ears. At three she went into the upstairs bathroom to pee and noticed in the mirror that her forehead was streaked with dirt and sweat. She wondered if it had been like that when she saw Joey.

"I don't give a damn what he thinks. I don't give a damn what you think." The strangeness of the new house and its institutional smell of paste wax from the former residents made the empty rooms seem even more gaping. Her voice startled her.

She wandered back to the library, then down to the kitchen. She looked out the window over the sink, and then went into the yard. Her hat was where she had left it. Picking it up languidly -- the heat had sapped her of her energy -- she noticed something fall out. She assumed that it was an inspector's slip that she had forgotten to take out, or a label that came off.

Kneeling before the peonies, she watched the lines of ants

going up and down the stems. A cloud passed in front of the sun. Irene put her hat over her face and leaned back against the tree, raising her legs off the ground so her baggy shorts would catch a bit of breeze.

It was not quite sleep. She was aware of the wind, but felt as if her own body was drawing it to her and that if she concentrated just a bit more it would blow stronger. She was doing this, moving it away from the trees and bushes that blocked it and towards her, when she heard the scream. She was certain at first that the scream was trying to break her concentration, to free the wind from her. But it wasn't on the same plane as the wind and it wasn't until she felt that she had lost control of the wind that she realized someone was screaming.

She was on her feet and running. The scream was breathless, wearing itself out to a high thin whistle and then starting again and then there were other screams choked with sobbing. She was now in a yard that she had never seen and it occurred to her that this might be another dream, that she had lost the wind and only moved into another dream. Coming around a hedge of lilacs with their brown flower heads, she saw them.

A boy, maybe nine or ten, was pulling a garter snake from a stone embankment. The screams came from farther off. In the shade of an enormous weeping willow tree, she made out four small figures. A girl, maybe eleven, was backed up against the trunk of the tree. Two other girls stood farther off, jumping from foot to foot so that they would be able to dart away. The back that was towards her was a few inches taller than the girls.

She parted the branches. "What's going on?" Her voice shocked her. It was louder and angrier than she'd expected.

A red-headed boy swung towards her, stepping back at the same time. A headless garter snake twisted up toward his hand in rhythmic jerks. Even in the speckled light under the willow, its end was a plastic red.

Disgust welled up in her. She drew her arm back behind her shoulder and brought the full force of her body behind it as she swung at the boy's face. He ducked and her hand brushed against his hair. The snake fell twisting into the grass. The three girls shrieked and fled. The boy fell and then scuttled off like a crab without looking back. Irene stood alone under the tree.

The snake twisted and rolled at the edge of the shade where the branches of the willow brushed the ground. She trod back through the hot afternoon air. There was another headless garter snake making figure eights by the stone wall where she had seen the first boy. She looked at the ground or stared straight ahead, afraid the neighbors were peering at her from behind curtains, from a stairwell window, or through a crack in a fence.

She trembled until she reached her own yard--expected to cry, but sat at the kitchen table and waited for one of the neighbors to call. She thought of an explanation. She had been sleeping and was startled by the scream and wasn't really awake when she hit the boy. It was as if the snake was part of her dream. Or maybe she should say that she had a traumatic experience once with a snake. Probably she would say what came to her at the moment and it might even be the truth.

The yard no longer felt like her own Eden. She noticed a few weeds that she'd missed in the peonies. As she sat down, she saw what had fallen out of her hat. It was a condom. She flushed.

"Damn smart-ass kid."

She dug a small hole in the peony bed and buried it. As she stood up, she noticed a woman at the edge of the yard dressed in a blue denim summer dress that had been sewn crooked. It made her one leg look longer than the other.

Irene smiled at her, but there was no response. She felt

her own smile stiffening, her cheeks rising and hardening. The woman's head was tilted slightly as if her thoughts were all on one side and it was pulling her head off kilter. Her lips stuck out.

"Hello," Irene said and her smile softened as she raised her hand to wave.

The woman stood for another minute. Then with a short brisk movement of someone who was used to giving orders she motioned to Irene to come over.

"Yes, what do you want?" Irene didn't budge.

"To talk and I don't have all day."

"Then why. . ." she didn't finish. She started again. "Would you like to come in?"

"No, don't have time. Thanks. Just come over here."

"Yes." Irene moved toward her.

"Did you hit my boy?"

Irene's mouth opened. The woman began a word, but stopped when Irene seemed about to speak. Again nothing came out.

"If you so much as lay a hand on a hair on his head, you'll have to answer to me and I'm not used to losing arguments. Just take the time to ask some of your neighbors." The woman held Irene in her gaze for a moment and then seemed to drop her like a rag into a bucket of water.

Irene sighed as if she were about to speak. The woman turned and looked at her again, then walked away.

After she shut the hallway door, she stood for a moment listening. She heard a lawnmower or lawnmowers far off.

When she went back to the library, she couldn't concentrate

on organizing books. Her clothes stuck to her body. She held a large volume of *Arts and Ideas* from her first year at college and had no idea what to do with it. It seemed like an unsolvable task. When she looked down at it, the letters of the title seemed unreadable. The sweat from her hands mixed with the dust on the jacket. She dropped the book and it banged on the floor. She laughed. Hearing her laughter gave her the sensation that she was spying on herself. She often felt this way when she was alone in this house. When she accused herself of spying on herself, she was aware that the accuser was not the observed or the observer, but what seemed to be yet another level of consciousness. This was when she felt most lonely.

The light for the answering machine was blinking when she went to call Tom to see when he was getting home. It was a message from him.

When they first lived in New York, he had called her from work and left intimate sexual messages. She had compared them to those that Prince Charles had left for Camilla. Tom claimed his were better.

"I'm going out bowling with the boys tonight, honey. Don't wait up for me, baby."

He never called her *honey* or *baby.* At first he tried using those sloppy endearments but she had ridiculed him in front of their friends. He had stopped and when he slipped, she only had to look funny at him and he edited himself. She assumed he was with some of the clients of the insurance company he had taken over when his father died. They probably called their wives all sorts of stupid names.

Getting annoyed about the message gave her an edge again. A few hours later she couldn't stop thinking about Joey, the snakes, and the woman and she played the message over again. In his Iowan incarnation, Tom seemed sturdy and dull, an antidote to the jigsaw which her day had been so far.

If someone had told her two years ago that she and Tom would move to his hometown in western Iowa, she would have laughed. That had been one of her favorite reactions to any question that presumed that their relationship was capable of being normal and suburban, not to mention quasi-rural. The months before Tom's father, Ralph, died had changed all that. What had once been a joke between them, Tom's hick background, had almost overnight become unspeakable.

Some of her favorite stories came from her first visit to Pendayhaz, Tom's hometown. "New York, that's a pretty big city." People referred to them as "the New Yorkers." How many times had she heard that? His father had taken them to a Rotary Club banquet so Tom could talk about business opportunities in the computer age, a speech he had written by summarizing an article in *The Wall Street Journal*. He had checked her clothes before they went and had pleaded with her to change her shoes and earrings. She had no idea that he knew the contents of her suitcase. He suggested first one and then another alternative. He asked his mother to loan Irene some earrings that Irene would have characterized as fifties cocktail if she had been browsing through a flea market.

One of the greatest lines was from an older woman who had asked, "You probably know that Jackie Kennedy's daughter lives in New York. Do you ever see her in the street or maybe the grocery store?" This line usually brought down the house.

During his father's illness, Tom went home often. He always came back a little changed. Irene felt as if she were on weak moral ground, her own artistic cynicism as opposed to Ralph's illness.

She became less demanding of Tom. All of his actions were the product of grief. When he was gone one weekend, she went out to a club, met an old boyfriend Sammy, and went back to his place. It had not been the liberating experience she expected. His litany of galleries where he had ins and of who was hot and shouldn't be, a language she herself was an expert at, bored her. While they were having sex, she studied the art posters Sammy had "altered." He made a wrenching scream to show the intensity of his orgasm, as she looked at a Rothko poster with a ship sinking under a band of red. The horse in "Guernica" had a merry-go-round pole sticking out of its back. A poster of Dali's "Time" was set in the window of Tiffany's with price tags on all the watches. Goya's "Colossus" ate an ice cream bar instead of a human head as melted ice cream slobbered from his mouth.

Tom had called the next morning to tell her his father had taken a turn for the worse. For some reason he mentioned the time of the last attack, "1:00 a.m., 2:00 a.m. Eastern time." She figured out that was about the time she was looking at the sinking ship. He mistook her confusion for grief.

It was only partially guilt. She had the sense that she was being spiritually watched and now had to atone. She had wondered if Iowa was by any chance an Indian word for penance.

The gallery job was getting iffy. She had to do something. They were hiring more and more people and the commissions were getting smaller and smaller. She didn't like to fight over customers and there wasn't that much to fight over. She had heard Eleanor, the owner, whisper to customers that when they really wanted to buy they should talk to her. "They can't change prices. They can only sell it for the stated price."

She sat leafing through books until it got dark and then went downstairs to find something in the refrigerator.

She was pretending to be asleep when Tom got home. Schlitz and Obsession she thought and smiled at the idea that she could identify the brand of beer. The perfume she was sure of.

Journal June 8

Day two and I'm still working on the title. I could call it The Observer, The Spectator. *I will watch myself change or wait for change or tell myself I am changing. What is it when we look around quickly into a mirror and think that we can catch ourselves unaware? We are always a second too late. We already know we are watched and change. The photograph gives some space for objectivity. Or maybe that's just equating surprise or a disparity between what is expected with what you see with objectivity. Is that me? I had a dream about Joey last night. It was probably the lawnmower and Tom snoring. You know how those things get mixed up.*

In the city there are always people around you and you feel like the stone in the stream, like those masses are water curling around you. Here the world is flat and quiet and I feel like I am ebbing out on all sides and have to form a crust or scab before I am all gone.

Being jealous was one of the stupidest things she could think of. If Tom didn't rub her face into it, if he took a minimum amount of precaution so she wouldn't know, she didn't care. To her, his discretion showed dedication to their relationship. But she wasn't in a city where she could entertain herself. It wasn't fair or was she just being jealous?

Tom noticed even before she asked about his night out with the boys and which one used *Obsession*.

"You know, in New York when you went out, I could always

find something to do, but here I'm at a loss."

He looked at her with humiliating concern. She stared into her coffee cup in a way that was mildly melodramatic, *General Hospital* in the 60s.

"Do you want to move back to New York?" She had never liked making decisions for groups, not even for the two of them.

"We should think about it. Maybe we should or at least to a city." She felt the rush to her head as if she were on the edge of breaking out of a bad dream or on the point of winning a race.

"You used to tell me about how shallow the people were. I thought that this was what you really wanted."

"At least there the people were shallow." She regretted it the minute it came out of her mouth.

"What is that supposed to mean? Comments like that are so unlike you." Tom stared at her with that hung-lip bafflement that made her get a vision of herself in the morning mirror.

"It was just stupid. Forget it. It's just that I don't know anyone. No one. Well, your mother, but I wouldn't call her a soul sister. I like her. She's nice." She lost whatever ground she had gained.

"People here are shy. You have to get to know them and give them a chance. As a goof why don't you join a church group? They're not really religious, more social. Do it as an anthropological study."

She gave her smile of defeat. "But we never do anything together since we got here."

He was quiet for a long time. She saw herself as a cloying housewife. The line seemed right out of Ann Landers. It occurred to her that the silence was to let the stupidity of her comment sink in.

"I have friends here. We talk about things and people you don't know. If I don't invite you, it's not to bore you."

"Well, try boring me." She wondered how they had gotten off the subject of leaving.

"I thought I did that enough already."

Journal June 17

There is a great spot in the yard for painting. God, summer light. If I could do some good ones, maybe sell them, that would be an option. Build up a little reputation. Like I meant to do before I started working in galleries and took my life "seriously," as Tom would say.

There's a triptych I'm thinking of doing. Maybe I need another journal for the paintings I would do if I were painting. Some way to get out of here. The first one would be a woman with a stony face opening a box. There would be lush scenery. Something like Rousseau, not real, too lush, maybe with corn stalks with the cobs growing without husks. The husks could be at her feet or covering her body. The hair from the corn is piling up around her legs. In the middle frame she has taken her face off and laid it in the box. Her head looks like a biology chart. Her skirt gives a cutaway view like those old diagrams of the sex organs. But there are strange fires and the face in the box is in pain. The last one, I see her as a skeleton. There is a stack of faces in the box, but all blank and the ground is covered with kernels and her face is on every one. Some of them have begun to sprout, but the roots are all out of the ground which is cracked clay shards with scenes on them, maybe desert scenes, colors of Navajo painting.

She was ready for a break from the unpacking which she only did half-heartedly. Opening each box seemed like resignation to what Tom claimed was "what she really wanted." The phrase itself would send her huffing around the house, slamming doors and cupboards until her fist ached. If Tom by accident (since he had figured out that those words alone would set off the cold distant anger in her) said it, he would quickly change the subject. He had won. She had not argued in the time allowable and now he could enjoy his victory without gloating.

She had ripped the tape off a box and gone to sit for a few minutes. When she walked back up the steps, she paused at the window on the stairwell and looked out on the yellowing grass and what seemed from the cool darkness of where she stood to be a light so bright and liquid that it had stuck to everything. Two weeks had gone by since Joey cut the lawn. She had no idea how long she had been standing there when the phone rang.

"Irene, this is Mom. What are you doing?"

"Unpacking. It's such a drudgery. It's driving me loony. I still don't know where to put things. Every time I do a little cleaning, I change things." She had stopped addressing her mother-in-law directly to avoid offending her by not calling her mother.

Doris ignored her completely. "Tom was telling me that you wanted to get involved in some church work. There's a circle meeting today."

Her first impulse was just to say that Tom had misunderstood her. She made a few guttural sounds, coughs and hmms and then said what she felt was an unconvincing, "Well, sure."

"Good." Doris had decided to ignore any doubt in her voice.

"What should I wear?"

"It's not church, but it's in the church."

In her journal, Irene wrote this at the top of the page with the comment underneath, "A Gertrude Stein hidden in the sticks." She knew that somewhere in her journal she had a few gems like that from Tom, but could only remember one. "It's not that you're tired, but you're really tired."

"Okay, I have an idea then. When is it?" From her experience with Tom, she knew that whatever answer she got would involve some interpretation on her part.

"They meet every second Tuesday night of the month. You should bring your Bible and a list of your greatest talents. It's an activity they are doing"

"Can you pick me up? When should I be ready?"

"Well, it isn't my circle. It's for the younger women. The pastor's wife is in it."

"What time does it start?"

"You can call the church and find out."

Journal June 25

I now have two journals. One for art ideas and one for just writing. Today when I got the New Yorker, I thought of a third one. I'll imagine what I would be doing if I was still in New York. You know, this life that might have been or that is happening simultaneously and yet I'm not aware of it. The road not taken taken. I wonder if it's too New Age. Right now I need to feel as if I have other selves. Like you see yourself in an old photo or I see a painting I did years ago and I think, what was that person like in the picture or who was it who did that painting. Did I have those ideas?

Doris had another great line. "Soon you'll be settled in and then you'll be at home." I told her, "Oh, that's so true."

Carla came over today. She seemed okay. I don't know about being bosom buddies.

T smelled of perfume again. Same smell. It's probably something stupid. And so what. It shouldn't matter.

Doris came over yesterday. I left for a moment and I know she opened the cupboards. I should have marked them so I could be sure. Are we falling into this mother-in-law/daughter-in-law thing? I'm being brought to life as a cliché. Or cliché as life. A bride of Frankenstein stitched together with old movie lines. I think I once saw a photo of Gaugin's mother-in-law. I could paint her and Doris as Tahitian beauties, one lounging in front of the Little Mermaid and the other in front of a silo. My journals are getting mixed up.

The center of the town had crept into cornfields and incorporated fence lines dotted with trees as parks in flat suburbs. Some of the streets were curved to add diversity where a straight road would have been more practical. There was nothing for the curve to avoid. The town itself had a hill, but had managed to keep all intersections right angles and all lots nearly uniform. Houses faced houses.

The church had reached a crossroads where it had to expand or move and chose to go out of town, beyond the few poor houses on the edge, beyond the new hardware store, and between two of the new developments. The old church was sold to a Pentecostal group and its white wood front was soon draped with warnings and threats of hell. Irene had a section in her journal entitled "Dire Predictions" and had written down "God is watching you. Are you ready for eternity? Have you ever smelled burning flesh?

Nuclear meltdown? Fear hell. Do you know who will be in hell or are you waiting to find out?"

She remembered the year she worked as a high school teacher in a Long Island suburb. She had been overwhelmed by a sense of despair, perhaps too many educational programs emphasizing the unfathomable expanse of space. She made her art class read *Dover Beach* before working on a representation in water colors of modern despair. The class and painting had been failures. When she got to the "eternal note of sadness" she had asked how they conceived of eternity. She repeated the question to five rows of dumb and bored faces.

Finally a pale-skinned Russian boy with a heavy accent had raised his hand. "I think eternity is a waste of time."

She asked herself "Are you ready for a waste of time?" every time she passed the church.

The new church still had the smell of cement and linoleum-tile glue. There were halls of classrooms with blinds drawn that looked like storage rooms for the half light they held. The rows of white pine pews reminded her of a minimalist exhibit she had seen in Soho in the mid-eighties. There were two large stained glass windows with the 19th century version of Christ done in a style she described to herself as *fauvist* cubism. It seemed to say everything and said nothing to her. The staff, the arm extended uncomfortably, the faltering feet pleaded for something, but it was not spiritual. She wrote in her journal, "Looked at church. Altar proves that god or God or Goddess is getting mushier. I can see nothing but emotion. Oh God, where is thy punch?"

She stood at the back of the church and felt a hot breeze from outside. Sod had been laid down the week after the building was finished. The few bushes planted around the edge were still scrawny and had a long way to go before their branches met and encircled the church.

She had always associated God with dank basements where Sunday coffees and dinners had left a vague smell. The servants of God, the angels, had been older women in hair nets whose faces were benignant and who moved with the awkward lurching take off of a heron or waddling run of a heavy goose.

Irene sat down in a pew. She remembered the hush when the minister swept up the aisle on hot August Sundays with his robes smelling of sweat and Old Spice that lingered in the air for only a second after he passed. The scent was born away by the turgid air that came in and out of the church like the breathing of a sleeping child. But he was always too verbal to be holy. Listening to him, not even thinking of the words, he seemed to weigh her down. On summer days her dress stuck to the pews and her legs made the sound of tape ripped from a wall when she stood up.

Her mother died when she was nine and for a long time she felt like the world could fall on top of her at any moment. In her dreams her mother was crying in front of the altar and no one could hear her because the air in the church was special -- it was impenetrable. She also felt like a freak, the girl without the mother. She couldn't stand to go to the church where her mother's funeral had been, so she stopped going.

Carla came up behind her. "How can you stand being in here? It's a hundred and ten in here. What did you think of circle?"

"It was interesting."

Carla gave her a blank look.

"I liked it." Irene said.

They walked to the parking lot which had rows of saplings along the edge. Several of them were dead and others had brown branches.

"When did the movie theater close?" Irene asked to make conversation as they drove through town.

"The last time?" Carla asked smirking.

"You mean it's closed before."

"Four times in my lifetime. Well, let's see, when did *The Bridges of Madison County* come out? Let's see, wasn't it in. . . Help me." Carla began to make a strange clicking sound.

"I have no idea. Was it any good?"

"Wonderful. It's about this guy who is older, fifty maybe, and he comes to Madison County, Iowa and falls in love with this farm wife whose husband is at a 4-H competition in Chicago with the kids and she loves him, too, but in four days he leaves and they never see each other again and don't tell anyone, but they are in love until they die."

"I don't even remember a few guys I was engaged to." Irene looked out the side window and wondered where they were going since they had passed the street her house was on several blocks ago.

"Well, it is kind of strange. Maybe that's why the writer made her Italian and him a hippie, so it would make more sense. You know that they had sex right away."

"Hm, that's not the part that sounds weird," Irene said. The clicking was beginning to annoy her. "Where are we going?"

"I just thought we'd drive around for a while. I guess the really beautiful and cool thing about the book, I read the book, too, is that they had this love affair that they had to keep secret forever and still loved each other. And it changed their lives." Carla gave Irene a warm lazy smile.

"What's that sound?" she asked when Carla turned back to

the road.

"Oh, I bet it's my false tooth. When I get nervous I start to suck on it. Some times Harold makes me take it out because it bothers him and I can't stop. It happened when I was in an accident. Angry at someone and just didn't pay attention to my driving. I hit it on the steering wheel. You know the tooth." Carla pushed the tooth out with her tongue.

"Oh sure, I see," Irene said.

Journal June 30

Last night I couldn't sleep and watched Tom breathe like he was a natural phenomenon, tide or sunset. I tried to remember everything that I could from when I was born until age five, got to about age three before I faded off, not to sleep. Got bored before sleepy. Of course I don't remember, but my father has told me about leaving his office at 1:30 in the afternoon and by four I was born. The girl. I've seen pictures of my two brothers looking darkly at the camera and I am propped up between them like those pictures of dead children from the last century. You can already see the way their brains are turned in on numbers, they seem to be concentrating, counting molecules of air. I always felt like I floated among them, that they were always elsewhere, nowhere. In the picture they look like they are a fake backdrop. I could never get traction, walked on words and images. I used to imagine that their feet did not just touch the ground, but that there was a part of them that was invisible to everyone but themselves that sank into the floor and earth, that if the world suddenly twisted ten times as fast as it normally did and everything not nailed down flew off, only their kind and things with roots would be left and that they were part of a secret plan. Hector was ten and Alex was eight when I was born. I told Carla that both of my brothers were autistic yesterday when we went out walking. She got one of those

Mother Teresa faces. I ran with it for about a half mile and then she asked me where they were. "One works for IBM and the other teaches math at M.I.T." The half mile was mostly her talking about cases of autism from her cousin who was a volunteer somewhere. She clammed up for the rest of the walk.

On Tuesday a storm came up while Irene was stretching canvas in the yard and it took one of the canvases and blew it against the lilac bushes. The others she had already set in the shed. She grabbed the canvas and turned it so it gave the least possible resistance to the wind, the edge straight into it, but she happened to turn it slightly and it caught the wind and almost threw her down. When she got close to the shed, there was enough wind break so that she could handle it. By the time she shut the shed and ran to the house it was pouring. When she reached the door she fumbled to get it open, then on a lark ran out into the yard again, hopping up and down and laughing. Her wet hair slapped against her face and she twisted her head back and forth so that her hair flung out sending a circle of water around her head. She rubbed her hands against her wet clothes, ran for a puddle that had formed under one of the eaves where the rain gutter on the house was clogged and jumped into it. Standing under the rush of water from the roof, she suddenly felt like an oddity, an animal that suddenly appears outside its normal habitat.

Inside she shivered, took off her clothes and wrapped a towel around herself. At the foot of the stairs, she turned and looked at the trail of water behind her. She had not turned the light on in the kitchen since it had been so sunny when she went into the yard, but now the storm clouds had darkened everything. She spoke softly and earnestly, "You ooze across the floor." Lightning gave her a better view of the pool of water where she had stood fumbling to lock the door, the trail of water with its intermittent puddles where she had stopped to listen to the storm. She looked at them as if they were marks of a stranger in the house, a trail that she had just noticed. She felt that she was not alone and in a loud sharp voice said, “I know you are here. Don’t think you can trick me. I know.” She laughed.

When the electricity went out, she was already lying in a warm bath. She remembered reading about people being electrocuted in their bathtubs, but couldn’t remember whether it was from lightning or from dropping a hair dryer or radio into the tub. She got up to look out the window. It was still raining hard. All the other houses were dark, but she saw the Crawfords out on their porch watching the storm. They sat without talking, lit by a gas lantern until the lightning penetrated them, made each of them seem like a cutout that had been placed around the porch in some stone-faced tribal ritual. Spying on them she felt as if she herself became a round ball with an eye that spun around the surface in search of evidence. She lay down in the bath water again and small ripples lapped her neck and chin. She turned the hot water faucet on to a trickle to keep the bath warm. Lightning flashed.

She heard the door open, listened to footsteps going to the stairs, Tom’s feet efficiently clicking up the stairs. The silence made her uncomfortable, made her seem suspicious.

“Irene, I’m home. Where are you?”

“In here, honey.” Tom tried the door and it was locked.

“Who are you locking out?”

“Force of habit.” She got out of the tub, wiped up the puddle of water next to the window. “Who am I locking in?”

Tom did not answer.

New York Journal

The idea is not to write about what I would be doing, but to write what I am doing in New York, this other life. Like I exist somewhere else. But then I wouldn't comment on it. But I can't go from here, the corn jungle, to Flatbush without a little warm up.

I remember that slat art that I'd see from the D train right before it went over the Williamsburg Bridge. It was like seeing a painting through a grating, but the train was going so fast that it was both its parts and whole. I would wait for it as a release from the dark tunnel. Then a few minutes later we would be out of the earth and crossing the East River.

Today there was a fire on the tracks and the train was late. We were stuck on the bridge for an hour. The air-conditioning was out and it was so hot. I got off at the Atlantic Avenue station and looked around antique shops. Lots of old stained glass. A woman got on screaming from a Bible at Hoyt Street and the whole car, it was rush hour, emptied out. What a city! I want to convince Tom to go with me to galleries this weekend. There's a new show at the Whitney. I've got to check the movies at Lincoln Center. Jens told me that they're showing Spanish movies from the fifties. I'd love to see Buñuel again. Looked through the rental section of the paper. I'd love to move to Manhattan. So much we could do this weekend. Sometimes it paralyzes me.

Where is this journal memory and where is it imagination? I'm not sure if this is going to work.

Journal July 8

Tom and I went to the Fourth of July parade, stood with friends, his, maybe mine. I had cramps so I wasn't in a great mood. Carla's husband was funny, not what I expected. Carla didn't know Tom since she was from another town, though she saw him play baseball when she was in high school. Harold decked out for the day--red shorts, blue shirt and white socks. He had a cap with a flag on the front. I told him he should be in the parade. Carla said if he had a couple more beers he might think so himself. If she hadn't complained about him always wanting sex, I would have bet he was gay. Well, then I thought she was, too. Thinking everyone must be gay is New York gallery syndrome.

Harold explained how the Tractor Pull queen and her princesses were all related, second cousins, even an aunt and niece the same age. They all had versions of a toothy smile bordering on buck teeth and long straight brown hair. Even a short article with a picture in the Des Moines Register. *Almost as complicated as the lineage of the Windsors, but no one smiled. The photographer at the paper must have had some good inbreeding jokes. Whatever gets you in the paper. Tom left us to do some hand shaking. Part of the business. Harold asked how I was adjusting. I think what he said was acclimatizing. I told him I was letting the hair grow on my legs for the winter, but he didn't think it was funny. "Mustn't be easy. But this is a great place to live." Carla was talking to Mrs. Crawford whose kids kept coming up to her whining for money. The 4-H float had some pubescent youth with calves, piglets, and a foal. A stray dog kept running up to the float and barking and the kids walking next to the float chased it away. It got kicked once and yelped. The unplanned is the only thing you remember. After it got kicked it didn't come back, but by then it must have been chased ten times. I started laughing and Harold gave me a strange look.*

The grass is growing after the storm. Saw Joey at the parade. He came up to talk to Tom. Didn't even look at me. I felt it was obvious how he was ignoring me. Tom asked if we had met, which was stupid of him since I had to have paid Joey. Joey, said, "Oh yeah, the paymaster" or something like that. I should have told Tom about that condom. He would have thought it was funny.

I was in the bath during that storm. I thought of myself as Elsa Lancaster in Dr. Frankenstein's brew waiting for the bolt of lightning. I guess she was on an operating table. Tom came in. I felt like I weighed a ton getting out of the water and my fingers were wrinkled. I unlocked the door and got back in the tub. He got turned on. I stood up in the bath as he came in, did my Venus on the half-shell imitation. I didn't expect sex. Sometimes it gets rid of all my tension, but I was still floating and felt so clean. Tom smelled like cigarette smoke and French fries. And I thought, who is this man on top of me? He was over-the-top turned on. Usually that would make me excited. I could have said no. The electricity came back on just as he was coming and it made me want to laugh. And then I told him I wanted to laugh. He thinks that if I notice anything while we have sex, I'm not into it. It should consume you. I once read that male cats bite the female's neck during sex and paralyze them during coitus.

Joey mowed the lawn once when Irene was gone. That day she and Carla went to a craft show in Des Moines. Carla picked her up at nine, honking the horn a few times and then coming in to get her. Carla brought a thermos for coffee but hadn't had time to make coffee, so they stopped at the Sunshine Café. Only two women were in the café sitting with their husbands and the rest of the clients wore overalls or jeans. The smell of coffee and Mr. Clean competed with manure and gasoline.

"God, I hate that place," Carla said "Especially in the summer. I mean it smells more."

As they drove by the Prairie Rose Theater, Irene noticed that though the title was still intact on the marquee, Meryl Streep had become Mer l S eep and Clint Eastwood was now Cli t   t oo .

As if she were reading her mind, Carla said, "I went to the last show. It was kind of emotional. I loved the movie, but not as much as the book."

"Hm," Irene said.

Carla talked on the way about cute ideas she had seen, doorstops made out of *Reader's Digests*, pillows made out of cleaning bags. Irene had a vision of a rash of deaths caused by the cleaning bag pillows and had quipped, "Lethal crafts," and Carla had explained they were decorative, just for the wall. Carla gave a shrug and said, "Trash-kraft, huh? Don't knock it."

"Do you really like that stuff?"

"In a way, the female ingenuity. I can imagine their faces, showing off what they did, looking at it, showing others how to do it like it was the easiest thing. That's why I collect the stuff. Corny with feeling, mostly the feeling I collect. The hours of concentration."

It took Carla a while to explain the crocheted turtles for covering soap bars, "something like a pre-loofa loofa."

"Do people really live thinking that? Cuteness, you know. Is cuteness a value?" This was a question Irene hadn't imagined asking Carla.

"Well, maybe thoughts just exist. Maybe they don't have to fit. Like Harold. Sometimes I think of we and sometimes I and sometimes him. About every two years I get this feeling like I am seeing him for the first time, like the dream where I see him and can't remember his name. Cuteness isn't so much a thought, more like a positive attitude."

Carla had been following a car that pulled to the middle of the road when there was no on-coming car. She pulled up to pass it a few times and it slowed down, but stayed in the middle. Carla clicked her tooth every other second. An on-coming car went by and Carla gunned her car and passed before the other driver could pull back to the center of the road. She laughed and gave the man the finger as her car pulled away.

"You mean that thought is fluid, not set." Irene took a deep breath and eased up her right foot from the floor.

'You lost me." Carla acted like she was concentrating on her driving.

"More like beer. It doesn't fit. They all exist floating in free association. It comes for a while, goes nowhere, then floats on down river."

"I guess so. Except for Mel Gibson."

"And cuteness drizzles on, maybe leaving its scent everywhere." Irene thought of Easter lilies, minus the nostalgia factor.

"Sometimes I get really heavy." Carla flew over a bump at sixty and Irene got butterflies in her stomach. "Wow, that's a lot to think about. You know, I have never seen any of your paintings."

Irene gazed at some cows in a feedlot and thought of Phillipsen, a nineteenth-century Danish artist who only painted cows. "Most of them are at my father's in storage, a few sold, and none of the ones I am doing now are finished."

"One of those artists who don't like to show their work until it's finished, huh?" Carla seemed pleased with herself at having guessed this.

"No, not exactly," Irene said. She could show Carla paintings in progress, the woman in the bathtub, the shooters at the gallery, the women whose faces were not yet distinctly blank, just unfinished. She could show her the message without its contradiction.

Irene spent most of her time looking at cutout wooden lawn ornaments that looked like cartoon animals, the backside of obese women in bikinis, palm trees and flamingos with sun glasses and a martini. "Art of public communication." Everyone with the same message, "We are fun people." What was her message? Locked up in her house for weeks, feeble attempts at sociability.

There was a section with Iowa theme art; corncob-shaped hair clasps, stuffed pigs, a shoe scraper in the shape of Iowa. Was it that important to be from some place? Was it the siege mentality, the reason derogatory words are embraced by those who they are used to insult? Or was it just copying places with bigger egos; New York, Paris, Los Angeles?

She picked up a clay plaque in the shape of Iowa with a pig, corn cobs, and a barn painted on it. There seemed to be some religious significance, three objects interrelated. The yellow glow around the edges was an aura or emanation from the green background. Irene walked absentmindedly between the tables holding the plaque as a talisman that made her invisible. A saleswoman, who wore corn earrings, a clay pig pendant, and a loose green A-shaped dress that made her look like a boxing clown that always righted itself, approached Irene. "Better get that now. Those are going fast. Real quality."

"I have too much stuff already." Irene's invisibility had disappeared and she felt like a shoplifting suspect. In stage exaggeration she held the plaque out at arm's length, turning it in the rotisserie of her gaze. She put it down.

Carla was waiting for her by the door to the auditorium. She handed Irene four place mats with needlepoint poppies in the corners. "Wedding present for that wedding I have to go to on Saturday," she said. "Aren't they cute?"

Carla took another road back and stopped before an

abandoned farmhouse. Pigs in a lot came out from under their lean-to shade and then returned grunting.

"I bet you're wondering why I stopped."

"To pee?"

Carla gave what Irene thought of as her oh-you're-being-silly laugh and got out of the car. "Come along."

They trudged through high grass at the edge of a cornfield until they came to a square patch of overgrown brush, mulberry trees dotted with black fruit, overgrown rhubarb, small bushy elms, feathery asparagus bushes with red berries. Irene wondered how well she really knew Carla.

"Do you see it?" Carla stood with her hands on her hips and her pelvis jutting out. Her pants were covered with burrs from the walk through the weeds. Irene noticed that her own suede sandals had picked up burrs and looked like short-quilled porcupines.

"I see something. What is it? Is it safe around here?" Irene found the suspense tedious.

Carla sucked in her stomach to pass between a large thistle and the branch of a mulberry bush. "This place was once in, I forget, *Photography Today*, or *Art and Crafts World*. It's like a minor Watts Tower. Well, really minor. Here's the Taj Mahal."

Carla carefully yanked back a morning glory that draped a mound of cement. The outside was encrusted with depression glass and chipped and broken Fiestaware.

"They used to give these glass plates away at the movie theater. It was almost like junk and this guy created the architectural wonders of the world. You know, the famous ones." Carla kicked some sticks and leaves out of the reflecting pool of the Taj Mahal which was filled with chips of blue glass. "He worked from pictures, so he just invented what the back looked like if he couldn't find it in a picture."

Irene caught sight of a low four-legged table with the roots of a mulberry tree pushing up one of the legs. On the ground lay the rest of the Eiffel Tower. There was a stout Empire State Building that had been chipped but survived. It was decorated in red, white and blue plates. The top of the Chrysler Building was missing a couple of hubcaps (gray colored plates). To Irene the only plan seemed to be to let enough room between the structures so a person could walk between them.

She sat down on the steps of an Aztec pyramid where the top block was decorated with yellow plates with plastic fork prongs as the rays of the sun. The cement was already hot in the dead July heat. Several flies menaced her head. Carla had begun to pull the shroud of weeds off the Parthenon, which had been built with blue cement and yellow and green depression glass.

"Imagine, he did all the work himself." Carla shook her head.

"No accomplice."

Carla didn't seem to hear in her earnestness in pulling out the weeds from the cracks in the floor of the Parthenon. "Yes, what an accomplishment is right."

"Let me take some of those burrs off you." Carla stood before her and Irene used her fingernails to pull the burrs off Carla's slacks. Her hands were sweaty and the heat was making her nauseous. A few beetles and centipedes moved across the foundation of the Coliseum.

"When I was in high school, it must have been just after the old bachelor who made this died, we would come here for drinking parties and smoke marijuana. There weren't all these weeds and you could sneak off with someone behind one of these miniatures. I was here the night Gordy Farkwell got drunk and smashed the Eiffel Tower with a baseball bat. It didn't break right away, but cracked. It became a thing like who could topple it."

"Now let me do you." Carla knelt down to start on Irene's shoes and then moved up her leg. Irene wasn't sure that there were burrs everywhere Carla's fingers pulled.

"When we were younger we rode our bikes here in the summer. The place was somehow secret. The old man paid some kid to come and weed around it, cut the lawn. We knew he was there. We imagined he would chase us if he caught us and it made the place more exciting. It still makes me feel funny to be someplace like this in the summer. You know, you're isolated here, the sun is out, and anything could happen. Once we took off all our clothes."

"Carla, it's so hot here. I'm dying. Let's go." Irene slowly moved away from the kneeling Carla and walked over the steps of the pyramid to the other side.

Carla moved a few steps toward her and stopped. "It is hot. A quiet, almost holy heat like you can feel the grass grow."

Irene disappeared behind Big Ben as if she suddenly saw something interesting. After a moment she said, "No Carla, it is just hot." She walked towards the path, passing a purple Saint Sophia and a yellow Sphinx with claws made from handles of red glass coffee cups.

In the car Irene relented slightly. "That was some place. The unbridled mind made cement. Surreal."

"It's really different, isn't it," Carla said as she took off the emergency brake and drove onto the gravel road.

"It's so American, too," Irene said to herself.

Painting Journal

I painted a few garden flowers, the kind I can show the church ladies. I want to do a study of them with their Bibles and hands out of proportion, or maybe super-realism, detailed down to the hair on the mole, with that dank fifties linoleum that is new and those milk chocolate brown metal folding chairs. That kind of realism takes too much time. I get bored before I get finished. I thought of taking photographs and circling elbows, moles, lips and doing detailed, almost microscopic paintings along the sides of the canvas with the photograph in the center. The disjointed surface, the person divided in our consciousness. Do our minds have all chins, breasts, teeth in separate files and we pull up the appropriate ones when we imagine someone?

I have an idea for a painting called the bather. Maybe I'll call it "Le Tub," sort of an ironic reference to Degas. I am in the tub as the lightning bolt goes through me. You see a cut-away view of the house and the plumbing. An emaciated man at one end of the plumbing blows through the pipe, the source, and at the other end on the sewer pipe a woman whose face receives a shock of water. She is bloated, tears on her face -- a cross between Bosch and Spenser's "Resurrection in Cockham Dean." The pipes wind around like snakes and lead to and from the bath. The dark back of a man can be seen coming up the stairs. The Crawford children are on their porch looking at lightning. The woman's face (it doesn't have to be mine) shows a vague panic and the lightning comes out of her mouth.

New York Journal

I went for a walk in Prospect Park. Tom's out of town on business. He seems to be gone more and more and I make my own life. I went from the park to the Botanical Garden. Sat in the

Japanese Garden until a hoard of school children (must be in some camp) started running along the paths, screaming at each other. From a few older people, volunteers, to ten-year-olds. Ended up at The Brooklyn Museum. I think I've found an apartment on the Upper West Side. Outrageous rent. Tom's not sure he wants to move. I am. Leslie invited me to her opening at that Soho gallery. Her friend Inez is one of the owners. She called to tell me her name was in a Village Voice *article, like she was a known standard, though of course if you're a known standard in the Voice, it's not necessarily flattering. I looked for the comment, but couldn't find it. Maybe it was an indirect reference.*

I had a fight with Tom so I just left to see a movie at The Angelica Film Center. He wasn't there when I got back. We punish each other with avoidance. "You don't know me and I will grow to know you less and less." But there is a whole world here. So much experience that you can burnish the exterior, never fall into the inner morass where you feel you need another to affirm and define your existence.

María Elena wants me to share a studio with her, really start painting again, and do what she calls corporate lobby art to pay the bills. She's got her young cousin Chago (short for Santiago, I guess) helping her. He's about twenty-five and we joke about a romance, June-August, 25-35, instead of April-December, 18-80. He's always asking what we're laughing about. Girl talk. María Elena can make it sound so insipid that he never asks for details.

Tom says that with my job, the apartment and everything else I want to do, taking a studio would be stupid. He tries to never say no -- just wears me down. Any sign of doubt -- that's all I ever have -- turns what he feels miraculously into what I feel.

At times on the street or hanging from a strap on the subway, I can long to see him, but even my longing becomes something visible and amusing. I analyze it like the faces in the car. His body parts: feet, hands, nose, mouth, butt, left shoulder, and then the gestalt reaction with the missing parts fading in slowly. I think it was five or six years before we got married, when we were in that studio on 106th that he asked me if I knew what his defect was. I thought perhaps it was a secret heart condition, a bizarre gene, a dark psychological secret. I had laughed. One of his eyes was higher than the other. I yelled, "Quasimodo," but he didn't think it was funny. Male self-perception. It was never mentioned again, but I always looked for it after that in pictures of him, not so much in the real Tom Marston. Real Tom Marston? It's hard to keep the past separate from the future or the simultaneous, whatever this journal is.

I spend more time with María Elena than with Tom. She wants to go to Puerto Rico next month, take me with. I could see the place my grandmother lived when I was ten. Never got to know her second husband very well. Only went there a couple of summers before he died and she moved back to New Jersey.

Journal July 18

Carla called to see if I had a good time at the craft show. I'm sure if I tried to talk to her about the approach, that she would have to be offended, have to deny it, so I play dumb. When I got back here and saw the lawn had been mowed, I felt suddenly cheated. I had wanted to confront Joey, but he had been here, cut the lawn and gone, like waiting for a lover and missing them while Carla removed burrs from the back of my blouse as if they were wounds she was healing, removing the signs of a passion that never happened, sticking her fingers through the holes in Christ's hands. Being the beloved is awkward, though great for the ego.

Her choice of scene for love, a compilation of childhood and adolescent transgression and the cultural nightmare of a depression society creating junk affluence, left me feeling both physically and spiritually unclean, and I saw myself twisted in her own mind, fitted into her memory rack playing doctors and getting high school hickies and going on drunken binges. The Eiffel Tower cracked to look like a cement clitoris.

This time they had let the grass get too long. In a few long damp places, it was thick and had begun to fall over.

"There should be enough gas. You won't have to go for gas." Irene talked to him through the screen door since she was still in her robe.

"I don't need gas. I need a goddam scythe."

"Well, figure out what you usually make an hour and the extra time it takes and add it to what we usually pay you."

Joey scowled at her.

"Can't you raise the mower? Adjust the wheels or something?"

He shook his head and walked away.

The grass was still wet from the dew and it shot out from the mower in clumps. The motor died for a few minutes and she went out to see if anything was wrong. The moist grass stuck to her shoes. The mower was turned on its side and Joey was scraping the bottom with a screw driver. Large pads of grass fell off.

He looked up at her. "If I don't do this, it gets heavy to push. I should have a hay baler."

"Listen, I'm sorry, okay. Do you want a break?"

He didn't answer her but motioned with his hand at the underside of the mower as if he wanted an explanation.

"In a few minutes? Maybe when you're done cleaning the mower."

He knocked on the door and came in. Irene was at the sink. She dried her hand on a towel.

"Sit down. I'll be a second."

She set the coke and two donuts on the table.

Joey had moved to the doorway between the dining room and kitchen. His face was red and lines of sweat had cut through the dust on his face.

"You like donuts?"

"They're okay."

"I have some." Irene opened leftovers that Tom had brought home from the office where they offered customers free donuts and coffee. Irene referred to the chocolate covered ones as having scabs, because their syrupy sweetness was anathema to her sense of what good food was and because she wanted to make them seem even more repulsive so in a weak moment she wouldn't go on a donut binge.

"Yeah, I like them a lot."

Irene peered into the framed light of the refrigerator trying to find the 64 ounce bottle of cola that she had bought for Joey.

"I really like them." His voice was loud and Irene, who had been lost in searching through the refrigerator to the point of having forgotten what she was looking for turned around startled.

Joey looked away from her, but stood so his erection bulged in his loose shorts. For a moment she turned back to refrigerator and stared at a large bottle of hot sauce as if it had to be remembered and explained.

"You do want something to drink, don't you." The words came out as if they were separate tall thin structures that were about to collapse onto each other. They both stood silently and then Irene looked up at him.

Later she remembered that smile and felt it might explain everything: iconic and cryptic. His eyes did not meet hers, but his face turned in her direction and his mouth was unashamedly open, his crooked teeth she thought were being flaunted. It struck her at that moment that he was only a child, seventeen at the most, and then almost like a smothering wave of heat she thought that hormones were ageless. A year later she would look back and think how pure the idea of animal desire was, almost like electricity. She would then realize that what she longed for were not any specific incidents, but the ability to see things so simply.

"Why don't you come over here for a second?" The smile was still on his face. When he scrutinized her furtively, she turned away.

"What is it? Why should I come over there?" She thought, *I could stop this now,* and closed the refrigerator door and walked. She stopped a foot from him and stood stiffly. In a flash of anger she thought of Tom and then currents seemed to course through her so she felt that thought had left her completely.

"I have to get something in the living room. Would you, please, move?" she said.

He shook his head. Irene moved slowly toward the dining room door and as she passed him he raised his hips so he rubbed against her. She stopped and turned around to look at him. He smiled sheepishly, but she would forget that he had and only remember the other smile. She walked back through the doorway and he put a hand on her shoulder.

"Let's go upstairs."

I can stop this now, she thought.

"Why upstairs?" It sounded to her as if she were speaking in a dream where words had no meaning, but only filled space.

He took her hand and rubbed it across his chest. It was cold and glistened with sweat and Irene's hand became wet and the chill sunk into her. *I can stop this*, she thought. He pulled her hand down to his crotch and she resisted at first, then looked into his face. He pursed his lips and looked down at her and then turned away as he rubbed her hand up and down along his cock.

She watched herself move up the stairs led by Joey. The scene was from overhead and showed only the shoulders and tops of the heads. The lighting was dark and the stairs were not the green carpeted ones of her house, but some dark stairway in a *film noir.* The silence of what she saw was the same as the silence as she moved up the stairs. She was both outside watching and aware that the film had a logic of its own that she could not enter or stop. It was liberating, exhilarating until Joey turned her around and jabbed his erection against her stomach. Without wanting, she noticed the light stubble on his chin, a few blackheads on his forehead, the curve of his buttocks. There were two scenes that flipped back and forth, this closeup that could only be now, and then the camera as the removed, indifferent viewer who saw everything in hazy black and white. The second scene had already become memory. There was no intermediate perspective. She sensed that she existed in that empty in-between and was forced to look at her and Joey as both objects in a film that could not be stopped and as minute parts. When he removed her blouse that she had spent ten minutes picking out, deciding whether it possessed the type of authority and seriousness that she wanted him to sense, she looked down at her own breasts as if seeing them through a camera shot.

When he led her to the bed, threading between piles of clothes she had left on the floor while she tried to decide what to wear, she felt that the observation had stopped. He undressed in front of her and she had a wild urge to stand up and laugh, grab her clothes and dart back downstairs, perhaps lock the bedroom door as she left.

"Tell me how much you want it." He pulled his shorts down to his knees and swung his hips from side to side. She wondered what part of her own excitement was the masking of desire.

"You like it quiet, huh?"

She pulled away.

"You wouldn't be here if you didn't want it."

This wasn't a seduction, she thought. No, the seducer tries to convince you of the power of your beauty, the need you have created, perhaps working the slow steps of desire, each pass warming up to the next. She had never been seduced because she always wanted to show that she knew all the tricks. She had played this game of "I know what you are doing, but you don't have to in order to get what you want," and out of pride at showing her rejection of sham, she had slept with a lot of men whom she wasn't attracted to. It was almost a pedantic mission.

What finally excited her, she thought after he left, was when he began to fumble, dropped the condom, tried to enter her and missed, went to lift himself up and one of his arms shot off the bed and he pulled both of them off the bed and they finished there on the floor. Several hours later she imagined the bed scene. The slow narrative of sparse words and images that she inspected from impossible vantage points years in the future, through the eyes of her father, Tom when she first met him and he seemed so innocent -- was interspersed with an intrusive image of fish pulled up onto a deck, their tails and heads cracking against the deck as they flopped in pure air. It was not a conscious image. It seemed to shoot in from nowhere and distance her from what was happening, but she had no explanation for it.

Journal July 22

I have begun to think that some day I will be in New York and I will be writing a journal about my life there and begin another one about my imaginary life here in Pendayhaz. What are the possibilities of place? I do here what I wouldn't do there. I am not myself here and am myself there. Or is it the other way around?

What the hell have I done? Lady Chatterly's lover and Lolito. He didn't stay long, but told me that he needed money to fix his car. Forty dollars. I gave him forty dollars. And twenty-five for the lawn. Writing it makes it sound worse. Do I write journals and paint to understand life or to create it into something foreign and objectified so I can bear it? Do I put up with Tom because I vent my anger at him in my painting? My relationships are objects and now this one even has a price tag on it. Then I can put it in a painting and sell it to someone else. Representation is objectification. It is shown and sold and its monetary worth becomes its meaning. Now I pay for experience and sell it in a painting.

When Tom got home he asked why Joey hadn't finished mowing the lawn. I'm sure I turned bright red, caught, but ran off like I had forgotten something and then shouted from the top of the stairs that I thought Joey said something about the mower being broken. The next morning he came to finish. I heard the mower as I woke up. Tom was gone. When I got up to look out the window, Joey had left.

I'm glad Tom won't be home for a few days. An insurance salesman's convention. When he gets home, I'll be glad to see him -- for about two hours. I can't deal with him and sort myself out.

Got the bill today on the credit card for the Bible I bought through that religious books catalogue. I didn't get the right Bible so it was hard to follow. Carla wants me to do altar duty with her. Put up flowers and trim candles. It makes my feminist blood boil, but here I am not a feminist. I feel like I am masquerading as someone I am not. Mostly because these people act as if whatever you seem to be is you. I probably have this all wrong.

Irene never showed anger, instead she showed boredom. Everything Tom did struck her as stupid. He bought her roses and all the vases were packed away. He brought her back perfume from a trip to an insurance convention in Dubuque and it was Obsession. Three nights in a row he came home almost at midnight from visiting clients, after leaving a vague message that he was going to be late and didn't know when he would be in.

She was rational enough to see these were minor offenses, and knew Tom well enough to know that if she mentioned them, she would be the loser. If she called him on the Obsession, she would be accusing him without proof. If she pointed out that there were no vases, she would be a shrew. If she brought up his late nights, like she did after the third night, she would get the lecture about the nature of his job and how it was giving her time to paint, which gave her horrible guilt about not painting.

Her gnawing resentment came from no great injustice. Since the source was nebulous and undefinable, it had no outward focus and so worked inward and left her depressed, holding a paint brush for an hour while her mind wandered, the paint drying on the brush, conscious at some level that she should use the brush or store it. She sat each day with an art book in her lap, her eyes and brain not connected as her eyes seemed to drool over a picture. She stared at Rauschenburg or Sigurd Polke, followed all the surface connections, the easy meaning that taunted any deeper significance, the Lichtenstein tear falling from the cheek, the Warhol soup label insistent on containing meaning.

Carla called one morning to ask Irene if she wanted to start walking in the evenings, maybe after supper at about eight or nine when the day had cooled off some. Irene woke up with a headache. Sitting at the kitchen table, she looked towards the living room because the light from the window made her feel nauseous. She expected it to be Tom, so changed her voice to friendlier.

"I'm not feeling up to it today. I've got one of those monthly headaches. What about tomorrow? I'll be better by tomorrow."

When she hung up, she wished she had kept Carla on the phone longer. She pulled the shades down in the bedroom and curled into a fetal position with Tom's pillow between her knees. His scent was aftershave, cologne, smoke that she imagined to come from The Too Sweet Bar, and a touch of sweat. The simple longing she felt for him would dissipate at the sight of him. Her mind disengaged from her body in the quiet dark room, the pain of her head and the ache in her stomach became objects that she observed from farther off, from the ceiling or just outside the cloth blinds that glowed yellow in the morning light.

She imagined the day building up to a storm, the heat and humidity as sand that piled up on her shoulders, hung on the trees, pushed insects into the grass and then was washed away by the afternoon storm. It was an oppressing and comforting pressure. She got up and looked at herself in the mirror. Tom's pillow had left creases in her face. She got her sketch book out of the "book room," as Tom dubbed it, objecting to the term library as presupposing order, and sketched the creases and dated the page. That was the image of the day. She liked leaving insignificant details in journals, margins of books to mystify herself later.

She lay down in bed again. The television was looking at her. Its square friendly face that had been designed to resemble the square scene of a stage, instead of the round secret shape of the telescope or binoculars or say the curve of horizon and the heavens. Her parents had had one with a door that slid across it and they had kept it shut when they weren't using it. As a small child, it had seemed to her that it was dangerous if unobserved and had to be controlled and covered. Alex had told her once that the small people in the television would crawl out if you didn't shut the door and would push their way into your head through your ears or nose. She remembered coming in once and finding the door open and the television off. It wasn't until she sat in school that she began to worry about it, cried most of the day and knew that there was no way she could explain to the teacher. They had called Hector who was still in grade school to come and talk to her. The teacher left them alone for a few minutes while she went out to check the other children during recess. His presence felt like an extra weight on her. He sat across an aisle from her in a desk that was too small for him and finally broke the silence to tell her to stop crying because no matter what it was, it had been proven that crying would not help. He left before the teacher got back and Irene brought herself down to a swaying hulk. Her mother had accompanied her neighbor Dorabel Jeharvis to a doctor's appointment and the school had been unable to find her father. Finally it wasn't the fear of the television that made her cry, but the shame at telling anyone why she was crying.

The remote gave her a sense of power that the first listeners to radios or viewers of television also had when they turned the button on or off. All of the voices insisted on being heard, only more noticeably on the religious stations.

When Tom was first trying to impress her, she could make him turn the television off by calling it the insidious stupidifier. "The insidious stupidifier is eating the last brain cell of Tom Marston. It has liquified his brains to gray mush and soon they will begin to drip from his ears like post-nasal."

Tom had comebacks. "Let's watch a couple of hours of tv, get stupid as cavemen and have sex," or "Igor needs his insidious stupidifier or he is liable to rebel against Big Sister." She thought herself that their sex was best after he had watched a few hours of sit-coms or football. She liked sex passionate but distant. The Discovery Channel did nothing for their sex life.

Irene flipped through the channels with the remote. She watched five minutes of a game show and then flicked to a soap opera. She pushed the mute button and watched the faces mimic anger, intrigue, deceit, confusion, hurt and evil. She turned up the volume and repeated the lines of one character for a while, then another.

"Joe needs our help."

Irene yelled at the screen. "I've heard that line a hundred times. Joe does not need our fucking help."

"I've given him all the help I can. He has to do it on his own now."

"Twenty-five times." Irene threw Tom's pillow at the screen.

"He needs to know that you believe in him."

"No, not that line for the thousandth time! Tinkerbell used it. Even Jesus Christ!" She switched to the next channel and imagined pulling the plug from the automatons on the soap.

"I am queen and with a tap on the button, you disappear. My country 'tis of thee. Sweet land of . . . " Her disgust struck random mental buttons.

Irene slumped over in the small sitting chair by the vanity and began to knead the folds of her stomach. She grabbed clumps of fat and estimated the weight. "Two, four, eight, ten, twelve. Thirty pounds from being a Botello. Forty pounds from Venus of Willendorf." She stopped the remote on an exercise channel where an intensely happy instructor with grotesquely overdeveloped thighs shouted encouragement. Behind her like phantom personalities, four women and a man mimicked her moves. Irene imagined hoards of lonely women in rooms darkly lit by television screens moving in time with "Trimming with Millie", arms twirling in ostrich flight, synchronized.

"*Wasn't that fun?*" The camera person made a wrong move and Millie's face bobbed on the screen before it came into focus large and porous.

"The lonely women of America in the buzz and glow from the tube answer, Yes. Oh, Yes." Irene left the television on and got back into bed and covered her head with the blanket. She opened her eyes and could see the contours of the blanket like a dark mountainous landscape. Pinholes of light entered along the seam. Covered like this and unable to see more than the dark interior of the blanket, she felt invisible herself. She existed without a body. Yesterday at the grocery store she had seen a little girl who had played peekaboo and had hid by covering her eyes with her hands. The phone rang and she felt discovered.

"Oh, Tom, it's you. Well, who else would it be?"

"You could try a little harder to make friends." His voice made her feel guilty.

"Is that what you called me to tell me?" She talked with her head hanging over the side of the bed.

"No, just to see how you are doing. What are you up to?"

"Unpacking. Digging in. Entrenching."

"Is someone there?"

Irene paused before she answered. "No. Why?"

"I hear voices." Tom didn't sound interested.

"The television. Thought I'd watch the weather channel."

"You've been unpacking for a long time, now. Will it end?"

"Sure."

"Why don't you dump everything in the hallway and then put it away as you make trails to the rooms. Pile it up in front of the bathroom and drink a gallon of water." Tom waited for a reply.

"I've been thinking about a painting, too. Doing sketches." She put one of her hands inside her underpants and felt the warmth of her body. "Well, how's work going?"

"Fine. I've got a heavy schedule for tonight. Tomorrow I'm going to Iowa City, so if there is anything you need, painting supplies, let me know."

"Tom, I can mail for that stuff cheaper and better."

"Well, I just thought you might like to think about it. I have to run. Bye."

Was he really going to a conference in Iowa City? Maybe she would surprise him when he came back and have everything unpacked and put away, but if she kept boxes unopened, she could show her ambivalence about the move, the move Tom said she had wanted. Was Tom so bad at interpreting her, or so good? That led to motives. Was his motive to make her happy or get what he wanted? Hobbesian selfishness. No consolation in having a name for it.

"Millie, I have bad news for you. Your show has been canceled. Too happy. And those vitamins you're trying to sell are poison. Pick up your last check, Miss Thighs." Irene clicked off the television as Millie was giving a poised head-tilted smile as *$39.95* throbbed on the screen like a hammered thumb.

"Now I control you. You don't control me." She lay in bed for another hour until she began to feel hot and clammy. What vague projects could she have accomplished to justify the disappearance of a whole day? Tom was working so she could create. She could stay home and paint so he could screw the woman who wore Obsession. The mysterious agreement.

"Someone invented the stupidifier. Something else to control or be controlled by. Sex, appetite, words, birth control, shopping, sex, social interaction, sleep, apathy, enthusiasm . . . sex . . . No, I said that one already. Husbands, partners, cell phones . . . Why invent more? Privacy, urban, rural, god . . . Tools to a better life. Tools to a bitter life." She rose from the bed and wore the comforter like a cape into the bathroom. "Las Vegas chorus girl or the last fat whore at the Moulin Rouge."

Irene's father once explained to her, as a child she had a terrible case of diaper rash and because of the pain, had refused to defecate. Her parents fed her prunes mixed in chocolate ice cream, prune juice in milk shakes, flax seed and she had struggled against them, twisting her legs against the diarrhea that would soak her diapers. She was toilet trained early. Her mother sat her on the toilet and invented stories, drew pictures of princesses and animals. The stories and pictures ended with a happy visit to the bathroom. Irene would try to keep her mother talking. She wondered now if her sense of safety and her sense of loneliness as she sat on the toilet came from her childhood. Perhaps her new journal would be everything she could remember or remember hearing about herself from birth. Or maybe a toilet journal. Thoughts from the toilet, or thoughts about the toilet, or thoughts in the toilet. The accumulation of data as an avoidance tactic. But avoidance of what? Definition, self-realization, identity or the knowledge that definition, self-realization and identity are only vague phrases best preserved by limited analysis? Or that they all exist, but cannot exist simultaneously? Irene smiled as she thought that this was all bathroom philosophizing that was profound until she wrote it down and read it later.

She lifted the edge of the shade and looked out onto the neighbors' yards across the alley. No one was outside, though laundry hung on the line in the Crawfords' yard. The shoulders of the shirts shrugged from the weight of water. A light slip moved occasionally at the bottom. "A sign of life," Irene thought and let the shade drop.

"I make and unmake myself. Eat and shit. By myself I forget who I am. I sit here and remember since I am not here."

She left the bathroom and stared at the screen of the television. She wondered how the remote got into her hand and while considering this she turned on the set. A wave of colors from a paint commercial flooded the screen and then a used-car salesman brought her back to reality. The prices expanded across the screen.

Journal July 27

Not a breeze. I put two boxes out today to unpack. There must be twenty left. Some are things Tom packed away when he was transferred to New York and some are mine that were at Dad's. A couple look like they aren't mine. Maybe Hector's or Alex's. Math books, old science projects. The brotherhood.

When Tom came home yesterday, I had just put up the easel in the yard, knew he was coming home and made a quick sketch and dashed some paint on. He didn't look at it. He went inside after he waved and I could hear him on the phone, not what he said, but intermittent muffled sound and silence. I told him on Tuesday that I was inviting Carla and Harold over and he made a big scene about having to see a client and my not consulting with him first. I thought it would give me a little push to clean up the house, get out of the bedroom before noon. How many times have I fired Millie? The other day when I was channel surfing I saw a replacement for Millie and howled with laughter. Only temporary. She's back next week. One of her ghosts behind her moved up for a week. The exercise princess.

Walked with Carla a few mornings. She told me about the problems she has with Harold. I call her problem the unexplainable. His unexplainable absences, his unexplainable clothes not purchased by her, his mysterious distance, sudden passion. I think her pseudo problems are just a way to get me to spill the beans about Tom, or so she can get an opening to tell me the gossip. Then she may think she has problems. Children, he doesn't want them. Been married before and has a son. His ex-wife now lives in Colorado. She wants to know if I think Harold is handsome. Testing my sexuality? As an artist what do I think? I could paint Harold as the missing Tractor Pull princess. Don't think Carla would get this or think it was funny if she did.

She asked what I did in New York, where I lived, why I moved there. Organized gallery shows, sold paintings, Lower East Side to Brooklyn, thought it was a good idea after college. Every answer is frosted with her pat, "I could never live in a big city."

Got some good gossip on my mother-in-law. Carla was, of course, concerned. Doris was having a fight with her neighbors the Craigs over their dog and the semi that John Craig parked in front of his house. They weren't talking to each other. I had expected something more carnal or more mercenary. Carla was trying to sound impartial, but didn't seem too hot on Doris. Would say nasty things, like "The man has to work, not everyone can go to Florida every winter, can't all spend our lives drinking vodka stingers." Then after every wild attack, she would add, "Oh, I don't know. It's hard to know who is right." I told her that that was what laws were for, so no one would have to decide what was right. She gave me one of her "I never thought of that looks," sort of false flattery, since I saw her use it on a woman at church, and five minutes later. She broke me up when she said, "Some of these old farmers' wives will believe anything."

We drive to the park on the north edge of town, leave the car by the football field and then walk along the road. Cornfields on each side. The rows are so straight and uniform. Once in a while an area along the road has been washed out by rain, but for the most part the fields seem to be the tissue or hair of a monstrous creature. I asked Carla to walk into a field with me at a place where the fence was easy to cross. I held the barbed wire down for her as she crossed and she almost fell on me. I still get these sexual vibes from her and felt for a nanosecond this sexual thing as she held that pointed wire just below my crotch as I swung first one and then the other leg over the wire.

The countryside is so flat and the cornfields hide everything. It's like driving through pine forests where everything is the same for miles on both sides. I know the names of every family on our walk, kids, times divorced, previous romantic involvement. I don't know the faces, but I know their house, what their car looks like, their taste in yard ornaments. A few have planted corn between the house and the road, so I have to read them only by their roof. Their lives are as bare to Carla as those with a clear view to the road.

We walked down adjacent rows and our bodies moving the dry coarse corn leaves made a rustling sound. I stopped to listen to Carla and then she heard that I stopped and waited for me. It was like being in a cave and I heard the sound of a car on the road, looked at the white streaks of an Air Force jet overhead. Carla had enough and wanted to know if I wanted to leave. She makes crass jokes about men and I get the feeling that she watches what she does, afraid of being labeled a lesbian. It made her nervous that we had gone into the field, not the private thing of the depression glass/ Fiestaware monument graveyard. She seemed game at first, but it was too much privacy. How do you explain in Iowa that you wanted to know what it was like to be in a cornfield in August, to be walking down the vein of the great beast? If you can't explain it, it must be wrong.

When we reached the road, Carla began gathering flowers, as if that was why we had left the road. A few days later I asked her to wait for me by the side of the road while I went in and peed. She was gathering flowers again when I came out. A car was parked by the road. It was Carla's uncle. He asked if I was fertilizing the corn. I said, no, I was taking a pee, and it looked for a second that he was going to try to explain his lame joke.

I really just needed a break from Carla's chatter. She was explaining to me her investment in Beany Babies and Franklin Mint plates. She began collecting Barbie dolls, too, but they took up too much space and if you don't have them in the original box, they're not worth as much. She told me I should collect Barbies since I have more room. Not having to take them out of the box was the clincher. I am having a lot of trouble getting things out of boxes.

The cornfield was sterile. All the insects must have been gassed to death. I felt like staying. There seemed to be such a force and structure to the field. Less time must have passed than I thought since Carla didn't say anything when I came out. Her uncle is only seven or eight years older than she is. She told me he ran a plant nursery in Crandall. Divorced twice. No kids. Wives took him for everything and then left him. Her version.

I see less and less of Tom. Mornings breakfast and the paper are between us like slabs of the Berlin Wall. He must be making a fortune. All those evenings at work. We're going to a wedding this weekend. His cousin is getting married. Doris has already told me what color to wear for the family reunion photo. I guess she plans it out. How orchestrated are any historical records? Maybe the Dorises themselves are the history, the rest is merely haphazard and not worth recording. Tom and I are staying at a motel for two nights. His mother picked the place. I know her by what she spends money on.

Tom smeared peanut butter on a piece of toast and then placed it on top of another piece and lifted it up.

Irene sat away from the kitchen table. She glanced up from the newspaper. "Great levitation act. You think that's how David Copperfield does it?"

"Nah. Velcro." He pushed his chair out from the table and scooted over next to her.

"I don't have to go in until ten." His eyebrows bounced up and down in wicked anticipation.

"And?" She could smell the peanut butter on his breath and when he stuck out his tongue, it was light brown.

"Don't touch me with that thing. God, it's amazing it isn't drawing flies." She raised the newspaper to protect herself.

"The naked tongue is so boring."

"I bet you grossed them out in fourth grade cafeteria." She jerked and laughed when his hand went up her thigh.

"They were standing in line to give me their pudding." He tapped at the newspaper.

"Stop."

"The naked tongue is so boring. It should always be covered . . . with . . . something."

She found his psycho imitation inane. "Put a sock on it."

Tom ran off upstairs to the bedroom.

"Tom, for christ's sake, no."

He came down with the toe of one of her anklets over his tongue and the ruffle sticking out of his mouth. He grabbed her knees and spread her legs and proceeded to move up one leg of her loose shorts.

"You are so stupid."

"Igor always does what he is told." His speech was garbled. The sock came off and he licked his way up her thigh starting at the back of her knee.

"You don't like that? You used to."

"I'm reading the paper." She flapped the paper out straight and grimaced as she tried to ignore him.

"Let's go upstairs." Irene put the paper down next to her chair and dropped her shoulders in annoyance. Tom took her hand and pulled her up from the chair. She had the look of resigned martyrdom as he led her upstairs.

"You know what you need?" Tom said.

Irene shook her head and looked off to the wall. "No, but I'm sure you are going to tell me."

"You need a new name, another self. I'll be Wyatt Earp and you can be Miss Kitty."

"Miss Kitty was on Gunsmoke for twenty some years and never got laid. Imagine running a whore house and never getting laid? That takes imagination." She gave him a peeved smile.

"Well, maybe instead of being Miss Kitty, you should be Miss Pussy." Irene thought this was slightly funny, one of Tom's better, but wasn't going to let him know.

"And who are you going to be?"

“No, not Wyatt Earp. I’m the man they kept in the cellar. The stupidified gunman. The one who got it for free to keep the girls in practice.”

“No one gets it for free,” Irene said. “There are no whores with hearts of gold.”

Tom had gotten her almost upstairs, but then Irene held fast. “Who’s talking about hearts, Miss Pussy?” He rubbed his crotch against her shoulder.

She felt like she was on the verge of a crying jag and pulled half-heartedly away. Tom gave a slight yank and brought her up to the top step.

“Let’s get naked here in the hallway, Miss P. The cow hands might come through any door. Any door. Any moment.”

He bent down to kiss her, then brushed his lips across her cheek to her ear, “Any moment. Any door, Miss P.” He slid one hand down her shorts and dextrously unfastened her bra with the other.

“Do you have a name?” Irene did not want sex to be forgiveness. “Let’s find out who you really are, what you really do when I don’t see you.”

“Oh, Miss Pussy, I’ve been down in that hole so long that I’ve forgotten my name. I am nothing more than a yearning. A hot tongue and a hard dick.”

“Anyone worth his salt at least has a nickname.” Her body did not react and she kept her hands at her side.

“You are thinking too much, Miss P. Let me turn on the insidious stupidifier.” He carried her to the bed, pulled the shades, and switched on the television to a channel where there was only static.

"Talk to me, Miss Pussy. Talk to your hog man. Let the stupidifier loosen you up. Feel its rays make you naked. Groan for your hog man who came all the way out of his hole for you today."

She sat on the edge of the bed, bent over with her hands clasped under her thighs.

"Let's go into the other bedroom with the cowhands. Give them a little free look." She had encouraged these fantasies of public sex, but now regretted that Tom knew so much about her inner self. She hadn't specified, had gone out of her way to include kinks and fetishes that weren't hers, but somehow he had guessed. Or maybe when he stumbled on one, it just seemed that he had seen through her. When he was undressed, he got a cowboy belt out of the closet and put it around his waist. The fat bulged around it. She wondered why her fantasies were to be invisible and to be seen naked by strangers, to be bodiless or seen as only body.

The role playing began one day after Irene talked to Dunner Stakk, one of the painters whose work the gallery was carrying. Dunner wore jeans that were thread-bare in the crotch and was so stoned that he hardly ever finished a sentence. He smelled of marijuana, tobacco, beer and coffee with a strange underlying scent of cleanliness, maybe scented soap or deodorant. He explained his paintings to her, pushing the small of her back gently to aim her at "Trinity," three black balls on a completely white canvas arranged to appear on the same plane. His hand at first was firm, but by the "Untitled # 4," it was wandering up and down her back, lingering at her belt. On the way home on the subway, she imagined what Dunner Stakk would have been like in bed. She smiled out into the crowd of commuters as she imagined herself as an orgasm "Untitled # 2,500." Ten years later she would see one of Stack's paintings in an art magazine, a dead golden retriever puppy with its tongue and ears cut off and next to it the missing ears and tongue. Next to the photograph of his painting "Dutch Floral Arrangement" was a snapshot of Stakk that looked exactly like the day that Irene met him and he fondled her back and brushed against her breasts.

The subway stalled between 42nd and 33rd and the lights in her car went off. She put her book bag next to her to separate her from the man next to her who slumped into the seat when the car slowed in the tunnel. In the dark subway car she imagined that Dunner had asked her over to his studio to sit for a painting. The paint on his fingers and under his nails gave his hands a cold otherworldly quality. He did a quick sketch of her with his brush, placing her body in that vague whiteness of the three black balls and then suggestively moved the brush soaked in red paint across her breasts. The train engines began to rev up and Irene crossed her arms in front of her. A woman with white legs covered by rough red blotches had her huge butt only inches from the tip of Irene's nose. The lights flickered and came on and the train jerked slowly forward, the woman's butt jerking the other way.

When she reached the iron gate in front of the brick three-story house where their apartment was, she couldn't remember whether she had taken the way home past the grocer's. Anyway she had to get something for supper. When Tom came home around seven, she already had her plan.

After supper and a bottle of wine, she suggested to Tom that they might possibly pretend they were other people. He could be Toulouse Lautrec and she could be a prostitute he was painting. Tom couldn't get into it. He put on an old beret that she had which was covered with paint and a painting smock. The props seemed to only emphasize that they were acting. She considered for only a second whether he should have oils, but luckily chose the watercolors. They pulled down the blinds in the front room and Irene lay on the couch.

"Tom, tell me what to take off. How do you want me? Talk

to me like you have a vision how I should look. What do you want to see?" Later she wondered whether it had really been her idea.

The next time she had been Catherine the Great and Tom had been a palace guard whom she had sent to her quarters and then forced to strip in front of her. This seemed to work best. The sex was always best when Tom took the role of the rebel or outlaw. She kept up the fantasy until they were in bed, visualizing the scene where Tom pulled out of her and his head was chopped off at the same moment. But the fantasy never lasted until orgasm. Tom would say the wrong thing, too hip. "Throne to prone. The right soldier can make any queen." He spoiled it for her.

Tom missed the point of giving himself completely to the fantasy. For him it was always a spoof, a joke and he couldn't keep his sense of humor out of it. It was humiliating for her to be reminded that she was playing Catherine the Great, or a Parisian prostitute, or a saloon tramp. "Enough of the metatextual," she blurted out once and felt both stupid and out of character. "Whatever that means," Tom had gasped and she saw that he was enjoying her anger.

Tom laid her on the quilt in the guest room. She remembered that the sheets for the bed were still packed away. "Tell hog man about all the men you've had in the bar."

"Tom, I don't feel like playing this."

"Hog man isn't playing."

"Is this hog man thing something Iowan? Corn and hogs?" She stared at him with her tired adult look.

"Irene, is there something wrong with you? Maybe you should see a doctor. This isn't the way you act."

"My mind was just moving some place else. I couldn't get

into it. Is that okay?" She sat up and tried to cover part of the bare mattress which was showing.

"It's not as if we have sex all the time."

"No, we don't, do we. At least I don't." She felt something inside her collapse. That wasn't what she wanted to say.

"You don't have to wonder why. That should be obvious."

"Everything here is obvious, but nothing means anything. The cornfields are in rows, the towns are in boxes, the yards are square, but nothing adds up. Order and figures in a row and no sum."

"How long have you been practicing this little speech? I don't understand you. What did you just say? What does that mean?"

"Nothing. It means nothing. I just didn't feel like it. My mind was somewhere else." She got up without looking at him and walked into the bathroom.

"I can't be around you when you're like this. I've got a job to do. I have to be up. I can't decide when I feel like it and when I don't. I've got to act like I care about everyone who walks in the door." Tom was now stomping around the bedroom, opening drawers and slamming them shut as he got his clothes for work.

"You don't have to screw them at nine in the morning before you finish your breakfast." She got up and locked the door as she was talking.

She heard Tom chuckle and then laugh louder. "A lot you know about business. What you didn't do at the gallery for a sale or a connection?"

"Let's talk about this later. I can't make sense. I'm sorry."

"Why can't we talk now?" She could tell by his voice that he didn't want to talk either.

"I'm not going to say another word, Tom."

From the bathroom window she watched Tom's car pull out of the garage and on to Pierce Street.

Painting Journal

The cornfield picture, rows of corn and a woman dressed in early sixties summer wear; pedal pushers, white lace blouse, hair flipped up at the ends, costume jewelry. She is looking between two rows of corn and at the end there is a door and behind a door a beast with a corn cob penis. You see her from above and the other rows she could have chosen and a replica of the corn satyr is behind every door. On a hill off in the distance is "Christina's World" by Wyeth, only the house has the same face as the corn satyr in every window and the field of grass little by little becomes corn. Christina is the same, but is wearing an ankle bracelet and a tiara.

I took my camera to the Bible study group and got a picture of five women, Eleanor Craig, Minnie Sorensen, Dagmar Fender, Kristie Crawford, and Lotte Chambers. My dark room equipment is packed away. Dad stored it for all those years. I checked out the basement and guess I could set up a dark room in the cold cellar. It has that funny smell of wet dirt. Years of sacked potatoes. I want to print on paper so I can paint over it. I might do a series of necks, hands, shoes. Hair would be with the circle on the hair, an arrow to a microscope on the edge of the painting and then a circle with a blow up of hair. What does our knowledge tell us? I want to paint the limit of our knowledge, the surface deep or shallow that insinuates understanding, but leaves us empty. The women will have little gaudy touches, attempts at expression or escape from the mundane, feeble attempts before the microscope, the statistic, the ultimate summation at the grave. The last painting, same women and a chart where they are set next to equal signs and their name on a gravestone. Definition and summation only shows that there is no definition or summation, but not that there is anything else. The reassurance of the equal sign.

Somehow I'd like to work "The Corn Painting" into "The Church Ladies," make them a series. I don't want Tom to see them until I'm finished. I don't want to hear, "Done before," "Oh, heavy stuff," or "Who is going to buy it?" "The Corn Painting" will be summer, lots of green, birds in the sky, sweat on the brow, expectation. "The Church Ladies" will be fall and winter, taking inventory, holding on, faith. Could do another church lady, circle the Bible in each hand and show it on the edge like each other part, but instead of blowing it up or adding detail, present it exactly as it is in the center picture. Unlike the body parts, it is always separate, always the same size, inscrutable. The viewers do not read the Bible.

Did sketches for some more flowers. Maybe show them to the ladies, or use them as an ornamental border for "The Church Ladies." At what level of consciousness do they exist? Another border idea, televisions with soap operas. Good one for the Bible painting. No men in the paintings?

Journal August 3

I have an image of myself as liberal, sensitive, irreligious but interested in religion, morally upright, feminist, painter whose agenda is to paint only what cannot be understood, make visual the riddle. In New York I didn't think about who I was, or maybe I was in a place where I could be what I thought I was. Here I have become another person. It's not just that I see this other side, but it is a side I smugly thought didn't exist. Old society ladies pay young boys for sex. The humiliation is part of the attraction. Selfless in lust. The parts of me that add up to something, that make me different from Carla or María Elena or Doris Marston don't matter. I don't even think I enjoy it. I am playing the part of the woman who is too obsessed to think and by playing the part I become it, and in flashes the observer, parts the curtains and I see myself playing this role with Joey and am never sure why. It only happened once. No telling how many times it has happened in his retelling. We are not in control of ourselves in the mouths of others. Why do people go to such ends to protect their reputation if it is not connected to their self? The struggle against others' conception of you.

That I would try to mislead people into thinking that I believe in big-daddy God, beard and flowing robes, eyes looking down always on women and men in their sinning prime, Adam and Eve in their twenties, I would never believe. After communion a few weeks ago, Carla and I were supposed to wash the glasses. I made some holy barmaid joke to Tom. Well, Carla gets out of it at the last minute and I'm stuck in the little study with the sink with Mrs. Kraus, all cheek bones and chin, one of those people who look like a caricature of a self that might have existed twenty years ago. I have to listen to her speech about how she feels closer to God, definitely big-daddy-husband type, washing up the communion glasses. Didn't seem to me as if she was doing much communing since she didn't stop talking. She told me the minister had even mentioned her comment in a sermon. If that isn't validation. I nodded and smiled. Stuck in a couple "Goodness sakes" à la Doris Marston.

Can I never be any better than my context? Today Carla asked me to pick up an Andrew Wyeth book for her in Des Moines and the clerk gushed about how moving the pictures were, and instead of telling her narrative painting bored me and that the only secrets or mysteries in his painting were all autobiographical, I beamed at her as if she had just made my day. I think I even said some garbage about how great his colors were. I picked it off the shelf when no one was looking, clutched it against my chest. Before I put it on the counter face down / price up, I had planned a little speech about how it was for a friend (doesn't this sound vaguely familiar like those stories about buying the personal vibrator at Duane Read's or Walgreen's), she picked it up and started gushing. I looked through it on the way home. I went through the same thing with Carla, mild false admiration which I want to be vague, no commitment, some shred of integrity.

I keep thinking about Joey. Is it guilt or desire? Every time I hear a motorcycle, hedge clipper or lawnmower I rush to the window to see if it is his lawnmower. Obviously I am looking for the chance to prove I will not fall again. Maybe if I got into doing a painting, I wouldn't think about him so much. T. S. Eliot was so chaste, but he must have felt that his actions were important, a whole culture dependent on the disdainful quiver of his upper lip. The limelight made him ascetic, but not especially good. Fascist, elitist, anti-Semitic, monarchist, chauvinist. I paint for an audience I imagine, a world they perhaps can't imagine.

New York Journal

Unbelievable. I went to a party with María Elena and met a woman there with my same last name. How many Langers can there be in the world? She just happens to be getting married and giving up a rent-controlled apartment. For a thousand dollars she said I could take over the lease and she would tell the landlord that I was her sister. She even gave me a picture of her family so I could do some cutting and pasting in Photo Shop. I'm her little sister so in the picture I have to put my head on her cousin's shoulders. I always wanted a sister. She wasn't that friendly, but for a thousand dollars she's going to invite the landlord up, show him the picture to explain who I am.

I'm showing at the gallery where María Elena works. (What would be a good name for a gallery? Usually just a last name, or specialization. Neo-surrealism, neon-surrealism, femi-realism. No Time Magazine pun for a name. Ugh! The clever of Columbia's journalism school. Punning 101. Modern Arthur.) A mixture of photography and painting. Detail. "Paintings that reveal the secret levels of perception through a play with the analysis of scope and pseudo-scientific classification." The Village Voice: *"The paintings reflect a recent trip by the painter to her husband's (ex-husband's?) hometown in Iowa. The paintings expose both the struggle to make meaning and the evasion of meaning in detail of a surface rural Iowa which appears deceptively clear and cogent on first view. Irene Marston-Langer has captured our late twentieth-century dilemma of a surplus/surplice of information that drowns any attempt to organize and understand it and has taken the place of religious mystery and the spiritual infinite." The brochure for the show. Going to Nantucket for a month to paint. Still not sure if Tommy boy is in the picture. Have to think about that one. It seems like in this journal we have parted forever. Testing the waters? "Mejor el mal que sabe," as María Elena says. Better the poison you know. But the repercussions on this level are minimal. He can fly up for the weekends. Some kind of reconciliation. I'm still not ready to give him complete freedom. Maybe Chago realizes he really loves me. It doesn't work that way, of course, only in the soap operas, and what is this?*

Journal August 26

I saw Joey again. He disappeared for a month. Someone else cut the lawn, a cousin of his.

Tom is talking about having a family, says my painting is going nowhere. He talks about our bodies' clocks, but I get the feeling that having a child with him now would make this relationship permanent, forever death. And I have always somewhere in the back of my mind thought of Tom as an interval. A child makes life so continuous and also gives a biographical purpose to your life that creates a sense of end. I am over because this child is here to replace me. A woman is never herself again. Whatever that means. Perhaps the selves I want to become are more difficult.

Carla says she wants kids. Harold says he's done that. Not quite the same need as the gynecologist who got hundreds of women pregnant with his own sperm when they thought they were getting a handsome, brain surgeon, football player, anonymous donor. All those overweight near-sighted offspring with the same crazy need to proliferate. The great thing about having a hazy memory is that the stories I have read and heard become over time polished to what reality should be like in order to be ironic, meaningful, tragic, absurd. There is never enough basis to weigh it down in detail, to explain away our innate absurdity until it sounds like a Sixty Minutes story. Did the guy have fantasies of creating a new racial type?

The last three walks with Carla have been dedicated to a woman's need to have a child. I plead my weak bladder to escape into the cornfield. I even take down my pants without going just to feel for a moment free. Writing it makes it sound silly and perhaps it is. It is definitely a bathroom experience, that aloneness and quiet and the sense of being hidden with the whole world around. And when I come out of the corn, Carla finishes the sentence she was on when I excused myself. It's as if time itself had stopped while I was in there.

Irene heard the clipping from the open window upstairs. She pulled the curtains back and saw Joey pruning the lilac hedge. When she got downstairs, she picked up the phone to call Doris, but Joey walked in.

"Your husband asked me to prune that hedge." Joey walked over to the doorway to the dining room and leaned up against the wall.

"This is crazy. We can't do this anymore." Irene had planned her speech. "I don't believe in this kind of relationship. It's only sex."

"You didn't like it?"

"What does that have to do with anything? I'm older. I'm the one in charge. I say that this cannot go on."

"One more time won't hurt."

Irene had moved closer to Joey as she talked. "You don't understand. I have decided not to do this."

Joey took her shoulders and pulled her into him and then began to rub against her. She knew that she had waited too long to react. *I can still stop this. I can still stop this*, she thought and wanted to cry, remembering that this had been her lame mantra the last time.

He took her hand and led her upstairs. He pulled her down onto the bed. He took off her blouse and kissed her shoulders and back. She imagined herself being worshiped, lying goddess-like on the bed. Or a statue that is carried to filthy hovels at night. She closed her eyes and felt his lips move from her knees up to her mouth and then to her ear.

"You know I've been thinking of that," Joey held his body over her. She waited.

"You know the money and all." There was another pause.

"You know, like the last time. Well it can't be like that."

"It was okay," Irene said. "It doesn't matter. Forget about it." The money had bothered her. It had made her feel ugly and old and she knew she wasn't desperate. Well, if she had been some place else, she would not be desperate.

"Well, I've been thinking," he said. She noosed her fingers into the curls of his hair. She was afraid that if her smile was too open he would see how much the question of money had upset her.

He kneeled between her legs and took out a condom. "You are so beautiful."

He kissed her, moved towards her lips again and pulled away. His hand moved up her leg and stopped. He was about to move into her and pulled back. His tongue moved up her thigh and stopped.

"You know," he said and moved his tongue farther up her thigh. She didn't want him to talk. She faced him and then closed her eyes. He stretched his arms up and put a hand on each of her breasts.

"You know, I can't do all of this for just forty dollars."

The air seemed to be knocked out of her lungs. She lay there for a moment stunned, limp. She stared at the ceiling.

Irene swung her legs around to the side of the bed and pulled a sheet around herself.

"I'm sick. I don't want to do this. No, I don't want to do this. I don't want to do it. I feel sick."

"It can be like last time," Joey said.

"No, just leave."

"Just money for the car."

"I really feel sick." Irene ran to the bathroom and slammed the door behind her. She sat on the toilet seat and cried. Twice she stood up to look at herself in the mirror.

She came out after Joey left. There was a note on the kitchen table.

I TOOK FROM YOUR WALLET 15 FOR THE HEDGE AND 40 BECAUSE I NEEDED IT.

Painting Journal

The perspective should be off. There is a carnival scene with a shooting gallery. The faceless dolls move along on the conveyer belt until they get older and bigger. When they are two-thirds down the range they are life size and wrinkled. Their faces show fear. They have the look of the Alzheimer patient who first realizes she is losing her mind, but they aren't over fifty. The shooter is a young guy with a muscle shirt and a big bulge in his pants. He has shot the last woman on the conveyer belt and she is falling into a pile of older women. A line of ugly grotesque men waiting for their turn are applauding.

Journal August 31

I saw Joey today at the supermarket with his mother. He acted like he had never seen me before and I asked him how the lawn business was. I think he said something like "Green. It's a green business." It occurred to me that the woman wasn't his mother. What kid goes grocery shopping with his mother? What do I know?

I was reading over the New York journal. Do I really want

Tom to leave?

Tom is talking about having a family, says my painting is going nowhere. He refers to the shed as The Image Dump. I told him we were all an infinite number of images headed the same place. He gave me one of those don't-be-stupid looks.

Carla told me that she has heard that Tom has seen his ex-girlfriend. That was the kind of thing I didn't want to hear from her. If I don't care, why should she? Don't I care? This woman works at the insurance office. I can't write it yet because it makes me feel too weird. If I don't write it, it might just slip out of my mind, might not be true. Well, it's Joey's mother. I have to check to see if it's the same woman at the grocery store. Maybe I can suggest that Tom have a company party. What about Labor Day? Appropriate, huh?

I don't know why Carla told me. Did I have to know? I knew there was someone, but I was all right until I knew who it was.

The other day I was going into the shed. The door had been open all night. There was a wren sitting in front of the mirror that's over that old sink. It was singing to itself like it believed that there was another bird there. I didn't paint that day. I went into my bedroom and sat in front of the bureau mirror and read my journals out loud to myself. I felt that as soon as I moved away from the mirror I would disappear.

Reasons Why I Should Never Have Married Tom

1. When we moved into the Brooklyn apartment together he was so obsessed about cleaning the stove that he scrubbed the numbers off the oven dial thinking they were dirt. First clear sign that I would always be seen as the unreformed slattern and I was living with someone with an obsessive-compulsive personality.

2. When we went to Cozumel, he pointed out things for me to look at while driving the rented motorcycle, doing corners as he pointed left and right. The more nervous I got, the more he did it.

3. Sex was too good at first. It had to go down hill. (It wasn't really good, but I felt in control.)

4. His mother came to visit us when we were living together and she and Tom whispered in front of me. I ignored it.

5. The first time I showed him one of my paintings, he asked if I really liked it. He claimed he liked the work I did in college better than what I do now.

6. He tried to get me to work full time as a high school teacher. (Does he harbor some death wish for me?)

7. When he is really pissed, "Nothing is wrong."

8. I was not wild about him at first, but thought he was safe and sound. The extent of the connection was only obvious when he pulled away and I was hooked.

9. He always knows how to get his way and I smolder, but never light.

10. He "liked" all my friends, but found excuses to never see them. I let him fill up all of my social life. Laziness? Convenience? Insecurity? Is an answer even necessary?

11. Jokes about his mother were taboo. He liked to tell my father things I said about him to embarrass me.

12. His male friends were yuppie jocks in Polo shirts who made sexist and racist remarks. Well, not all of them.

13. He knew no gay men or lesbians until he met me.

14. He actually wanted to get married.

New York Journal

Today I told Tom to take his things and leave. María Elena said she would move in with me to share the rent. We get along at the studio, though she's a little neater than I am, but my mess doesn't seem to bother her. She kicked Chago out of the studio. I didn't get all the details. But he's gone. It seems better.

María Elena and I are thinking of going canoeing down to the Delaware Gap. I did it a couple of times with Tom when we first met. I went to a lecture on Judy Chicago. All women. It was wonderful. We're both through with men for a while.

The city is so hot and filthy. August grime. I met some co-workers from the gallery at Riverside Park for a picnic. We went to a bar afterwards. Some guy tried to pick me up who was young, attractive and rich. It's good to know I've still got it, even if what I've got is bar pick up stuff.

I want to see films from when I was young. Are they the same films? Sometimes I'm twenty minutes into them before I know I've seen them before.

Tom says he might go to his parents house first before he comes back to look for a place to stay and get another job. He wants me to believe that it was his idea to leave me. His job won't give him a leave of absence.

I want to see my father. Maybe for Labor Day. Tom always gets nervous when we're there. I should say got nervous.

That Saturday afternoon she sat with a *New Yorker* at Tom's desk in the guest bedroom. They brought the desk with them from Brooklyn thinking Tom could use it when he worked at home. Ralph had worked in a basement office except for five hours a day he had spent downtown in a little storefront office on the corner of Wilson and Main. Of those five hours, one was consumed daily at the Sunshine Café. He crossed Main Street for a cup of coffee and a roll every time a client, who could almost be anyone within a few miles, "popped in." The little hallway of the office was always dimly lit, like the waiting room of dentists' and doctors' offices in the fifties or the lobby of the Benson Funeral Parlor in Pendayhaz. The Christmas after Ralph died, Doris gave them a picture montage. Irene had seen the same frame and cut out mounting at The Pottery Barn. Doris called it Ralph's Life. Ralph in short pants in front of the family farm. Ralph in business school in Dubuque. Ralph in front of the storefront office. Ralph in the Sunshine Café surrounded by friends. Ralph on a fishing trip before the war. Ralph in the service. Ralph wearing a grass skirt on July 4, 1961. Ralph in his office with a big sheepish smile. The office picture always interested Irene because it was cropped so that you only saw the arms of the secretary spread across her typewriter. This wasn't the first one that she had seen like that, but when she had joked to Tom that it looked like his mother was getting rid of the other woman, he had looked at her with his cheeks raised in amazement so that what was left were two glaring brown slits for eyes. With this picture Irene had taken the frame apart and scrutinized how the picture had not just been set in that way, but that Doris, she assumed, had cut away the rest of the picture.

The desk in Brooklyn, which had stood next to the old bricked-over fireplace, had looked like a museum piece of twentieth-century American normal life. You weren't supposed to touch it and you didn't really want to touch it either, just like in some museums. Irene didn't have a desk in Brooklyn. She had a large table in the bedroom where she piled up books, kept stacks of articles, ads, illustrations, and magazine and newspaper reproductions of paintings and the piles grew and slid into each other. At that point she was doing paper collages and then painting over them, letting bits and pieces of the collage show. In a fight where Irene had brought up the famous "oven dial incident" -- just the day before she had been trying to bake a quiche for supper and had to guess the temperature, Tom rushed up to the table, thrust his arms out as if he were trying to push it out of his consciousness, and screamed, "Why do I have to live with this?"

Irene had caught the intensity of the argument and in a burst of emotion, that carried her into the small living room-kitchen, had pointed at Tom's desk. "This, this, this." It took her a while to form her emotional disgust into words, "This is dead art, a museum piece of middle-class absurdity. This, this, this has its lips so fucking closed that it doesn't belch or fart but fills up with moth ball air." She felt stupid as soon as she said that and before Tom could give one of his sardonic howls of laughter—he was already giving her that dumbfounded sneer—she rushed into the bedroom and screamed, "This is performance art. It says something. It's alive!"

Tom had screamed, or at least as much as you could scream in a place where you heard your neighbors cough and wheeze, "What?" This meant both "What does it say?" and "What are you talking about?" Unable to answer, Irene locked herself in the bathroom, turned on the faucet at the sink to the right force so that the pipes gave their usual whine and turned the shower on, aiming the head so that the water hit the shower curtain directly and made a light thundering sound and sat down on the toilet seat, ignoring the neighbors' pitiful banging on the pipes until she heard the front door slam.

Doris and Ralph were newly married in a bronze framed picture in front of the letter tray. Another copy of this photograph was in the center of the "Ralph montage." Doris's deep lines in her cheeks were mere dimples, her hair curled so it looked like a carved frame for her white rouged face. A version of the familiar I'll-show-you face, but with a broad triumphant smile, hardened in the photograph. Ralph looked straight at the camera with the same expression he had when Irene and Tom visited him after his first heart attack. The sheepish smirk was detached from the intense diffuse look of his eyes and the stiffness of his face. Irene recognized the same upward curve of lips that Tom had, the same stance with his arms and hands hung at his side like wooden weights. Ralph's pants billowed out from his narrow boy-waist. The rented tuxedo's sharp square cut that contrasted with the real contour of his body, apparent in his naked neck or hands or slim waist under the cummerbund insisted on the primacy of that moment now forty-five years old. She looked for Tom in Doris's face, clicked off in her mind the cheek bones that were high and round, the gentle almost flat curve of her chin. Perhaps Tom in drag would make it easier to see his mother's genes. Or perhaps the present Doris without the neck scarf, the ball-shaped hair, and the layer of skin toner would show more of Tom.

Irene had never opened the drawers of the desk, not even when they moved from Brooklyn. Tom had not seemed mysterious. You could tell who he was by his worn, but clean and pressed jeans. The desk's tight-lipped neatness said everything. When she met him, he had what she described as 1970s Playboy boudoir techniques, an almost unvaried routine that finished off with a frenzied missionary position. After the loonies of her past, artists who never bathed (Greg, Finn, Chuck) or bathed constantly (Myron), men who never had money (everyone mentioned so far), borrowed from her (everyone mentioned so far and Lance), stole money from her (Hobbs, Finn, Tyrone), stole ideas from her (everyone previously mentioned), sold her things to buy cocaine (Finn) or to buy a dress (Hobbs), she found Tom and knew exactly who he was. She had never had the least interest in looking through his things. His lack of openness about his past, she took as having nothing to say. He told her what were the important things to him: his baseball trophies, he had worked two years for his father after high school, gone to college on a baseball scholarship, moved to New York when the bank he was working for transferred him. In the first three months she knew Tom, she would sometimes write out the questions she was going to ask him and then predict his response.

"Why did you take that offer to move to New York?"

Tom would say, "It was a great opportunity in my career. I wanted to see a little more of the world." Possible funny answer, "I didn't know how weird it was."

Tom's answer, "I was looking for you." Funny answer. Upon pressuring the answer was just as she had expected.

"How did it feel to be a teenage sports hero?"

Tom would say, "You don't even think about it. Winning is so cool. It's a real rush. It's like focusing on some point on the horizon where you know you are going to be able to fly and then you keep moving to that point and when you reach it, it's true, you float off. Wow." Possible funny answer, "You get laid a lot, so I guess it feels like an orgasm."

Tom's answer, "Cool. You don't think about it. That was a long time ago." I almost got that one perfect. Even when I don't get them, I'm so close.

"Did you have a lot of lovers before you met me?"

Tom would say, "No, maybe a couple. No one important." Possible funny answer. "You taught me everything."

Tom's answer, "You know, the usual." Except for the wording, I got that one on the nose.

When she read it over later, it occurred to her that her questions and answers sounded like those from *Cosmopolitan* or

Redbook. How much did people's words tell you about them? And being able to predict them seemed only to show that she knew the public product.

When she brought up her past to him, the boyfriend who threw all of her things out the window when they broke up (Tyrone), luckily it was a first-floor apartment, or Hobbs who stole her clothes and brought tricks home, with whom she sometimes also had sex, since Hobbs liked men who thought they weren't really gay, the types María Elena referred to as *bugarones* and her Danish cousin Jens called *trække drenge*, though that really meant hustler, Tom didn't want to hear about it. She seldom got more than a sentence out before Tom said, "Do I need to hear this?" She wasn't supposed to answer since it wasn't really a question.

In the beginning when they were with her friends, Tom would become withdrawn, or slightly too friendly or interested in their opinions and interests, take their bragging or showing off so seriously that it embarrassed them, and especially Irene.

The desk contained very little and had been moved without removing the drawers. The right drawer came out slowly because the sides were warped. On top of a pile of papers she found Tom's high school yearbooks, all four. A mixed emotion of relief and disdain came with the thought, "Just like Tom."

"Tom, I read you like a book," she said when she found his senior picture. The boys' pictures were framed by footballs, baseball bats, or cars. The girls' pictures were framed by roses, hearts, doves or dolls. Under Tom's picture, baseball bats, of course, it said, "He breaks the heart of women, any age. Great player on and off the field, huh girls? Uhhh? Ladies?"

She stared at the picture with dull consciousness, thought of herself attaining a state of meditation where some secret knowledge would filter in like light through a curtain, but had a nagging sense that she was drifting through the morning. The forehead seemed broader, the skin over his cheeks stretched like a drum, shone like a billiard ball. A queer desire came over her for the boy in the picture that had not known her, who was to know her, that made Tom suddenly more desirable because the whole Tom was unattainable and perhaps never existed, only the parts. In a romantic flush, she pictured herself embracing Tom so all versions of him melted into an image marching into the future, like an assured worker in a Chinese communist poster. She imagined the moment of wholeness he felt, sexual ecstasy.

All four yearbooks set Tom into the sassy assured tone of teenagers. She lingered over pictures of him as a homecoming attendant, student body member his sophomore year. There was a note someone had written in black ink that someone else, she assumed it was Tom, had tried to blot out by scribbling over it in blue ink. She kept going back to it again and again, finally went to the window to hold the page up to the light and try to read it from the back. At first, she couldn't decipher anything, and then it became more and more obvious to her that it said, "Soon more than just the girls will be calling you big Daddy." The signature sometimes looked like "Pete," other times like "Luke" or "Carol." She thought that she saw the woman who had been with Joey at the grocery store in several pictures, but when she looked for the name, found that they were four different girls.

The morning was almost gone. She stretched when she rose from the desk, walked to the window that looked over the back yard. Several children were playing in the ditch which was fed by the rain sewers under the streets. It had been dry for a week. She thought she recognized two boys from the incident with the snake.

After lunch she went out to the shed to work on the cornfield painting. Painting leaves, creating insidious monotony, what Irene told herself was the "suffocating life rhythm" exhausted her. After a couple of hours, with breaks for coffee, she put the canvas back in the shed and threw a light sweater over the t-shirt she painted in.

When she and Tom came for Christmas one year, she had visited the library, a small box-like building with Carnegie in cement relief over the entrance. It had four stacks of books, was open three afternoons a week and Saturday morning, and its collection consisted mostly of donations. Georgette Hyer took up almost a whole shelf. Laura Ingalls Wilder books took up a fourth of the children's section, sometimes five copies of the same book. Someone had given a complete collection of Horatio Hornblower. The art books were mostly teach yourself something or other. This was the magical place where knowledge had finally been limited. All you needed to know to be knowledgeable here were in these few bookcases. Why the important cultural documents were Georgette Hyer and Danielle Steele and a few Mark Twain and Clare Booth Luce, no one could tell, but then no one could explain any religious mystery. There were six hardcover copies of *The Bridges of Madison County.*

She had walked to Ralph and Doris's from the library that day feeling like an alien in a world that had solved the problem of exploding information. Like the characters in the science fiction books, she would ask the wrong questions, be surprised at what others took for granted, be whispered about and stared at, cause terror and curiosity. If the science fiction was Ursula Le Guin's, everyone would talk to her in some mix of phony Elizabethan and caveman dialect, lots of compound words. Other-place-woman for herself. Tower-town for New York. Rock-donut for bagel. And there might be some interesting sexuality, cow orgies, chicken love, aprons and overalls instead of latex and leather.

Since she and Tom moved here, she often went to the library, but usually left without a book. Today she was looking for Grant Wood, thinking she would put one of his scenes of rolling hills in the corner so her vision of Schopenhaurian procreative horror would be thrown into artistic stasis. The force of vision sucked off into dreamland which made the vision even more frightening, like a dream where you wake up to another dream, but everything is too normal, sinister in its superficial integrity. Or where a syrupy surface covers murder and torture.

Irene recognized today's volunteer librarian from church circle, but couldn't remember her name.

She smiled, "Why Irene, how nice to see you."

"Just thought I'd get out. Something has come up the last few times there has been church circle. Haven't been able to go."

"We just call it circle, not church circle." The woman gave her a smile tinged with disapproval.

"I'm looking for a book. Grant Wood."

The woman missed her cue to offer assistance. Irene noticed the name plate on the desk. "Olive, could you tell me . . . where the art books are?"

"Oh, I'm not Olive. She's dead. The library is named after her, but it's not official since it's the Carnegie Library. But we keep the name plate. As a gesture. Why should you remember my name anyway? There were so many people there that day. I'm horrible with names. Can't remember anything. Never could."

Irene thought she had missed the woman's name again.

"That's interesting. Where are the art books?"

"You mean the books on how to embroider? There might be a watercolor book. One of the volunteers offered to tape some of those programs on television about how to paint, but no one ever did. No one has asked for anything like that."

"No, it's books with paintings. You know, Grant Wood. The

Iowa painter."

"Oh, I thought Grant Wood was the author. Now I feel so stupid. Of course."

The librarian had only one book, Famous Iowans, with a few of his paintings. American Gothic was there, of course.

"Oh, sure I know that painting. Wasn't it in an ad for insurance or something? Maybe on television. Did Carol Burnette do something with that?"

"They use it a lot. It's like an icon."

"Wow, an icon. Didn't know."

For a second Irene felt that she was going to remember the woman's name. Then she recalled distinctly that it was Patty. But, of course, it wasn't.

That sternness of American Gothic was far from Harold, Carla or Tom. She would have painted them with the same house in the background, but maybe with a tennis racket, golf club, a martini, a Walmart shopping bag, a t-shirt with an arrow and "I'm with stupid" printed on it. Maybe paint all three of them together, or in Iowa State sweatshirts, instead of the original pair, no dry coupling. And the painting would show a head with a large camera at the bottom of the painting. The three of them always consciously unposed. Local pride and no color.

Patty-who-wasn't-Patty's fingers were large and swollen. She took the book back from Irene without a word and flipped through it. "I wonder who gave us this book? I bet it was Ladette LaRue. She inherited a lot of books from her uncle who was a professor at the university. Most of them we couldn't use. Too technical. He taught history."

Irene waited for the chance to take the book back. "Mamie Eisenhower was from Boone, you know. I read once that she got so sad when birds sat on Ike's statue," the librarian said as she stopped and gazed at a page that Irene couldn't see.

"Sat? Sat?" Irene asked.

The librarian nodded. "Now that was love." She looked up at Irene who took the opportunity to slowly pull the book out of the librarian's hand.

On the way home she stopped at the corner to look at a school bus pass by. A child on the bus stuck her tongue out at her and another pressed her wet lips and red cheeks against the glass, then they dropped back into their seats laughing. Irene's explosion of warmth at seeing the bus full of small children was followed by a tinge of uncentered despair. Her own feelings, she thought as she walked home, were manufactured of expectation.

She opened the book on the kitchen table to the page of Mamie Eisenhower dressed for a D.A.R. meeting and looking like what W.C. Fields would call "a well dressed grave." Perhaps Mamie in one corner and the Grant Wood rolling hills in the other. She could title it "Famous Iowans." Tom had already begun to call her "the corn belt basher," a lame version of her own "corn belt booster."

Irene was more aware of time in the fall. Children walked past her house to the grade school two blocks away. First came the group that played along the way at around 8 a.m. and then as 8:30 approached, the stragglers rushed by the house. At noon the town fire whistle went off. In the afternoon the high school students cruised the streets of the town and Irene looked at the cars that passed, at times seeing Joey leaning over the steering wheel of his old Buick or imagining she saw him as the passenger in other cars. The girl in Joey's car, bleached white hair, tight clothes, cheap effusions of bangles, body piercing that Irene could only imagine, lounged across the front seat, her chin at the level of the window. On warm days she had her feet up on Joey's lap and her head lay half way out the window. She looked older than Joey, at least at twenty miles an hour in the frame of a car window, and she had the look of someone who still believed that what they wore made a difference in the world, not just in the way they looked. When Irene wrote this in her journal, she had underlined "made a difference" twice as if it was the key point in the line.

The quiet now seemed almost deathly after the children had gone in the morning with their book bags, intermittent games of tag, girls screaming, boys and girls shouting, and occasionally the crying of a child that would bring Irene to the window.

On Wednesday she had been sitting at Tom's desk when she heard the cries first high and pitched, and then muffled, more like hulking. A child was pushed through the broken hedge of bridal wreath up the sidewalk to her front door by two larger children, a girl whom she had seen that day under the willow and the boy with the snake. She couldn't be sure it was them. They moved out of her sight and seconds later she heard a loud pounding on the front door, then saw the two older children bolt up the sidewalk, the boy tripping and catching himself with one hand on the cement stair like a football player on the line, and running on. The girl dropped a pencil bag, scurried back shaking with laughter and dread to pick it up. They both were gone.

The small boy fell and scrambled to his feet. He gave a horrified look back, his face red like he was choking and his shirt pulled out of his pants, probably when he was dragged to the front door. Irene automatically pulled back from the window and when she looked a second later he was gone. She saw him farther up the street past the hedge running knock-kneed as if the devil himself were after him until he came within ten feet of the older children. He stopped , cupped his hands into a megaphone, and yelled something that Irene could not hear, and tripped on breathlessly. Just before he disappeared, he turned back and looked at her house. She imagined that he tried to see her, or some imagined persona that was supposed to be her.

The day was a perfect 75 degrees, a little warm in the sun. On her way to the shed she sat down in a pile of dead grass and broken leaves that she had raked together the week before. The stillness made her uncomfortable. She called it the silence of being seen. Leaves had fallen since she had raked and been blown into the tangled lower branches of the bushes along the house and alley.

It took her a while to find the painting she wanted to work on, a self-portrait that she had begun when she was in her early twenties and had painted over for years so that only a few brush strokes were visible from the first painting. She had been careful to leave a few patches of hair, the square buttons of the coat from the first painting. Tom had asked her about the painting. By the time he arrived in her life it was impossible to recognize her. She told him that it was a project in paint as texture, paint as veil since she made a point of never completely covering any of the earlier versions. She stretched the paint out so bigger fingers were backgrounds to smaller ones, a tiny nose lived within the new sharp jutting curve. Today she felt like giving the whole painting a light yellow wash, a sickly glow.

It didn't turn out the way she had hoped. There was something romantic about the yellow that bonded everything together. She had gone in when the noon whistle blew, had cold leftovers. She took an old brush that hadn't been cleaned properly and painted crude brown lines that cut up the canvas but thinned out and disappeared before they reached the edge. She painted a small rough brown border in the lower left-hand corner and in it a crude likeness of the whole painting, the mirror reflecting the mirror hidden in the whole.

When she came in for a break, the stillness in the kitchen bothered her and she went upstairs to Tom's desk. She scooted the chair over to the north window to look at some children playing in the ditch that was a continuation of the rain sewer culvert. First a girl in the red sweatshirt and jeans disappeared into the culvert, then two boys in ragged t-shirts and finally another girl who glanced around as if she were checking to see if anyone was looking. Irene pulled back from the window and when she looked again she saw the girl's legs as she crawled away. She thought of the Brueghel's painting, "The Fall of Icarus," where all you see are two small legs sticking out of the water. It occurred to her that the flat cornfields were like an ocean, but there seemed to be no life. Or what there was had just disappeared into a vein in the ground. Perhaps one of her own veins.

Painting Journal

New painting idea. The paintings start with an idea, but the act of painting is to remove the idea, so the idea is seen in its carefully outlined absence. "The Fall of Icarus in Iowa." The air is full of rocketing corn silos, each with a pair of legs that protrude out the back. Five or six have hit the ground and sunk in, only the bottom of the silo and the legs showing, but several have no legs. The bottom of the canvas is crudely divided by red and black strokes of paint, almost like waves and the part below gives the story of Icarus and Daedalus in five frames; imprisonment in the labyrinth, the making of the wings, the fitting of the wings, the warning, the flight, and the final one the surface of the sun. Though I want to do these fairly crudely, the colors in the bottom frames should lift the top portion, make it seem to fall back into the canvas and Icarus's face should be recognizable since in the upper part I want his upper body to come out of culverts, cow tanks, up between the roots of trees. I will pair this with a painting of Icarus at a computer, the background black and his face lit by the computer and on the screen a glossy photograph of "The Fall of Icarus in Iowa." I'd like to show them six feet apart facing each other, hanging from five rods that connect them. The rods are balanced on an arch so the paintings move slightly up and down and they are so close that it is impossible to get a complete view from a distance.

The day before she had begun a list of the people who signed Tom's yearbook. After writing down the names, she went through the Penndayhaz phone book looking for them. Most of the last names were still in town, but only two correct combinations of first and last names were in the phone book. Harold was one of them.

She painted until four and then went upstairs again. The children who had crawled into the culvert now gathered leaves into the ditch and leaped into them. Mr. Crawford crossed her lawn to talk to them. She imagined that he was worried about the leaves blocking the water near the fence and flooding his yard. After he walked away, they took a few handfuls of leaves out of the ditch and left.

She wasn't sure whether the ditch was in their yard or not. There wasn't any marker and she couldn't remember seeing Joey cut the grass there. Near the trunks of several small willows she bent down to pull up weeds, walked to the opening of the culvert, peered in, pulled a few twigs out. It was smaller than she had imagined. She couldn't place her arms vertical with the ground, instead had to crawl with her hands stretched out in front of her. It was probably only twenty feet to the road and she could see light. She stopped and tried to move backwards. It seemed to be possible.

What would she do if Mr. Crawford came back to clear the ditch or the children came back? What she was doing was stupid, not wrong. She stopped to recognize the smell of wet dirt and slow decay of grass and leaves. Her palms landed on some larger rocks and she tried to move gingerly over them. She felt a cobweb on her face, pulled back and hit her head on the top of the culvert, then shivered in disgust. She picked up a small stick beyond the web and waved it before her and crawled on for a few more feet and waved it again. A few yards in front of her she could see sickly light and hear voices.

"Jimmy's coming." She couldn't tell whether it was the boy or girl she saw who was talking.

"Can you hear where he's coming from? It's all echo in here."

Irene froze. Her back was beginning to hurt, but she was more afraid of being discovered.

"We could throw stones."

She heard a stone ping down one of the other culverts.

"He would have yelled if he was down this one. Let's get out of here."

Irene heard shuffling pant legs and feet against the tunnel as the children moved off. She waited until she could no longer hear them before she crawled on. Now she could understand that the light she saw came in through the street gutters into a square cement space. She could just barely stand with her neck bent. The ground was covered with a fine muddy sand and she could see the prints of the children. The voices came back again. Her feet moved silently across the sand as she hunched down, set her hands behind her and sat down.

"My mother says she's a witch." She tried to focus on where the words came from, but the sound echoed against the cement and seemed to come from nowhere.

"Maybe she's worse than a witch. Have you watched her

paint? It's nothing I've ever seen."

A car moved past the gutter and blocked the light for a second. There was a long silence. Irene let her head drop to her chest.

"Why doesn't she have any kids?"

"She must eat them. She grinds them up and makes them into paint." This sounded like a girl's voice.

"If only we could catch her. We have to watch her. See everything she does."

It seemed like the voices came from different tunnels and communicated through her.

"It must be some kind of spell. That's what Joey says."

Irene began to sweat. Her stomach knotted. Her head dropped into her crossed legs and she could smell the cool rot of leaves and humus in the muddy sand, as if the smell when it is just about to rain had been fermented in the dark cavern.

"I don't want to talk about Joey. He stole my Gameboy. His mother's a witch, too."

For what seemed a long time there were no more voices. Irene heard dull thunder and the wind begin to rise. Another car passed and sent a cloud of dust into the cavern that filtered down onto Irene. The thunder was louder.

Irene heard scraping and rustling coming from one of the holes. Before she herself could move back into the culvert, a boy came out. He screamed and jerked back when he saw her, his head thumping against the top of the tunnel. The thunder clapped again.

"It's okay. I'm leaving. I dropped my keys down here. Came to find them."

The boy panted and whimpered. He had backtracked into the tunnel so Irene could no longer see him and it seemed that he was trying to control his whimpering and breathing so she couldn't hear him.

"I'm leaving now. Don't stay in here. It's going to rain." Irene got into the spread crawl position and put her head into the tunnel.

"Don't stay in here. It's dangerous." Her words echoed into a muddle. She moved quickly without worrying about the small stones and broken glass on the bottom of the tunnel. When she came to the end of the tunnel, there was already a trickle of water falling out of the culvert. She crawled in the ditch until she came to the row of lilac bushes and stood up. Through the branches she saw some children running on the sidewalk along the street, trying to get out of the rain.

She considered waiting until the storm came before she ran to the house. The child came out of the tunnel and Irene recognized him as the boy who had been dragged to her house a few weeks before. His face was red and wild, his head bobbed with the heaving that was a mixture of gasping for air and sobbing. He ran a ways toward her in the ditch, tried to climb out, and fell back. The boy howled kicking at the leaves in the ditch. Irene moved from her hiding place. The boy was unaware of anything except his despair. It seemed that she had reached the boy by being pulled by a cord. She picked him up and brushed him off. He could see nothing through his tears and limply let her stroke leaves and dirt off him. She helped him out of the ditch and he stumbled on for a few feet before he turned back to look at her. She stood silently trying to imagine what he saw. He sobbed as he stumbled up the hill to the sidewalk and then stopped and turned around. With the back of his arm he wiped his tears away until he could make out Irene's form at the bottom of the hill. He stared at her like certain wild animals when they are surprised in the woods. Then he ran off in a jerky trot.

The windows were open and the curtains flapped in the storm wind. She closed those in the living room and dining room first, then in the kitchen. She could hear the Venetian blinds flapping in the upstairs bathroom and the swoosh of the long curtains in her and Tom's bedroom. The sky broke and it began to pour. The rain came through the screens in a pulsing spray. When she finished closing the windows, she lay down on the floor. She listened to the phone ring, heard a siren for a tornado warning, closed her eyes and saw a bright circle of light.

New York Journal

Today I was stuck in the subway, a fire on the tracks or something. The lights went out for a few moments and I felt alone, though could feel the people next to me, hear groans and sighs, whispering. I closed my eyes when the lights came on and floated away. I had just been to the Met to look at Rousseau and Chagall and Chirico and some early Arp. Both cold distant horror of the imagination and the naive possibility. The paintings seem to all be about space, expanding, hidden, circular, falsely two-dimensional on a two-dimensional surface.

María Elena says love is dead for her and she lives in a culture of rock songs, boleros, tangos, merengues where love is apotheosized. What is good about merengues, cha chas and all that heavy percussion stuff is that the singer is talking about commitment, cheating, revenge and the music is talking about your feet moving and blood pounding. Its message is sex. There is no one text in the song. The text of words, of what is going on in our lives, the reasonable or emotional level of language, and then the text of the music which is sexuality and which twists and deforms the surface so the music joyously enfolds the singer, who talks of ripping out her heart and giving it to the man who has possessed her.

I had sex with Chaguito, though haven't let María Elena know. He is calculating. After the first time, which was when he dropped by to deliver some family things his father had for María Elena, he asked me if I would talk to María Elena about him sleeping in the studio until he could find a place. Then we could see each other more, he said. He seemed too young to be hung like that, as if a penis should come with age. It was such pure sex, removed from anything except ego and his attempts to make it seem romantic, which were transparently self-serving. His confession that he had wanted me since he first saw me, which he wanted me to feel was a revelation on the level of killing his mother, came right before the request to talk to María Elena. You know that whole act, "I want to tell you something, but . . . " and then you have to drag it out of them. Who knows if he has fucked her, too. But it made me feel sexy and powerful to know that it wasn't just my body he wanted, that I was in control. Every time he brought up staying in the studio, I changed the subject.

María Elena and I are having a show together. We are each doing five paintings then doing five other paintings as reactions to the other's paintings. New York is so stimulating. To get all the stimulation into the work, you have to do a hundred paintings at a time. There is no one picture. The eye is less likely to drift into the mud of the soul.

We got some grant money to cover rent, materials. Chago makes the canvases. He could do a year's supply in a couple of days, but it gives me an excuse to call him up to come over so I can torture him with vague talk about his sleeping here. I guess he's even considering the West Side Y., and has been sleeping at friends', which means he has fewer and fewer friends. María Elena told him to go back to the island, live with his mother in Bayamón.

Tom wants to move back. He's called a few times. I guess Iowa was not what he expected. To go back to him physically would solve a few of my financial and social problems. I don't think

Chago knows that we split. But what makes me leery is that I see an endless emotional web that I have freed myself from and one strand could land me in the maze again. There is never a new start, not even with a new man. That was the mistake I made with Tom, thinking that we began like two figures in a romantic painting who are completely in the present moment and ready to move from moment to moment into the future, letting the previous one slip from under them as they move to the next. Timeless naivete. How do you reconnect anyway?

Jens is in New York for a month living with a boyfriend here. He says he prefers faithless love to loveless faith. I told him the two are not mutually exclusive. From his description of back-room sex in New York in the early eighties, I think they created both a religion of the penis and socialized infidelity.

The afternoon walks had become sullen. Carla made half-hearted attempts at conversation.

Carla would say, "Why look at that!"

Irene would respond with a listless, "I see."

Carla's neighbor Jane Fargonet came with them a few times and Irene felt encapsulated in a glass bubble, able to hear, but not to be heard. Jane asked a few perfunctory questions about her settling in, made a vague invitation to dinner and then fell into prattle with Carla that seemed like a foreign language that Irene perhaps had studied so she recognized words, but couldn't get any meaning, and eventually under the strain she had drifted off.

Occasionally Jane tried to bring her back in, "You know, that's the son of the Truewells. They live in that house with blue trim next to the Gordon's." Irene nodded emphatically so she could be left alone. After two days Jane discovered that she had shin splints.

With nothing to talk about, the pace increased to a fast walk and Irene had lost five pounds in three weeks. She went walking even when Carla had something else to do, which became more often. After several days walking by herself, Irene was glad to see Carla again and acted interested in the articles Carla had read in *Redbook* or the *Oprah Winfrey Show* she had seen.

"This woman just stood up in the audience and said that she had never felt loved by her mother and started to cry and then it all came out." Carla was out of breath and the phrases came out in a broken pant.

Irene subtly increased the pace. "I just don't see why public confession is so wonderful."

Carla fell back a little. "It was like she was getting rid of it. Like it had become everyone's when she shared it."

Irene stopped for a moment to wait for Carla. "And what if she felt that at that moment and the next moment felt something else. How do you get all the pieces back?"

Carla huffed past her, "Huh?"

"It's like mass hysteria."

"That's not how most people feel." Carla let Irene pass her again.

"No, you're right."

"Those shows are full of experts. Just full." Carla's difficulty in breathing stopped her from saying more about the experts.

The sun on the western horizon cast long yellowish shadows. The corn stalks had begun to turn whitish tan and from where she stood on the hill, Irene could see the shadows between the rows and the glistening dry tassels that still caught the sunlight. "Isn't it funny that the male part of the corn is the tassel and the female part is the corn?"

"Not ha ha funny," Carla said. "All the guys have the big corncobs, huh?"

"Not all," Irene said and went into her stride.

"I don't really know about all, that's true, but the few I have known." Carla made no effort to catch up to Irene.

"And men spread the rumor that it doesn't matter." Irene was now ten feet ahead.

"Isn't the idea we walk together?" Carla stopped.

Irene glanced over her shoulder, then walked back to Carla. "Yeah, I guess it is."

They finished at the corner of Main and Buckeye. Carla sat on the retaining wall of the corner lot. Irene wondered later why she told Carla about the tunnel.

"Something funny happened to me yesterday. I was walking back from the store and I dropped something and it fell down the rain gutter. Well, later I went to find it. I put on these old clothes, got on my hands and knees in the culvert and crawled to where the rain gutter was. There were kids in there playing. I thought, wow, this is dangerous. Then it seemed they were talking about me, or maybe they were. "That crazy woman who paints strange nothings." They were just voices, almost like voices in myself."

Carla stared with what Irene felt to be an uncomfortable level of interest.

"It was really nothing, but I haven't been able to think of anything else all day."

"Did you find what you were looking for?" Carla looked suspiciously at Irene.

"Well, sort of. Yes, I did, but it was so stupid. It was a letter from my friend María Elena, the one I told you about, but I had read it before."

"Why did the kids talk about you? What else did they say? Anything?"

"They said one of their mothers said I was a witch." Irene laughed.

"I wonder who that is. Don't you think we should try to find out?"

"No, we shouldn't." Irene's own tone of voice jarred with Carla's warm whisper.

Carla wanted some fall pansies and mums for her garden next to the grape pergola. Actually Harold wanted them. He made the decisions about the garden and Carla did the planting and maintenance. The day before Irene and Carla had run into each other while they were walking and it had been awkward. They both blurted out confusing excuses about why they hadn't called the other one before going out for a walk. So it was out of embarrassment that Carla had invited Irene to go with her to buy pansies and chrysanthemums for her fall flower garden and with similar feelings that Irene had accepted.

That day Irene had been painting "The Fall of Icarus in Iowa" and had the painting so clearly in her mind that she didn't want to stop and with each stroke she saw what the next options were for color or composition. The painting pulled her on. After three hours she wanted a break to get perspective on what she had painted and got into her sweats and walked almost to the road past the high school when she saw Carla. Her concentration vanished and the next thing she knew she was spending the next day with Carla away from "The Fall of Icarus in Iowa".

Irene had gone to the shed as soon as Tom left for work to

look at "The Fall of Icarus in Iowa." The morning had an edge, cold and still, that the sun removed along with the cold dew. She and Tom had managed what she called in her journal "perfect stranger sex." She was never good in the morning, always part of her body and mind still belonged to sleep, which meant that in a way she accepted him without thinking, and her movements were not passion, but the result of limiting discomfort. Tom fell off her like a leaf and lay dead next to her. It was what María Elena had called sex of the mollusks, or *fruit de mer* if the guy had an accent, or *mariscos* if the guy was Latin. She made up a gay version for Jens, *mariscones*, a blend of *maricón*, which vulgarly meant queer, and *mariscos*. Irene had occasionally been jealous that Jens seemed to find María Elena more interesting than herself.

A large cut-out cherry, which Irene assumed was the source of the cherry-cough-drop scent in the car, swung from the rear view mirror. Carla had covered the dash with Stick-ems with inspirational sayings. Irene interpreted them all, or least the ones she could read without encroaching on Carla's space, as meant for her, or maybe some of the older ones were written with Harold in mind. "Being alone is better than not being wanted." "You owe yourself all the love in the world." "If you don't find light at the end of the tunnel, maybe you are in the wrong hole." "Before I was a man, I was an arrow, a long time ago." "Tell all your troubles to your friends and they aren't yours anymore." Carla turned on the radio and hummed along demonstratively. The second time through the Stick-ems, which were scribbled in pencil, Irene felt car sick and concentrated on staring far ahead. She opened her window and leaned over to the door to take a few deep breaths of fresh air. A farmer had spread manure on a field and the effect of the fresh air on Irene's stomach was mixed.

"It's so good doing something different." With a sinking feeling Irene thought of the painting sitting in the shed.

"You just keep yourself too too too locked up, Irene." Carla said "Irene" long and drawn out, as if she were talking to a child.

"Too, too, too, too, too locked up, Carla." Irene tried to keep the parody out of her voice.

"I have this great opportunity to sell jewelry and accessories at home. It's like a Tupperware thing, but with pins, bracelets, charms. You have a little party and then show the stuff. And people who come get points for stuff themselves if they sell to their friends. So you have everyone selling for you. Everyone. Just imagine."

"Well, who buys it if they are all selling?" Irene stared straight ahead.

Carla's shoulders slumped slightly. "People buy more because they get something free, even if it's for themselves. Don't you get it? And they sell to friends. And if you are one of the first people to sell and you have other people selling for you, then you get a whole bunch of free things."

"And I get to be one of the first." Irene rolled up the window.

"Really you are. I thought of Jane, but her husband doesn't want her to do anything with business. He's old-fashioned, and you know he's an official at the bank. But she thought it was a great idea." Carla twisted slightly in her seat and pulled herself up straight again with the steering wheel. "And you have that experience at the gallery, so Tom can't have anything against you selling stuff."

"But I didn't like it. And I don't know anyone here. Who would I sell to? My mother-in-law who already has the crown jewels of costume jewelry?" Irene laughed and looked over at Carla.

"Well, it was just an idea. You might have fun at the party, meet some new people who you could sell to."

Carla took one of the Stick-ems that Irene couldn't read off the dashboard and crumpled it up and stuck it in the ashtray. For a few minutes neither of them spoke.

"Wouldn't those people be trying to sell to me, too? What if we just sold to each other, like a bunch of girl scouts with too many cookies?" Irene could see the sign for the nursery.

"It's something we could do together," Carla said and turned into the parking lot for Toby's Green Fingers Nursery.

"Oh, it's just a name. Lyle had this kid working for him who took a market research class at the university and as a project tested names out in Crandall to see what names they thought were friendliest and most reliable, and Toby won. It was a joke at first. They started calling it Toby's among the employees. Lyle changed it and told people there was an outside owner. Funny, huh?"

"So there's no Toby." Irene was glad to be out of the car and away from the cherry scent.

"Well, there must have been somewhere for all those people to feel so good about him." Carla laughed at her own joke.

The aisles between the plants were just wide enough so the two of them could walk side by side.

"When I walk into a nursery and it's so warm and tropical, it does something to my blood. My shoulders want to move backwards and forwards like I am coming on to someone. Like this sexual sex drive." Carla turned to Irene and shook her shoulders like George Bush Senior imitating Celia Cruz.

Irene chuckled and then laughed. "Carla, what other kind of sex drive is there other than a sexual one?"

"There' the your-husband-has-been-nagging-at-you-for-a-week sex drive, and the . . ."

"Is that the drive for him or for the teenage bagger at the grocery store?"

"He's nagging for sex. That's the drive." Carla grabbed a red mum and turned it around to check for dry stems and flower buds. "Do you like this color?"

"It looks fallish. Maybe as an accent with lots of yellow." Irene was trying to act interested.

"Hmm." Carla pursed her lips. "That's just what Harold told me to get. Lots of yellow and a few red. I would have gotten a lot of red and a few yellows. Or maybe whites."

Irene loosened her sweater. She felt like she had to drag the heavy air into her lungs. The wet peat moss smelled like a hot damp forest floor.

"I've heard that my uncle Lyle is an old goat. One of his wives was from Kentucky. She used to say that he was hotter than a two-peckered billy goat. Wouldn't leave her alone."

Irene responded with a wan smile.

"My mother once told me to never lie, unless it was about him being my uncle." Carla loaded several mums into the shopping cart without inspecting them.

Irene had expected Carla to laugh, but she stopped the cart and turned seriously to Irene. "I think he likes you. He mentioned you to me after the time we were on the walk. You know, when we went into the cornfield. Or maybe it was just you who went in to pee. Nothing much, but I know how his mind works."

When they turned into the next room, Lyle was standing with a mister connected to a water hose. Carla blushed, but Lyle hadn't seen them. He wore a white kirtle and large white rubber gloves. He stood in a halo of mist charged with sunlight.

Carla raised her eyebrows and clamped her hand over her mouth. Irene smiled back. Then Carla gingerly pulled the back of Irene's blouse and the two of them quietly turned back into the other hall.

"Don't you want to see him?"

"Not yet. Not right after I was talking about him. And I feel like I should warn you. You know I didn't think about it." Carla was trying hard to look interested in some pansies that she had passed up before.

"Harold would kill me if I got these. Wrong color. But they're nice, aren't they?"

"Yeah, that's what I thought the first time I saw them." Irene's voice was slow and stagnant like the air in the hothouse.

"And now?"

"Well, they are sick looking. The color though, I like the color."

Irene had seen Lyle coming towards them with the kirtle open like a flack coat and hadn't said anything.

"Girls finding everything you need?"

Carla's head jerked up and stared alertly at him. "I knew I'd see you here today."

"Didn't recognize you, Carla. You've lost weight."

Carla kept the shopping cart between her and Lyle. "Some. Not much to speak of."

"How's Harold." Lyle had moved so he was on the same side of the shopping cart as Irene.

"Fine, just fine. He told me to say hello if I ran into you. He always says, "Buy from Lyle.'" Carla looked at him as if the conversation were over.

"Always a discount for relatives." Lyle paused for a few seconds to separate and emphasize, "and friends."

Irene moved slightly away from Lyle.

"You moved into Mrs. Fliplak's house, didn't you. Lot a work to do on that yard." Lyle's face took on what to Irene was a humorously serious aspect.

"I like run down. Old roses, old peonies, old bridal wreath. Makes me look younger."

Lyle ignored her comments. "And from what I hear your husband is busy. Very busy."

Irene was shocked for a second. "Well, uh . . . "

"Very busy with work." Lyle leaned towards her with a smile that seemed purposely ambiguous. "And you might need someone who knows about yards here to come and give you some advice. It's part of our service, if you buy the plants from us. We have a great crew, too. And classes."

"I think your garden is nice the way it is. It's charming." Carla's voice echoed and both Lyle and Irene turned to look at her.

Lyle took a pen out of his kirtle and began writing on a small card. "You want more information, we're here to help. Just call. And if it's a question of price, Toby's flexible."

"Well, I'll have to talk to Tom. We already have someone who does the lawn. Not a professional."

Lyle pressed the card into Irene's hand in a way that made her jerk back. "I'll see what he says," she said.

"Can you show me where you keep the good pansies?" Carla pushed the cart forward and placed half of her body between Irene and Lyle. "Irene, could you find two more good red mums over there."

Carla stood impatiently as Lyle gave Irene a slow-motion version of his best merchandising smile and then turned to lead Carla into the other hall.

Carla's voice seemed to be everywhere. Irene wandered up and down the aisles. She picked up a scented geranium and pinched off a leaf to smell it and then looked at a tag to see what she had smelled. *Lemony Roses*. She put the leaf into the pocket of her jeans. When she got to a small table of cyclamens in the corner, she looked back over the large room which was empty and silent except for the hum of the ventilator fan and Carla's voice."

"Lyle, you have better than that . . . Don't you have a bigger one? Look how tiny it is . . . You call that a stem? . . . It's so wobbly it wouldn't stay up for five minutes . . . Where do you keep the good stuff? . . . Oh, I like that. Oh, yes, yes . . . Can you read this on Harold's list? If you get close enough you won't need your glasses. Not even with glasses, huh?" She never heard Lyle's answers, imagined some of them as being another plant for Carla's inspection.

She picked up the first two red mums she saw. Carla pushed her cart towards her. Two boxes with pansies sat on the bottom rack. They were putting the mums in the back seat when Lyle pushed a dolly with two bags of bark up to the trunk of the car.

"I think this is what Harold wanted. Bark. Bark, bark, bark." Lyle laughed.

Irene thought the joke was so stupid that she giggled thinking an adult man would tell it. This only encouraged Lyle to laugh louder. Carla looked at them with her shoulder raised and

Irene realized that Carla actually thought she found the joke itself funny.

Carla strode to the car door, sat neatly down and started the engine. Lyle jerked his head and pressed his lips together as if he were shaking off the laughter. His face remained set in a fat-cheek smile for the few moments before he offered Irene his hand. He held her hand in both of his and Irene laughed and jerked her hand back, but he kept a hold.

"Oh, it wasn't that funny," he said and winked at her.

"Well, maybe not. I'd better get into the car before Carla drives off." She had to pull her fingers out from the tight cup of Lyle hands. He stretched his arms out so she had to back up to get away. She suppressed a snort of laughter by converting it into an obviously phony cough.

"Remember, if you need any . . . " She closed the car door before he finished.

"God, he is weird."

"Yup," Carla said tersely and turned her head to the left as if looking for oncoming traffic.

"Carla, no car's coming. You can go."

Without looking over or answering, Carla gunned the car and swung wide into the wrong lane where a car was coming. The car honked and Carla righted the car.

"No use for that. That horn. Who does that guy think he is?" Carla's eyes were locked on the road.

"It was a woman."

"I know that," Carla snapped and there was a silence that lasted for five miles.

“Lyle is such a Jew,” Carla said and Irene didn’t understand at first since she had been thinking of “The Fall of Icarus in Iowa.”

“Is he really Jewish?”

“No, but he acts like one.” Carla was defensive.

“How do they act?” Irene had been through this with Tom.

“You know, he tries to get every penny out of you he can. Kind of low-handed.”

“It sounds like every good business person in the world.” Irene’s voice trailed off and she avoided looking at Carla.

“You can’t know everything. Did you ever think of that? You can’t. That’s one thing that really bothers me about you.”

Irene realized that she didn’t care about the conversation. “Sorry.”

“You have to watch your reputation. It’s different for we women. It’s not like for men. It’s different.” Carla’s eyes were red and she sniffled.

“Yes, I know or am learning.” Irene sighed, but Carla chose to ignore it.

“There was a friend of mine. Not someone I knew very well, but a friend. Her husband didn’t pay much attention to her. I can’t tell you her name. You don’t know her. And she had someone working in the yard, someone you know, I think. And she and her husband left town.”

Irene couldn’t speak for a moment. “Well, what happened?”

“I can’t tell you. I promised her that I wouldn’t tell anyone. But I am telling you so you know.” The anger was apparent in Carla’s voice.

"Know what, Carla? What is it you want me to know?"

"You can figure it out if you want to. I can't be any clearer, okay. And it's not what I want you to know, okay. It's what you better know." Carla barreled through the intersection running a stop sign.

"Thank you, Carla. I appreciate it." Irene's voice was conciliatory, calming.

Carla relaxed a little. They seemed to miss the curve in the highway and went off on a gravel road.

"Is this a new way?" She turned slowly to look at Carla who looked back for an instant too long and the right wheels pulled slightly towards the ditch.

"Sorry," Carla said and looked ahead again. "It's that I have to talk to you. Can I see the card Lyle gave you? I have to see it. It's important." Carla tightened for a moment and then dropped her head onto the steering wheel.

"Here, let me get it. Sure."

Carla brought her head back up.

"It's in my pocket, I think. The blouse pocket. No. No. Let me try my jeans." Irene undid the safety belt and stretched out in the front seat so she could stick her hand into her pocket. She pulled out the scented geranium leaf and the crumpled card from Lyle.

"Let me see if this is it." She spread it out against her thigh and read, "Toby's Green Fingers Nursery, Lyle Bucker, General Manager." On the back side Lyle had written his home phone number and "Call any time. Love to talk about your bushes."

Irene held the card out in the empty space between them. Carla slowed down to take it. She glanced between the card and the road a few times and then put the card in her pocket.

"As a friend I have to tell you something. Because you're a friend, I think I can. Are you my friend?" Carla sniffled through the last four words and reached out the hand that had held the card and grasps Irene's shoulder.

The car languidly swayed down the middle of the gravel road. They were approaching the top of a small hill. "Yes, Carla, you are my friend. My really good friend."

Carla drew her hand back and steadied the car. "Tom has been seeing another woman. Men are such pigs." There was a long pause as if this confession had overwhelmed her. "I heard that it was even before you moved here, when his dad was sick. The night his dad died he wasn't there. That's what I heard. With her. They say the whole night. And then he brought you here."

"You're really a good friend, Carla. Thank you." The car had started to sway back and forth across the road.

Carla stared over at her with bleary eyes. "They say that's why Tom left town the first time. Because of her. But now she's divorced. Married young. Had to. And her son's no better. The stories I could tell. You must really be upset about this."

Irene knew she had to really be upset or Carla would keep her captive in the runaway car. "I don't know what to say. I'm stunned. Speechless. I have to work through it."

Carla seemed in control again. With her tongue she pushed her false front tooth out and then sucked it back. The sound usually made Irene nervous, but now it seemed to be comforting, as if Carla were a pressure cooker and was cooling off with little spurts of steam.

"I'll take you home and then we can really talk. There is so much more to say."

Irene hummed a distant affirmative and Carla held a steady fifty-miles-an-hour until she turned back onto the highway. It seemed like the sun had suddenly come out. They passed the row of three billboards announcing Pendayhaz to the world. "Landmen's Bank - Pendayhaz banks with us. Community banking." "Sleep-Rite-All-Nite Motel. Privacy and friendly faces. Our customers come back night after night!" "The Good Shepherd Lutheran Church. Is God in your life? One block off Main Street. Turn right on Presley Street. Come worship with us."

Irene was tensely aware of Carla during the silence of the next five minutes. Carla bit her lips a few times, sucked her false tooth in and out, and sighed deeply. When they reached the Pendayhaz town limits, Carla glanced over and smiled. "It will be all right. You can fight this."

"Yes," Irene said and remained serious and distant.

Carla waved at Mrs. Collins who was taking a break from washing her screen windows with a hose.

"Maybe I can come in when we get to your house. We have to talk." They were only two blocks from Irene's house.

"I really need to rest. I have a painting I need to finish. We could talk tomorrow." Irene avoided looking back at Carla.

"I am probably your only friend here. I defend you all the time. If you knew what people were saying about you. I thought I should talk to you before." Carla's voice began to sound the way it had on the gravel road.

"Carla, I can't control what people say about me, can I?"

Irene was startled when Carla braked fast. "It's not for me I want to talk to you. I promise you. You believe me, don't you?" Carla reached across the seat for Irene's hand.

"Well, yes, I suppose maybe I do believe you." She looked up and saw Tom's car parked in their driveway.

"Tom's home. I'll tell Tom you said hello. I have to go."

Carla hadn't noticed the car. After Irene shut the door, Carla shouted, "We have to talk. Remember."

Tom was lying on the bed upstairs with the lights off.

"You okay?" Irene opened the door but didn't turn on the lights.

"I guess so. I just needed to get away. I've been going a lot. Maybe you could make supper and we could have a night at home."

"I had a hard day with Carla. I'm going to have a glass of wine. Then I'll go to the supermarket." Irene stood looking into the room. The paper blinds glowed with the afternoon light. She now could see Tom better.

"What happened? Carla try to get in your pants? Or was it a hard day because you let her in your pants?" He made a sound between a grunt and a laugh.

"Of course not. You have the strangest ideas." She noticed that he continued to stare at the ceiling even when he spoke to her. "Maybe I should try to get into her pants. A little less vanilla sex might make this place more alive."

"Maybe. Maybe not." Tom's voice sounded almost disembodied.

"What happened? Love left your life." Irene shut the door softly.

"Something like that."

She was sure she heard correctly and opened the door a crack.

“Well, we had sex this morning, didn’t we,” Tom said. He seemed to talk from a momentum that had nothing to do with her.

“Yes, we did,” she said and walked down stairs.

Carla’s car was parked in the lot of the grocery store and for a moment Irene considered going home again. She saw Carla near the meat section, went around the aisle and then came back because she had the feeling that Carla had seen her already. She was halfway down the aisle when it became obvious to her that Carla hadn’t seen her and was talking earnestly to someone she couldn’t see. Carla’s voice hushed at the approach of the shopping cart and when she turned to look at Irene, her face went red. Jane Fargonet peered around the corner and gave what Irene called the Bozo the clown smile, a strange combination of lip puckering and lip spreading.

“Hi, Jane.”

“Why hi, Irene. You heard about my shin splints, I hope.”

Irene shook her head in consolation.

“Everything all right at home?” Carla asked with seeming unconcern.

“Yes. I have to hurry. I have a man at home to keep happy. And if I can’t do that, I should at least feed him.” As she walked home with the package of linguine, the canned pasta sauce, and some fresh mushrooms to liven it up, she felt a little guilty for playing the fawning housewife, then wondered what Carla and Jane would make of her comment about not keeping Tom happy.

Tom had the television on so loud that she could hear it in the kitchen. He jumped from channel to channel, put in an old porno tape that she thought they had thrown away when they moved from Brooklyn, and then either turned off the sound or turned off the television for a few minutes. When it came on again with the news, the water for the linguine was boiling and she washed and cut the mushrooms and put them into the sauce.

"Tom, it's ready in five minutes."

He came down in sweat pants and a sweatshirt that exaggerated the fifteen pounds he had put on since they had moved four months ago. He sat at the table like a sick child, answering only when she asked him something directly and eating with his eyes pointed at the table. He thanked her for dinner and went back upstairs.

Journal September 23

Does past happiness become false when what made you happy once no longer makes you happy? I used to love consoling Tom when he got home from work feeling a failure. Now the consolation seems only maternal, not wifely. And I don't want to be his mother. Let Doris have it.

Tom is having girl problems and if I have had to put up with his distance and abandonment in this wilderness, why can't he keep his despair to himself, like I have? At least he had enough sense not to tell me the details. I'm sure I can count on Carla to do that.

It's funny that after the stranger sex we had yesterday morning, he gets laid low by whoever she is. Then that dig about Carla. Is that what he wishes on me? I would love an Adrienne Rich or May Sarton, especially here.

Her Uncle Lyle seems to be out of a forties movie, the silly affected suitor who is menacing matrimony with our heroine if the misunderstandings between the young couple are not straightened out. Or maybe this is the mechanism I have for understanding Uncle Lyle. He did not attract me a bit until Carla took the card (God, how can I write this?) and suddenly I felt that I would have sex with him, just to free myself from her. Does this make sense? No.

The other day I was going to pay the grocery bill in cash and checked my wallet to see if I would have forty dollars left, the Joey money. I've thought about it and decided that the reason I like Joey is that I feel completely out of control, demeaned and reach the animal level of tribal fetishism. But then I have to plan, to make sure that I have forty in cash in case it happens again. I tell myself that it is like the smoker who must always have a full pack so she doesn't get desperate, which will lead to smoking. I need those forty dollars in my pocket book so I don't get desperate, so when he comes I can tell him no because I am in control, not short of cash, but ultimately so I can just not tell him anything and he screws me.

A couple of boxes that I had forgotten about arrived, one with old letters and another with the plates and cups from Brooklyn. It was like getting a present, not like the boxes that have been sitting in the upstairs closet and in the corner of the "book room" for four months. The Bavarian china cup I got when Ed died was broken and I put it in the middle of the kitchen table so Tom would see it when he got home from work, not knowing when that might be. Part of me wants him to know what I have lost moving here. He was more concerned than I had wanted, and I remembered how sad he seemed to be when Ed died, and that he insisted on talking at the memorial service. He had all kinds of suggestions for repair, even getting a professional to do it, as if there were cup repair specialists. Probably are. Said he knew an archaeologist. If that didn't give me a feeling of my worldly transience! I told him that it was too early for my life to be reconstructed by archaeologists, though I wanted him to insist. While we were talking, I picked up the pieces of the cup and took them out to the garbage can next to the garage and dropped them in. It was like the air had been knocked out of both of us. I wanted to pick it up from the trash, but I wanted to hurt him even more. It's the same feeling I get when I think that I lost the album of photos of my mother as a girl. How do you get that back? And what are the album and the cup? Just symbols of life's incompleteness. I stood next to the trash and thought that life was loss and experiencing and creating new things to lose. And I started to cry because I was angry at Tom and at myself and too stubborn to pull the pieces out of the trash, keep them in an envelope like the old letters.

Some of the other cups and plates were chipped. I put them away. I wanted Tom to be reminded of what this move has cost me. He came down from upstairs when I was putting plates in the cupboard, in the little space left after the wedding present china had been installed. I worked myself up so that everything became the focus of restrained grief. He watched me for a while and then said, "Well, you'll feel more like at home now." I lost it and started crying. In one of those I Love Lucy crying jags, I screamed that "those things would only remind me that I had lost my home, that what had been was gone and could never exist again. I was dead." He didn't fight back. I wanted a fight. He came over and held me and I cried even louder because now I felt completely lost. I thought, "I am being comforted in my grave." He took me up to bed, lay down next to me for a while, then went out when he thought I was asleep. Who does he go to tell about his troubles with his crazy wife?

Irene noticed when she came in from painting in the morning that four people had called without leaving a message on the machine. She thought the calls were probably from Carla. For the last couple of days she had screened her calls and only answered Carla's calls when Tom was home. Then she would invent some reason for Tom to talk to Harold and hand the phone to the bewildered Tom

She heard Doris's voice on the machine and picked up.

"I don't want to hear any objections. I talked to Charlene at the beauty parlor and got it all set up, and I am paying. That wedding is coming up. And I was thinking the other day that I hadn't really given you a welcome present, not a personal one, and what a better one than an afternoon at the beauty parlor."

"I'm busy today. I started on a box: linen and things like that, which were my mom's. I don't know why my father gave them to me now. I'm sure I don't remember any of them." She had started on the box before she went out to paint.

"No, no, not today. On Friday before the wedding. You'll love Charlene. She's a doll." Irene had seen the sign at the Meadowlark Mall, "Charlene's Beauty Plus Unisex Salon."

"You don't have to do this. I feel like my hair . . . " When Doris broke her off, Irene saw a steamroller coming towards her and couldn't get her feet to move.

"I insist on paying. Remember, my treat."

Irene remained silent.

"She'll do whatever you tell her to. Find something in a magazine and show it to her and she'll do it just like that, that is if you have the hair for it."

"Hmm," Irene said. She was gathering her anger.

"I told her perm, facial, highlights, manicure. Like a makeover."

"Doris, ah, Doris," Irene raised her voice to make Doris stop for a moment.

"Irene, honey, I have to go. The natural gas man. Friday. Remember, Friday at 1:30. All-expenses-paid vacation for an afternoon."

The receiver seemed to have been transfixed to lead. Irene let it rest between her knees until she got tired of the pulsing buzz of the off-the-hook signal.

She went out to the yard again. The wind had come up while she was on the phone and blown up dust and small leaves which had stuck to the wet paint on the first of the triptych "Stony Faces," which Irene had taken out after not working on it for a few months. She picked the larger leaves off the canvas with her fingertips. "Oil, dirt and leaves on canvas," Irene said louder than she expected. She put the canvas in the shed. As she was leaving, she noticed that one of the panes in the window of the shed had been rubbed so that there was a peep hole in the years of grime. In the tangle of ivy and tall feathery asparagus bushes in front of the window, she found a rusted folding chair with one leg rotted to a jagged stump.

She went back into the shed and stood still in the darkness. She took her hair out of the band that held it back and bowed to let it fall over her face. She gathered a handful and sniffed at it, thinking she could pick out Tom, the paste wax smell of the house, the shampoo, and that it was all distinct from the paint and old grease of the shed. She had gone into the shed with the intention of smearing the panes with an old brush from the inside so that it was impossible to see through them. Her hair rested just behind her shoulders when she threw her head back and then she surprised herself.

When all panes were clean on both sides, she placed "Le Tub" and "The Carnival Shooting Gallery" on the large workbench so they faced the window, and set some work lights up that she sometimes used to make the paint dry faster, so that they illuminated the paintings.

In the house she stripped to her underwear. She turned to the back of her sketchbook where she had drawn a series of caricatures of Doris, inspired by Roz Chast cartoons.

Doris Shows her Jewelry to Queen Elizabeth II on Her Visit to Iowa

Doris Fights with the Neighbor over the Truck Parked in Front of Her Yard

Doris Gives Her Own Oracular Gems to the Dali Lama

Doris Gets Turned On by a Special China Pattern for Good Friday (nails, thorns, blood and cat of nine tails)

Doris Flies South for the Winter

Doris Catches Hubbie with the Secretary

Expressions of Doris

Worry / Is my jewelry visible from space?

Anger / My daughter-in-law refuses to buy Thanksgiving dinnerware with pilgrims and turkeys, won't even accept my old ones.

Joy / I went to a cocktail party with the girls and everyone else had the same pant suit on.

She doodled on some of the ones she had done before, gave Doris angelic emanations for "Doris Gives Her Own Oracular Gems to the Dali Lama," added a few winged wheelchairs off in the corner of the "Doris Flies South for the Winter." Then in lettering that was bolder than she had used on the other cartoons, she wrote, "Doris as Delilah in the Beauty Plus." She drew a row of women sitting in beauty chairs and each had shorter hair than the one to the left and as the hair got shorter, it seemed to mount on their heads. Doris was dressed in a harem costume, and her head was turned madly towards the front away from the customers in their chairs.

That morning Tom had asked her to rake the leaves in the yard, or start. The Crawfords had raked their yard the Saturday before and had complained to Tom about the leaves blowing into their yard. She put her hair up in a bandana, found the rake in the cellar. The garden tools came with the house, and the shaft of the rake was stained and chipped. Irene made a long line of leaves around the west side of the yard and raked it towards the house. Every few feet she would rake the long line of leaves together and put them in a garbage bag.

Mrs. Crawford carried a basket of wet clothes out to the line. Irene waved.

"Chuck always says clothes smell better when they're hung out," Kristie Crawford said, walking over to look at Irene as she raked.

"Men always think whatever is more work for us is better." Kristie said this as if there was nothing humorous about it.

"I think he's right about the clothes on the line," Irene said.

"Sometimes I throw one of those scented fabric softeners in the wash and dry the wash in the machine and tell him it's been on the line. I don't mind doing it now, but when tax season comes around and I have a lot of work, and it seems that it always rains a lot between March and April, and it always rains when my mind is in the middle of someone's form, and I don't hear a thing until the clothes are soaked." This time she laughed.

"If only I could put fabric softener on these leaves and make them disappear?" Irene leaned the rake against her shoulder and looked at her red palms.

"Some things you just have to do. Well, bye." Kristie walked away abruptly and disappeared behind a sheet on the line.

After the fourth garbage bag, Irene went inside and called Tom.

"Tom, I've been raking the yard. I thought that would make you happy."

"Well, I guess so." Tom sounded like he was writing or reading as he talked to her.

"I already have two blisters," Irene also disengaged from the conversation, looking blankly at her hands.

"Huh, I think . . . I think . . . maybe . . . "

"I didn't want to bother you. When are you getting home? Should I cook?" Irene wanted to hang up.

"There are some gloves in the trunk in the basement. The one under the steps," Tom said.

"Oh, well what about cooking?"

"I could get Joey to help you with the raking." Tom seemed to suddenly have finished his other task.

"Well, I guess so. You mean on Saturday. Remember the wedding." She almost barked the last sentence.

"Oh I know. After school one day. I'll ask his mother." Now Tom sounded like he was in a hurry to get off.

"Why not him? Why would you ask his mother?" Irene had walked to the kitchen sink and turned the faucet on with her free hand and held her blistered palm under the cold water.

"His mom works here. Didn't I tell you? When Mrs. Benson has a doctor's appointment or something. She's here maybe two days a week." Tom sounded nonchalant.

"That's handy," Irene turned the faucet up and put the receiver in the sink.

"What was that? Something's wrong with this line," Tom asked.

"Did you hear me? I said that was handy." Irene turned the water off.

"She's great at filing. That's what there's most of in this office."

"Her nails or sticking things in boxes?" Irene grimaced at her own stupidity.

"Got to go. I hope you can live without an answer." After he hung up, Irene imagined him saying, "Bitch," like he would when he hung up the phone after a difficult customer. An especially annoying woman might get the male version, "Asshole."

She called him back, "What about dinner?"

"My mother said something about going over there. She thinks you're mad at her," Tom said with the same distant voice.

"About what?" Irene sounded surprised.

"About not helping you out more with settling in. I told her she was crazy. Oh, Luce says Monday is fine." Irene could hear Tom's garbled voice give instructions to someone. She picked out the phrase," "Mrs. Gooch, no hurry."

"Luce? Who's Luce."

"Joey's mom. Lucille Towner. Should I pick you up? Mom said six-thirty. I probably have to meet a few clients later tonight, so I told her early. Luce, don't put that away yet."

"I'll walk over on my own. Give you and your mother a little time to talk."

Irene set the bags of leaves next to the garage. She opened the trash can to pull out a preliminary sketch for "The Fall of

Icarus in Iowa" that she had thrown out that morning. The chair next to the window looked like there were fresh footprints, but it was a school day and still only one o'clock. She taped the paper to the top of the chair, but the sides were so rusty and dirty that she doubted whether the tape would hold.

Her head jerked up when she heard knocking coming from the front door of the house. On her way around the shed, Irene tossed the tape in at the door. It seemed that she had spent hours, days within herself, and now had to find the way out to communicate. The knocking continued in insistent bursts that she imagined were masculine. When it stopped, she waited and turned the corner. She stopped to laugh softly when she saw Lyle at the door peering in at the small window next to the door.

"No bushes in there," Irene said.

He turned slowly to look at her with a smile that broadened. "Irene, I was over to the Bundgaard's and decided to stop and give my pitch."

"Pitch away." Irene wondered why Lyle hadn't acted more surprised at being caught gawking through her window.

"Maybe we could walk around your yard so I can get an idea of the possibilities." He looked at her searchingly.

Irene turned her back to him and walked away to keep from laughing. "This way."

"Do you know the Bundgaards?"

Irene posed for a moment as if she were running a list of names through her memory bank. "I think I met Sharon Bundgaard. Is there a Sharon Bundgaard? Well, someone Bundgaard I met at the Lutheran church."

"They live a block away from Lucille Towner. Farther out." Lyle now hung almost over her shoulder as she walked down to the ditch.

“Who is Lucille Towner?” She stopped short and Lyle grabbed Irene’s shoulders to steady himself.

“Excuse me. I thought you knew who she was. She works . . . Well, they say she . . . I don’t really know how to say this.” Lyle was gathering force.

“This is where the property starts. I’d like to put something here to hide the ditch. What would you put in here?” Irene strode away to the opening of the culvert.

“I’d have to think out the whole thing first. I don’t just plant plants, I plan experiences. I don’t look at them as plants. I look at them as light. You have to think of what they look like in cloudy bright or dusky shadow.” Lyle had pulled a necklace out of his shirt and played with a silver peace sign.

“I really want that ditch covered.” She walked the length of the ditch and then turned to climb the hill back to the rest of the yard. When she turned back, she saw that Lyle surveying the area, kicking up a little dirt as if he were testing it. She went to the porch that faced north and sat to wait for him.

He staggered towards her as he tried to walk while making a rough sketch of the yard.

“I like my jungle,” she said.

“You deserve paradise,” he said and Irene laughed.

“I’m afraid that’s not what I’ve earned.”

“I have to come back to the Bundgaards on Monday. I could stop by with a few suggestions and some estimates.” He moved his eyes up from the sketch and stared intently at her.

“No, not Monday. Maybe another day. Monday’s not good.”

"I guess I could talk to the Bundgaards. Monday was my idea. I don't like to let projects stall." He took a little appointment book out of his pocket and made a note.

"Mind if I say something to you."

"There probably are a few things I wouldn't want you to say."

His tone of seriousness wasn't funny anymore. She looked at her watch to avoid his concerned stare, then stood up like she was about to go inside.

"Have you ever read *The Bridges of Madison County*?" He craned his long neck in an attempt to face her.

"Well, no. I saw the *Doonesbury* cartoons about it. But I guess if I had read the book they would have been funnier." She walked in the shade of the house to the kitchen steps where he had been knocking earlier.

"You should read it. It sold more hardcover copies than any other book. Well, more than any adult book."

"More than the Bible?" Irene exaggerated her surprise so it came off more as astonishment than as a challenge.

"You are just like Francesca. Sometimes I catch myself about to call you Francesca. I learned a lot from that book. I took pictures for a few years after I read it. Looking for the light."

"Hmm. Nobody has ever told me that before." Irene had moved to the top step and had the screen door open.

"Not the movie. Not Meryl Streep, but the one in the book. There's only one Meryl Streep."

"Yeah, Meryl Streep, I don't do accents and seldom talk into the back of my hand." This line was from a drag queen who had been a friend of Jens. It was lost on Lyle.

"Great actress. But the book is art. It's art for art's sake, like Robert Kincaid."

"Who?" Irene said and opened the screen door.

"Don't you remember? He's the guy in *Bridges*."

"Oh." She opened the door and let the screen door shut between them. "Call before you come over," Irene said and shut the door on the smiling face of Lyle.

Journal October 19

I met Carla on the way to supper at Doris's. I was thinking about her, feeling guilty about being less supportive, but she is so needy and so manipulative that I'm afraid everything would come out wrong. I would be put in the situation of going to bed with her or hurting her feelings forever. I find some things about her attractive, or did until she began obsessing about me.

She told me that she "saw Lyle's car crawling through town like a catfish looking for garbage on the bottom of the Mississippi." Where does she get those lines? Maybe from her ex-Kentucky aunt. I didn't tell her about my little visit. She mentioned again a little getaway with the girls. A group of friends she has. I would be a lot more comfortable with Carla in a group. I asked her if she had a copy of Bridges *and she offered to drop it off tomorrow. I told her about the beauty appointment and she thought that was really funny. She said we had a lot to talk about. That "a lot to talk about" always scares me.*

When I got to Doris's house, she and Tom were deep into a conversation about her taxes and property. She must have written out fifty questions and memorized them since she kept him talking all night. Not once did I hear, "When Ralph was alive . . . ," which is her usual whine. I kept getting more and more anxious about not talking to her about the hair and finally I blurted out, "Mom, I can't go to the beauty parlor on Friday and I feel like my hair is mine." I sounded so stupid that I immediately wanted to erase it from their minds. She and Tom both gave me a look like I had just fallen through the ceiling. It didn't even seem to be what I said, but like they didn't know I was there until that moment. Tom asked what I had said and I told him I was talking to myself and then I got up and wandered around the house, sat for a while on the screened-in porch and leafed through Good Housekeeping, *then got cold and brought it in to the living room where I could still hear them dawdling over their wine, clink as the glass touched a plate, and talking taxes like the stock market report on a station just out of range. I turned to the garden section—new plants for fall. And I imagined walking into one of those gardens where each section is a room with hedges and pergolas and walls covered in vines. It is the comfort of the maze, which is like the comfort of the wings that let you hide far up in the sky until you get too close to the sun. Now, if I had to live in a maze with my father or Doris, I might do anything to get out.*

When I met Carla I was meandering through town (heading straight for Lucille Towner's house in a roundabout route to Doris's). I'm sure I've walked by it twenty times, but it wasn't on Carla's and my route. I'm surprised she didn't try to change the route of our walks so we passed this Lucille woman's house and Carla could use it as the cue to pull out all the town gossip.

The stickers on her dashboard were another color, may have to do with what self-help book is in ascension, horo-self-help. I never got to Lucille's, thanks to Carla, on the way to Doris's, but . . . When I turned to go in the other direction, I felt almost relief. On the way to Doris's I wondered why I had been going to look at this woman's house in the first place. It was good at dinner to be left with my own thoughts, Joey on Monday, Carla, the Garden of

Eden with Lyle, Lucille Towner, my mother-in-law tricks me out of my hair. It occurred to me as I leafed through the garden section, that the only reason I wasn't sitting there stewing about the hair appointment, and I guess I did a few times while I sat at the table and that was why I blurted that out, was that I couldn't keep my mind focused enough, not even on my anger.

I gave Doris her daughter-in-law kiss and Tom his marriage peck and walked home. They both protested lamely, perfunctorily about my walking home and leaving early, but I said that I had missed my exercise the last few afternoons and had promised my father to call him. This was more for Doris's sake, since I'm sure that Tom didn't buy it. Tom chuckled nervously at my quip about checking out the nightlife in Pendayhaz and Doris's mind was still in tax evasion and only managed fleeting blinking confusion. I stopped at the end of Doris's sidewalk and thought about me out there and them inside. I didn't see them as being any more connected to each other than I was to them, but I saw it as symbolic. I represented formal alienation and they were the signs for a mock up in a sociology text of human communication, those horribly staged pictures that I remember from high school texts. Standing there for no reason at all and being slightly aware of eyes and my own lack of excuse, I had a welling feeling that I had found the sadness and beauty of the world as I looked up into the stars dimmed by the street lights. I shed a few tears of ecstasy and my eyes were dry again by the end of the block. Knowing that my feet without conscious instructions were taking me to the block where Lucille Towner lived made everything less cosmic. Or maybe cosmic minus the s. Keep the m. Pure masochism.

No one walks alone in this town, other than the deranged and perhaps people under sixteen who have a definite destination. One late afternoon when I was out in the yard, an old man came up to me and asked me if I was his wife. I had noticed him walking back and forth on the block. Tom said that it was Carston Gregor, an old farmer who lived with his son and daughter-in-law. A month later in July, right after the fourth, I saw him go by in his underwear, and a minute later the woman with the crooked A-frame, Mrs. "I'm-not-used-to-losing-arguments" went by. She stopped and looked at me as if she were going to ask me a question, then looked farther off down the street and trotted away. They must have taken another way home since I didn't see either of them come back.

I wished I had on sweat pants so I could pass as a late-night exercise walker. I didn't go fast, but kept my face braced forward with purpose so it looked like I was going somewhere. Maybe five cars passed me. I saw Joey's car parked off the driveway in the lawn. Positive identification. As soon as I saw the house, I felt embarrassed. Cheap one story with a small flat lawn and a couple of elm stumps in the front. Soap opera. Think if I watched that stuff I would have already had hundreds of confrontations with this woman. I would have the plot, just stick myself and her into it. I heard an automatic garage door start and jumped off the sidewalk behind a tree, (I see myself now and cringe) and a blue Mazda pulled out. Maybe it was a Mitzubishi. It whipped out of the driveway and backed into the street, taut quick car movements, automotive foreplay, I thought. "Oh, there goes the part-time secretary to the meeting with the client to take notes. Shorthand. Short hand job late at night." Funny. Real funny.

I walked all the way home telling myself I was going to call Doris as soon as I got home, ask where Tom was, tell her to cancel the appointment. I was puffing myself up, planned to rush into the house without thinking and call. Good plan. There was a note stuck in the screen door from Joey. "OK for Monday. 3:30." There was a business card, too. I thought maybe it was a joke from Joey, felt myself sink when I saw it was Lyle's. On the back he wrote, "You call me. In a universe of ambiguity, this kind of certainty comes only once, and never again, no matter how many lifetimes you live." More dashboard philosophy, I thought. Some people are certain all the time. I couldn't call Doris. I put Joey's note under the phonebook in the kitchen drawer and went back to look at it after I watched the ten o'clock news.

Thursday Irene worked on the Grant Wood section of "The Fall of Icarus in Iowa." It was getting too chilly to paint outside until way after ten in the morning and it usually was windy. A few days the week before had been perfect, but one day it had rained and another day dust and leaves kept blowing into her face and she gave up after an hour. She called Tom to complain and to mention the appointment his mother made for her at the beauty parlor. She really had nothing to say.

"Tom, you could have come into the bedroom last night. I wasn't asleep when you got home." She didn't know when he got home.

"I didn't feel like waking you. I wanted to sleep alone. You know how it is."

Irene mouthed Tom's last sentence to herself. "I guess so," she said. "You left early for getting home so late."

"I have a lot of work to do. Mom needs some things done. And the wedding is coming up so I can't work this weekend. What are you up to?" Tom said.

"I was trying to paint but it's too cold. At least today. And that was why I came here." She was embarrassed by the melodrama.

"Came where?" Tom was confused.

"You know, when we moved here, you said I would have time to paint. I could paint." Irene was hesitant.

There was a marked silence and then Tom laughed.

"Some days I can't think of any reason why I came," her voice was getting weepy.

"I'll check into some place downtown for a studio. I have to go. Not today, though, I'm busy." Tom hung up. Irene felt overwhelmed by time. She got into her nightgown again and watched television. The sky was cold and gray. At three she called Carla to walk, but she wasn't home so she left a message. At three-thirty she got into some old clothes and went out to the shed. The lights were still on and it was warm in the shed. It took a while before it dawned on her why she had left the lights on. The paper on the chair had several sizes of footprints and was ripped at the edges. She put "Le Tub" and "The Carnival Shooting Gallery" away and took out "The Corn Painting" and the first of the "Church Ladies." While she was changing the paper on the chair, Carla walked up behind her.

"Oh, you scared me," Irene said and hurried to hide the chair behind the asparagus bushes.

Carla remained silent and expectant.

"It's silly, really, but I noticed that some of the kids were peaking into the shed, using this old chair, so I put paper on the seat and when there are footprints on the chair, and I know they have seen what is up in the shed, I change it. Like a peep show. Maybe more than is good for them."

"I've never seen your stuff," Carla said.

"Well, look. The light from those lamps is lousy. I bought them to dry the canvases, but take a look." Carla followed Irene into the shed.

"Those look like photographs in the center with paint on them." Carla moved close to the canvas and then backed up to take it in again. At the gallery they had called this style of viewing the yo-yo buyer.

"It is. Don't you recognize some of the women from church, the circle."

"Oh, yes, of course. Mrs. Lawton from the library. And this one, is it Hanny Priggle? What does it mean? Oh my god. This one is really weird. It's like no one is connected. Very interesting. And different. Yes, different. Does it mean something?" Carla pursed her lips, tilted her head, and looked searchingly at Irene.

"No, no it means nothing. It encourages interpretation and frustrates it, because we have created a system of meaning to control experience that finally overwhelms experience. Meaning is imposed, perhaps necessary, but you always have to understand that it is artificial. And then the system we create creates the experience. How do we separate them? Can we? When our line of interpretation is interrupted, there is a chance that we become aware of how it functions, how it promises understanding, but recreates itself over and over again." Irene avoided Carla's unflinching gaze. She ended her speech with her fingers interwoven in her hair Greta Garbo style.

"That's all very interesting, but what I asked was, what does it mean? Like the corncob is sex, right. I can see meanings, but you must have one you are shooting for. It seems like you start with an idea and then get another. And I know it's art so I don't understand it. If I understood it, it wouldn't be art." She gave an apologetic smirk and ambled towards the door.

"Let me change my shoes and we can walk." Irene crossed in front of Carla and jogged off to the house. When she came back Carla was standing cross-armed outside the shed. Irene walked in front of her and locked the door.

"It's good you have something to do." Carla's voice was condescending.

"Yes, it is." Irene walked off towards the street.

"Do people buy those or are they a kind of therapy?" Carla had almost caught up to her.

“I hope people will buy them, but I can’t paint thinking whether they do.”

“No, true. It’s kind of a Robert Kincaid thing.” Carla lunged up beside Irene.

“A who thing?” Irene stopped in her tracks and swung around to Carla.

“A Robert Kincaid thing. You know, in *The Bridges of Madison County*.” Carla glared back at Irene. “It was a compliment, okay?”

They made it past the high school without saying a word. Irene had slowed her pace so Carla could feel the silent treatment.

“When you asked to borrow *Bridges* yesterday, I found it and started reading it again. It’s about two people who have an affair and no one ever finds out until after they’re dead and they still love each other. They love each other so much. And it’s kind of a forbidden thing.” Carla was out of breath when she finished.

Irene slowed her pace again. They walked silently for a minute. By the shaved cornfield Irene stopped. “And the woman’s husband is fucking his secretary.”

“No, that’s someone else’s story, not Francesca’s story.”

Irene tried to control her laughter. When Carla saw her back shaking, she thought Irene was crying and placed a comforting hand on Irene’s shoulder. Irene turned around.

“Sorry, Carla, but sometimes life has so many absurd coincidences. It’s not you.” Irene composed herself and walked a few feet in front of Carla.

“Maybe I could understand, too,” Carla said without trying to catch up to Irene.

“Well, ages ago this guy tried to seduce me by telling me

I was like Francesca." Irene repeated, "ages ago," for Carla's benefit.

"I'm not trying to seduce you." Carla forced out a bewildered laugh.

"Aren't you? If you say you're not, then you're not. And I never said you were." Irene strained to pull away, but Carla had broken into a trot to keep up.

"Someone has to open your eyes."

"Who appointed you?"

"I'm your friend, Irene. I'm your friend." Carla stopped to catch her breath. Irene walked on and when Irene finally looked around, Carla was gone.

She called as soon as she got home. "Carla, I'm sorry. I know about Tom fooling around, or as much as I care to know. I know you were just being a friend."

"I was," Carla said tentatively.

"Let's walk again next week. Not Monday, I have the lawn boy coming over to rake leaves. I'd rather be there to see he does a good job."

"Okay. Bye," Carla whispered.

New York Journal

María Elena wants to rent a car and take a trip up to Vermont, the fall leaf thing. I told her there were enough leaves in Central Park, but I want to get out of the city for a while. Even when I'm gone for only a few days, I come back and everything is new. Maybe she can convince Jens and one of his boyfriends to go with us. James, for example.

My painting is opening up, figures are disappearing, magnificent spaces made of lines and colors that foreground or distance shapes. It is feminine and architectonic, the human figure is there as observer and creator, turning the flat surface of the canvas into canyons, cathedrals of color. María Elena and I bounce off each other, inspiration and adventure. If we go to a good gallery, we tell each other.

Last Saturday Jens and I went to a drag show at a small club, A Night of Firsts, where first lady (female) impersonators put on skits between Jackie B. aka K. aka O., Nancy Reagan, Beth Truman, Mamie Eisenhower, Mary Lincoln, Betty Ford (pre-recovery). Top Girls *in drag with no apologies to Caryl Churchill. Jens said that the good thing about it was that even the big, the fat, and the ugly drag queens could get parts. Mamie must have been six foot seven. Mary Todd Lincoln was a five-foot two-hundred-pound black guy. For once, María Elena didn't want to go out with us.*

Tom thinks María Elena and I are having an affair. I told him it was as likely as he and Jens getting it on. He said he doesn't even like Jens. I said, "What does that matter? We had sex for years." My cleverness makes me stupid. Two friends of María Elena, Carmen and Doris, have been joking with us about our "relationship." Now when they mention it, María Elena says, "Oh we tried that already." They laugh and then get a suspicious look on their faces. Jens thought it was funny when I told him. I would have told that to Tom during better days, but now he would freak out. And it seems to be in my interest to keep him calm.

Friday morning she told Tom about the appointment while he was reading the *Des Moines Register* sports section (Irene claimed it was in that group of sports sections where a woman or gay man did not function as photo editor since the pictures of athletes were uniformly sexless).

"I have shortened it from Charlene's Beauty Plus Unisex to simply Plus Sex."

Tom rustled the newspaper as if it were laughing at the joke. "Don't you think Beauty Uni would be more like it?"

"Yes, but I don't know what it means. I guess you'll finally be getting the woman that your mother always wanted you to have. At least considering I'm what Charlene has to work with." She stared for a few moments at the raised newspaper.

"Why don't you leave my mother alone?" Tom wasn't engaged in the conversation, had barely looked at her since she came downstairs.

Her mouth opened a couple of times to speak. She ran upstairs without saying another word and lay on the bed waiting to hear Tom leave. When the door opened, she sat up to answer if he said goodbye. The door shut.

Journal October 22

Today Tom moved to the other side. Even with all the shit that has happened between us, it was always his mother on one side of a vague fluid line and the two of us on the other. Today suddenly I felt like the line had become dark and straight and that I had never been on the side with Tom, like I woke up in a dream and discovered that all my life I had red hair instead of brown and had never noticed it, that feeling in dreams that makes you question everything else.

I have the urge to cry without the energy to do it. And I don't want to cry over Tom, but over how I have misunderstood our relationship. All those pictures I have cut out from People or Versace models in old New Yorkers that I was going to show Charlene to confound her, the hip joke, now seem like jokes I don't understand and can't explain. Yesterday I thought they were hysterical.

Only a few times since she moved to Pendayhaz, had she borrowed Doris's old car, the Oldsmobile Cutlass. Doris now drove Ralph's last car, a Cadillac Seville. The extra key for the Cutlass hung on the key rack Tom had hung up in the kitchen so Irene could keep track of things. Doris referred to the Cutlass as Irene's car.

"That shed would make a great garage for your Cutlass, but I guess you need it for painting." "If you drove your Cutlass more, I might see you more often."

Irene always called it "your mom's car" when she talked to Tom. "Your mom wants to put her car in the shed." "Driving your mom's car I feel like I'm paddling a barge down a canal."

When she walked over to Doris's to pick up the car that afternoon, Doris was gone and Irene found a Stick-em on the steering wheel of the Cutlass. "I'm glad you found the time. Enjoy. Mom-Doris."

Charlene's Beauty Plus Unisex Salon was in the Meadowlark Mall, which besides Charlene's, included Sam's, a shop that did typewriter and cash register repair, sold used appliances, and had recently begun to sell computer accessories, The Giver's Corner, a gift shop that specialized in bird feeders and lawn ornaments, and a True Value Hardware store. Charlene's was in the corner closest to town and her daughter's pink MaryKay Costmetics Cadillac was parked in front of a large sign hanging from the roof of the shop that said "Charlene's Private Parking."

Two female and a male beautician were standing behind customers. Two women she didn't recognize sat under hair driers; one stoically concentrating on the air in front of her and the other reading *Cosmopolitan*.

"You must be Doris's daughter-in-law." Charlene put her cigarette down and came out of a small business office off the receptionist's desk. Irene caught a glimpse of the low slick red vinyl sofas with a patent leather gleam. The shop had rattan sofas and chairs with large cushions upholstered in fabric with hibiscus and birds of paradise. The walls were covered with green plush wallpaper and tourist posters from Mallorca, Guadalajara, Cancún, and Acapulco. Irene absentmindedly touched the ficus in the entrance to see if it was real.

"I am so so busy today. I have all my people in working. Homecoming and that wedding. When it rains it pours. I did eight people myself this morning." Charlene, who had the pinched face of a cute parakeet, clicked by in her low pink pumps and went to confer with the male hairdresser.

Charlene clicked back to Irene. "Louie says he can take you in about twenty minutes. Doris wasn't one hundred percent positive that you would be in. She said you probably wouldn't mind Louie. Some of the ladies don't like him, so I always ask first." Charlene had the habit of shaking her head back and forth like Betty Boop and exaggerating a dimple, that was now a deep line, by raising her cheeks.

"Don't see any problem." Irene smiled back.

Charlene slipped back into the office and picked up her cigarette. She scrunched up her nose and frowned. "Don't like smoking in the shop. If customers want to, that's okay, until they make it illegal."

Irene sank into one of the rattan chairs with a puff of dust. The smell of permanent solution seemed stronger when she sat down. Outside it began to rain.

"That'll keep the dirt from flying around," Charlene said

coming to the edge of the office with her cigarette extending behind her so it didn't cross the threshold. "Supposed to rain through Monday. When it rains it pours."

"Through Monday?" Irene asked and left The *National Geographic* she had picked up in her lap.

"That's what they say. Through Monday. What do they know? National Guesser Bureau." Charlene snubbed out her cigarette in a tall metal floor ashtray, poking the butt nervously and intently as if she were chasing an insect with it.

"Hm," Irene said and opened the magazine to an article on butterflies.

Charlene stuck her head out from her skinny neck and pursed her lips in what Irene took to be a preamble to confidentiality.

"Now Louie is very good. I have nothing against him. What he does, he does. But sometimes he gives you more information about himself than you really want to know. Just say you don't want to hear it." One of the hair dryers turned off and Charlene lowered her voice. "Just say, I'm not interested, or I got a headache, could you hurry. He's doing me a favor, but I don't mind telling you this."

"Thanks," Irene said without adjusting her voice to the new sound level.

Charlene winked with both eyes and walked without clicking her heals on the floor to one of the women who sat under a hair dryer.

Charlene came back when the young girl with her hair up in French curls walked cautiously to the counter as if a false move might make her hair topple. Louie swept up to Irene and escorted her to the chair.

“Put your purse on the counter, or better, hang it from the knob on the drawer.” Louie waved his hand to the counter in front of the chair.

“I’ll do the knob,” Irene said.

As she was sitting down, Louie looked at her seriously and asked, “Now is Irene like Charlene. I always wondered this. Is Arlene and Irene like Charlene, like women’s names made out of men’s names.”

“I don’t know about Arlene, but I don’t think Irene comes from Ire.”

Louie lifted up her hair in his hand and draped a sheet around her. “You know, like my name. Lois and Louise. They’re different and the same.”

“No, don’t think so,” Irene said. “It means peace in Greek.”

“Your family Greek?” Louie asked showing interest.

“No, no Greek. Swedish, Italian, Danish.” Irene hadn’t been in one of these conversations with a stranger for a long time.

“Wow,” he said as if he were impressed.

“Anything special you want, maybe,” he said as he inspected her hair without apparently paying any attention to her face.

“Maybe something with attitude. Something easy to take care of, a little wild, but not so wild that I would need to have my nose and nipples pierced to make it look okay.” Irene acted as if she weren’t checking Louie’s reaction.

He laughed through his nose in little sniffs. “I came programmed today to do eight hours of the Charlene special. Whoa! Let me change modes.” Louie shook his head like he was a robot and then wheezed at his own joke.

“I’m getting this done for my mother-in-law. I don’t want to make her happy.”

“Oh, yeah, yeah, yeah. You’re Tom Marston’s wife, huh?” He seemed to be only interested in her hair.

“That’s me.”

“He was a hunky guy when he was younger.” Louie grinned as if he knew he might be going too far.

“I’m afraid I got to him too late.”

“And I never got to him at all,” Louie said and took her chin to turn her face left. They both laughed. “I’m from here, but I moved away, about twenty miles. Bigger town. Crandall. I work for a couple shops. Like to start my own place. I’m going to school in Des Moines. Computers. Computers, that’s the future.”

“Probably,” Irene said disappointed at the turn in the conversation. She thought people had stopped saying computers were the future. Was that the line in *The Graduate*? No, it was plastics.

Louie thinned her hair, gave her short bangs that slanted towards her temples. “It’s not a Charlene special. When Charlene’s not looking, I’m going to give you my card. If you want to come to my house, I can cut your hair cheaper. Don’t tell Charlene.”

“Thanks. I won’t.”

Louie slipped the card into her purse. “There are eyes everywhere,” he said and Charlene suddenly appeared behind them. Irene had smelled the old smoke before she heard Charlene sashaying.

“The Mexican girl who comes in on Fridays to do nails couldn’t make it today. Her car wouldn’t start because of the rain she said. Rain didn't start until five minutes ago and she was supposed to be here two hours ago. You'll have to take a rain check."

"That seems to be the theme today, rain," Irene said.

"Louie, Fern Gregor is waiting. She didn't want you. I told her she'd have to wait two hours for anyone else." Her chin seemed to recede even more and her nose stretch out so she looked more like a chicken than a parakeet.

"I'll do my Warren Beatty in *Shampoo*." Louie sent a sour smile to Charlene and then looked over at Fern Gregor who had her lips out in an angry pout.

"No, baby, just shut up and cut. Keep thinking, shut up and cut." Charlene strode almost on her tiptoes to the front and then with a bow and extended arm ushered Fern Gregor over to Louie.

Irene said hello, but Fern Gregor didn't break her pout to answer.

"I have some of those little fold up rain bonnets. Only two dollars. Should I put that on your mother-in-law's bill?" Charlene looked nervously at Louie while she talked.

Irene checked her wallet and found that she had only forty-five dollars in cash."Could I write a check for the bonnet and get a little cash?"

"Oh, sure,"Charlene said and waited for Irene to write it out.

All three hair dryers were on again, but Charlene lowered her voice. "I've been in the beauty business a long time so I been around a lot of those guys." She nodded towards Louie who was silently testing Mrs. Gregor's hair by lifting it and letting it fall. "You might like them, but you can never trust them."

"Hm," Irene said as she took twenty-five dollars in change.

She walked over to Louie and handed him a five. As she left she waved to Charlene who was reclining on the red vinyl sofa in the office. She lifted herself up on an elbow and waved back with her cigarette.

It was still raining so she drove the car home instead of taking it back to Doris's two-car garage. She looked at herself in the rearview mirror, taking off the two-dollar rain bonnet for a better look. The rain seemed to hit the windshield like melted wax. When there was a lull in the deluge, she made a run for the house, fiddled with the key, dropped it, and shivered when she finally got into the dark kitchen. She took out forty dollars from her wallet and put it in the sketchbook between two caricatures of Doris.

New York Journal

There are a few complications with the apartment. It looks pretty sure that I'll get it. I met the landlord, but he returned my check for the first month. Where do you get a forged birth certificate? Tom knows how to pull off a scam, but I don't trust him. Never trust a disappointed lover. If they can't fuck you one way, they will another.

Both María Elena and I have some private commissions so I guess we have money for the time being. María Elena is talking about getting a part-time job, a little security.

I got off the subway after my stop and walked down Flatbush to Atlantic Avenue. The weather was wonderful and there seemed to be twice as much sunshine in Brooklyn as in Manhattan, openness. How close can you get to the center before you stop moving, before you lose the centrifugal force of the edge. And how far out of the center can you get before you spin out or only see a blur. Huh? With that sentence I think I just flew out to Elizabeth,

New Jersey.

Chago went back to P.R. He's back. I called him to help me one of the days María Elena was at her part-time job. He told me he was happy where he was living now. But I still think he wants to crash at the studio. I want him to know that I am in control. I told him I didn't care whether he loved me or not, whether or not he was going to die without me. I told Jens about him. He showed up as Chago was leaving to get a glimpse of the young stud. Jens promised not to tell María Elena, but I can't always trust him, so maybe I want her to know. He didn't think Chago was that cute or that young. Sour grapes.

This New York is not the dream world I imagined it would be. Makeover of the past? A future without conflict would be boring. The comforting realm of past refashioned or erased and possibility. The past is the impossible, the future is possibility.

"Sixty percent chance of rain all weekend and a fifty percent chance the beginning of next week. This system seems to have stalled over us for the time being and is dumping rain that we really need." Irene turned the television off.

Tom got home at seven-thirty. Irene had prepared chicken curry which Tom would eat, but didn't like.

"Do I sniff revenge," he said.

Irene opened a box in the extra bedroom and began unpacking it so she looked busy. "Curry, Tom. What you smell is curry. Revenge is a Midwest hot dish, slash casserole, that seems so innocent because it smells of nothing and then tastes like nothing, too." Irene concentrated on sorting the contents of the box so she could avoid looking at Tom.

"You're on my mother again. Take it out on your faithless

husband and not on his poor mother."

"Huh? Your mother? She's impervious." Irene thumbed through a notebook and then tossed it into the small wastepaper basket next to the desk.

"We don't even have to eat, now. The wedding rehearsal dinner is at eight. Your hair looks weird. It'll grow out, right?" He turned away from her.

"I'm going to eat. And why do you and the rest of the town have to constantly bring up your sex life to me?" She looked up from the box to see how Tom would react.

He was already at the top of the steps and stopped. "It's not working out, Irene. It's not working out." He plodded slowly down the steps.

"Whatever that means," she said when she knew he couldn't hear.

When she came downstairs there was a dirty plate on the table with a little curry and rice left on it. Tom sat in the living room. "Did you eat crow?" she asked.

"No, it was good. It was a change. Was it really crow?"

"So, you think my hair is weird." She put rice and curry on a plate and put it in the microwave.

"Who did it? It doesn't look like a Charlene-do." She was glad that this was a kitchen living room conversation and they weren't facing each other.

"No, some gay guy named Louie did it. He seemed to know you, or at least your body."

"Oh Louie Peterson. I used to beat him up in the locker room after gym. My gay bashing phase." Tom spoke with a nonchalance that upset her.

“Was it like a thing between the two of you?” She took the plate out of the microwave and set it loudly on the table.

“No, it was usually a group thing. Five or six of us would get together and make Louie eat potato chips we stepped on, or smear his dick with Ben-Gay that they kept in big jars in the locker room. The older guys did it to us, so we did it to the younger kids and to Louie. You know, when in Rome. Peer pressure.” Tom seemed to be talking between sentences in the magazine he was reading.

Irene stared down at her plate. “He told me when you were young, you were a hunk, but he didn’t say of what, you know, a hunk of shit, a hunk of, you name it.”

“Hey, I straightened out. I went on to become a Republican.”

Irene laughed. “You’re sick, Tom, sick.”

“Do you want to take mom’s car back? I’ll follow you and give you a ride back. We better get ready for the dinner.” Tom went to the doorway.

“As soon as I finish eating.” She lowered her head and began to eat.

She was glad to be alone in the car with Tom following. She said, “This is as connected as we get,” and then felt melodramatic. “Keep our relationship to meetings at stop lights where we both know the rules.”

Journal October 25

On the way to the golf club where they had the reception, Tom passed the old bank building on main street where the discount store is now and pointed to some second floor windows. He says that I could get a studio there cheap and he might even be able to get me some commissions if I did cows and sunflowers and rolling hills. He must have been looking around in the shed, because he told me he liked the corner (Grant Wood) of my corn painting. Maybe he's right. I'm good at copying other styles. Find out what's selling around here and do it. Then I could slip a little subversion into each painting.

I was glad to see Doris. Kristie Crawford came up to say hello. Most people here I nod to, but don't talk to. "They're so shy." I used to think of Garrison Keillor every time Tom said this. I tried to explain to Tom why I didn't like Keillor; hokey, perhaps a little sinister by creating a feeling of superiority in a bunch of Midwest provincials by holding up for endearing ridicule an even more provincial Midwest fantasy small-town past. María Elena and I listened to it one Saturday when we were painting. She didn't get it at all. Only true Americans can appreciate Keilor. They could make it part of the naturalization test. The rehearsal banquet was bordering on becoming a Prairie Home Companion skit. *There must be a book of speeches you can buy for these activities. Or maybe they are like fairytales, repeated so often that you have to tell them to children to get a fresh audience. There was the Ann-Landers-communicate speech. The supposedly funny most-marriages-fail-because-one-of-them-squeezes-the-toothpaste-from-the-middle speech. People laugh like they've never heard it before. The trick is to say it as seriously as possible, but Doris's brother Richard did the toothpaste speech and kept interjecting his horse-snort laugh which was the only funny thing in the whole evening. Jens had this goofy boyfriend Clark, who insisted on telling jokes and always ruined them by laughing uncontrollably right before the punch line. I thought of him as Uncle Dick spoke.*

Doris didn't say anything about the hair, but I felt out of place. I'm sure because of the hair Tom made an even bigger deal about what I was wearing. I put on a black sleeveless dress with a black shoulder cape. It looked great with the hair. Black fishnet stockings and low heels. A choker that looked like a tattoo.

"Getting ready for Halloween in the Village?" He said that as he came out of the bathroom in his underwear on his way to the guest bedroom where he keeps his clothes now. Then there were a couple of "Oh Gods" addressed to the air. I ended up wearing one of the suits I used to wear to the gallery, trendy but conservative. A cheap imitation of money. Maybe I'll put the black dress on again on Monday to rake leaves.

During the open bar, Tom disappeared. I followed Doris around, always a foot behind her so she would do the talking, ask people if they remembered me, then we'd move on. Almost a social stations of the cross. There were a few women there whom I met the first month in town, went to their houses for coffee, got the house tour, vague gossip, recipes and never went back. Clara Henderson, Jane Lambert, Sandy Hessbesser. Those were the meetings with "Oh, I've been so busy. You have to come over again some time (never)." I didn't call them back after I went to their houses, had really no place to invite them, other than my own private warehouse. They bored me to tears. I must not have felt much of a need for boredom at the time.

About an hour into the open bar and more country western music than Doris could handle, Uncle Richard came up and said that Tom had left and Doris was supposed to take me home. For the oh-God third time Richard asked me if I didn't think his speech was pretty funny. It gave me an opportunity to practice insincerity which helped cover how pissed I was at Tom. There seemed to be a pity party of women who clustered together at a table by the trophy case and followed me with their sheep eyes as Doris and I left.

Doris told me she was disappointed because the color of the dress I was wearing for the family picture after the wedding was wrong so I couldn't stand next to her. Really, it was the right color, blue, but the wrong shade, navy. After the picture, I pleaded a slight case of the flu, not too far off. Tom took me home and went back. It was raining again.

Tom and I had a chilly breakfast. At one point he started yelling about the clutter on the kitchen counters. "How can you live like this?"

"What's this? A guilt fit?" He put the newspaper over his face for five minutes, then asked if I wanted to go to church. I didn't answer and five minutes later he was gone. Usually I get the lecture about fitting in, my being there is good for business. I was expecting him home to change and go out and play golf, his Sunday thing. He seems to live in this David Hockney world of good clothes and golf clubs, of pictures that accumulate but don't connect. It definitely is not Norman Rockwell. Maybe all worlds have to be fictionalized to exist.

I keep thinking that the solution to my life will happen at 3:30 on Monday if it doesn't rain. Instead of under the cover of rain, this has to be under the cover of fine weather. Perhaps my life is like The Crying of Lot 49, *the story stops at 3:00 p.m. on Monday and no one ever finds out what happens. I and everyone else in this story become completely fictional. All the loose ends remain loose, unlike real life where some loose ends become solutions sowing more loose ends, or like detective novels where mysteries can always be explained. Jens had a friend visiting once, an English lesbian who wrote murder mysteries, and I happened to tell her that I hated mysteries. The characters were meaningless after the plot was solved. It was a glorified GRE analytical question. I didn't see Jens again while she was there.*

Now if I wrote about myself in third person would I know myself better? Could I write about myself as a minor character in someone else's life? The Doris Marston story where I appear as a social liability at wedding rehearsal dinners, my hair part of their own parody of the New York sophisticate. In another chapter I can be the daughter-in-law who will not become her buddy. In the Joey Towner story, a picaresque novel, I am the lonely abandoned wife waiting to be hustled. And the Carla story where I play a more central role, at least in her inner life. And don't forget the Tom Marston story. Here is where I am the obstacle in the happy resolution of true love. I am becoming only a character in other people's lives. Housewife syndrome. Maybe it started when Jens got sick and María Elena and I. . .

Irene had heard the knocking before but thought that it was the Crawfords working on the deck they were putting up next to their red beech tree. When she finally realized that it was the front door, she closed the notebook and went downstairs. Fern Gregor was pacing in front of the steps to the kitchen. When Fern climbed the steps again, her fist raised to pound the door, Irene flung the door open so for a second it looked like Fern was about to hit Irene.

"I want to talk to you. I want to talk to you now. And you better have some answers." Fern had a big nose and baby fat cheeks with webs of blood vessels showing through her pink skin.

"It was probably wrong, but I told no one about our little talk several months ago. I am not a gossip. But I can't have it. You leave the children alone."

Irene thought of the chair and the paintings. "Well, I have a right to privacy. If kids come into my yard and sneak around peeking at my things."

"I don't know what you are talking about. All I know is that my youngest son Joey came home crying an hour ago and I finally got him to tell me that you chased him into the rain sewer and kept him in there. He was crying so much that I couldn't get it out of him. Scared to death. You're a grown woman. He's a kid. I'm going to talk to your husband." Fern Gregor's head twitched as she spoke.

"I haven't been out of this house all day. With people like

you . . . . " Irene stopped herself from saying any more.

"Like me? Like me? What is that supposed to mean? You're the one who hits strange kids, chases them. People say, they say . . . . " Words abandoned her.

"I repeat. I haven't been out of this house all day. The way you talk about people, it's no wonder your kids are scared." Irene was trembling.

Fern retreated a step. "Do you swear to that? So help me if I find out from a neighbor that they have even seen you on these steps, you're in big trouble."

"Listen, I don't know why your son thought that, what you and everyone else has been telling him about me to scare him, but I wasn't out today. You come over here and make a fool out of yourself, waste my time, threaten me, and . . . " Irene couldn't think of anything else to say.

"Just leave my kids alone." Fern faltered a little as she walked up the sidewalk. Twice she stopped as if she would say something else, then finally shook her head and walked away.

Irene noticed that one of the arms of Fern's sweater seemed to never have been finished. Her brown pumps were faded and the heel on one of them was gone.

She sat on the steps breathing deeply. When she got up to go in, she saw Kristie Crawford in her yard, was going to ignore her, but raised her arm to her waist in a feeble greeting. Kristie sauntered towards her, slowly swinging one leg out, then the other, as if she were approaching a strange dog. "Got hell from Fern, huh?"

Irene felt she was going to cry and wished that Kristie would go away. "Yeah, guess so."

"Her husband drinks," Kristie said in a stage whisper. "And

her father-in-law is senile. Five kids. Doesn't have the patience for kids. Finally gets the kids out of diapers and now the old man. Whew!"

Irene shook her head gravely.

"All I want to say is, you know," here Kristie bobbed her head from side to side as if she were picking from various possibilities, "is well, with a grain of salt."

"Did you hear what we said. I mean what she said?" Irene asked as Kristie backed off in a reverse version of her approach.

"Let's just say, she's not soft spoken, okay, okay?" Kristie gave a perky smile and on her second "okay" turned and walked away.

When Irene calmed down, she called Doris. "Have you seen Tom today?"

"Oh, Irene, we missed you at the wedding reception."

"I wasn't feeling well. Tom, do you know where he is? I need to ask him something?"

"Maybe I can help." Doris's words came out as if she hadn't talked for a long time.

"Ah, no, it has something to do with taxes. My taxes." She knew that Doris had, or pretended to have a dread of anything connected to taxes and called Tom constantly about bank statements and bond reports.

"Well, then it can't be too urgent. Those aren't due until April." Doris spoke more clearly.

"You see, I had everything out and . . . "

"Of course. Well, you know me. I'm a complete loss at those things." Doris sighed as if this depressed her.

“So you haven’t seen Tom.” Irene tried to keep her tone neutral.

“Oh, even if I had, he wouldn’t tell me where he’s going. You’d think he could stop by once in a while. That man has no patience.”

“Well, if you see him . . . “

Doris cut in, “I will. But he hasn’t even come over to pick up his shirts.”

“Didn’t he get them on Thursday?”

“I wasn’t finished.” She remembered that Tom had planned on picking them up.

“When he runs out of ironed ones he’ll be over. I have to . . . “

“Well, let me go then.”

Irene listened to hear Doris set the receiver down and then put her own down.

She went upstairs to look at “Ralph’s Life.” Ralph holding baby Tom. Ralph and Tom at Tom’s college graduation. Ralph and Tom in the office together. Ralph and Irene at her wedding.

The box she had sorted on Friday while she talked to Tom was still in two piles. It was impossible to figure out what criteria she had been using and she filled the box again. She happened to glance at the wastepaper basket, pulled out the appointment book and put it on the desk.

She opened the notebook, looked at the last incomplete sentence, then wrote on the next line, “A relationship is only as stable as the least interested partner.”

Carla was surprised to hear from her. "Well, yeah, why not. If it clears up, we could go for a walk. I just had a long talk on the phone with Pearl's Jewels, that company that does home jewelry sales. I can tell you about it. How does four sound?"

The dashboard had bright red Stick-ems, though a couple of the sayings were the same as when they had been yellow. "You are what you produce." ". . . he was still watching the light." " . . . she reached to find them, somewhere north of Middle River in Iowa."

"How was the wedding?" Carla asked after a minute of silence.

"Okay. I didn't stay for the reception. The rehearsal dinner was enough."

"Hm," Carla seemed intent on her driving. She pulled into the football field parking lot where Carla wanted to start the walk today. "I've been reading *The Bridges of Madison County.* I love that book. You have to read it. It would change you."

"You think so?" Irene was already regretting that she had called Carla.

"I finished it last night and stayed up a few hours writing out Stick-ems from the book. I must have a hundred. I know those sayings are going to help me make my jewelry business a success." Carla puffed as she did warm-up stretches.

"I didn't know it was that kind of book." Irene took the stretching far less seriously.

"Philosophy, life, feelings, it has them all." She grunted as she did a forward lunge.

"That covers a lot," Irene said.

"Your hair, it's different."

Irene surveyed the sky for signs of more rain. "Yeah, I went to Charlene's like Doris wanted."

"But I mean different different. You know, really different." Irene stood very still as Carla stared into her face and lifted Irene's hair in her fingers.

"There was this gay guy at Charlene's, extra help. He did it. I told him I wanted something to get revenge on my mother-in-law." Irene stepped back and walked towards the road. Carla stood for a moment looking at Irene. Irene reached the road waited for her.

"He told me that he knew Tom from high school. Said that Tom was a hunk." Irene slowed her pace so Carla could keep up.

"God, he told you that. He told you that at Charlene's? What did you say to him?" Carla stopped and let her mouth drop.

"I told him I wish I had known him when he was hunky. I got him too late." Irene walked backwards as she spoke to Carla and then turned and walked on.

"That was funny. Doesn't seem like old Tom is having much trouble attracting women with his unhunky body." Carla laughed confidentially.

"Who knows?" Irene was dismissive. "Do you know Louie Peterson?"

"Oh yeah. What a fag!" Carla laughed again.

"Tom told me he used to beat him up in the locker room, in his gay bashing days. It must be hard being gay or lesbian here." Irene slowed down so Carla was next to her.

They walked slowly and silently until they reached the first corner of the section. Irene looked over at Carla as they turned the corner.

"Well, if you parade it in front of everyone's face the way he does, of course, it's hard."

"Of course," Irene said and hoped that Carla could hear the anger in her voice.

"But, you know, it's not something you have to share with everyone. I mean people who aren't like that don't go around talking about what they do in bed, do they? I think it's fine if it's kept quiet." Irene walked ahead for a few minutes and then turned to wait so she could observe Carla. Her face was intent and she looked off at an abandoned house that had sunk to one side. When she reached Irene, she beamed a quick false smile.

"Have you heard anything about the weather tomorrow? I'm supposed to rake leaves with the kid who cuts the lawn." Irene followed a few feet behind Carla as she picked up the pace.

"It's supposed to rain real hard tonight and then be clear tomorrow. That's what it said on the radio on the way over to your house. Who's helping you?" Carla was more relaxed.

"Joey Towner. Lucille Towner's son. She works in Tom's office. You know her, don't you," Irene said and paced away from Carla.

Irene managed to leisurely read Carla's Stick-ems on the driver's side before Carla reached the parking lot. Carla climbed into the driver's seat.

"I always need that last spurt. It makes my lungs work," Irene said and slid slightly down in the seat.

"It's in the glove compartment. Get it." Carla sucked on her false tooth.

Irene was confused, but Carla's voice was harsh and brittle. Irene struggled with the knob and when it opened a dog-eared paperback edition of The *Bridges of Madison County* fell out on the floor.

"It is the most beautiful and truthful book I have ever read. It was a bestseller everywhere, Europe, Japan. Everywhere." Carla's voice lost its power and broke.

"In Iran?"Irene asked and inspected the cover.

"Look on the back. I think it says everywhere." She reached over to help Irene find the blurb on the back cover.

"Oh, here it is," Irene said and Carla looked towards the road again.

"One hundred and sixty-five weeks on the bestseller list."

"One hundred and sixty-four," Irene said correcting her.

Carla shook her head and sniffed. "Read it and you won't be so concerned about numbers."

In a moment they were before Irene's house. "Okay, I will," Irene said as a kind of goodbye.

Tom had come home late, crawled into bed with an irritating nonchalance and his skin had been cold and wet from the rain. When he touched her again, he was warm and sweaty. Then he left their bed for the guest room. The next morning she acted like she was asleep until Tom left. It had rained so much the night before that the ground was spongy and her shoes made rhythmic sucking sounds as she walked to the shed. The sky was high and the easterly wind had picked up wet leaves and pasted them to the side of the house. As she was trying to go to sleep listening to the rain pounding on the roof, she had thought of Fern Gregor and decided to put the chair next to the trash barrel. She thought of the rain from the night before as she pulled it out of the mud where it had sunk several inches under the weight of the children.

She had taken the painting notebook with her into the shed, looked at each of the canvases that she had begun, and made notes for changes. It was the type of activity, like making shopping lists, that she did when she didn't want to think about something else.

After lunch she made her bed and then went outside to walk around the yard. A few low areas were still too wet to rake, where Mrs. Fliplak's son-in-law had removed some diseased peach trees when he was trying to sell the house, and in front of the old entrance to the cellar. At two o'clock the yard looked drier, though around the cellar it hadn't improved much. Taking a shower, she laughed at herself when she thought of ironing her blue jeans. She put on Outdoor Makeup Skin Toner that she had bought in Crandall. On the box it said, "Active Beauty. Glow in the great outdoors." "Radiate raking," Irene said as she dabbed her face and neck with small dots of toner from the tube. She looked at herself in the mirror. "You are going to eat him up." She saw herself as a woman-tiger in a Francesco Clemente painting: elegant, artificial, self-consciously sexual.

She went out to the yard at 3:20 and took her rake out of the shed. Her hands were still sticky from the hand cream when she put on the garden gloves. She began a long row of leaves. She raked the thick layer of leaves that had collected in the flower beds along the east side of the house. The soil under them was rich black and full of centipedes and oval beetles. She suspected that some of the leaves were from last year since they were already packed into wet clumps. A large clump slid away from the wall and she crouched down to smell the fresh earth. She knew it was partially an act and also an attempt to make herself concentrate on the moment, to relax into it. As she stood up she looked at her wrist watch. 3:50.

She left the rake next to the line of leaves and sat down on the kitchen steps. Her hands felt cool when she took off the gloves, but soon became cold. Fern Gregor hurried by and came back a few minutes later. Kristie Crawford waved as she loaded the kids into the car and as she drove by stopped. “Good day for raking. Maybe a little wet.” Her kids stared straight ahead as if they were suffering from their mother’s constant social interactions.

It was 4:15 when she picked up the rake again. Instead of continuing the line of leaves, she began to rake it into a pile.

“You started?” She didn’t know how Joey had gotten behind her without her hearing him.

“You startled me. I thought you had decided not to work.” She pulled the rake in long energetic strokes.

“Let me get a rake. They’re in the cellar.” He lifted the rickety double wooden doors that folded over the old entrance to the cellar.

“Is there water on the floor?” Tom had made a big deal about the flooding when he was negotiating to buy the house.

“A little,” Joey said. She heard him push in the door that had been put in when the cellar was expanded to a basement and a stairs was built from the kitchen fifteen years ago. She started to tell him to go through the kitchen. Tom warned her about opening that door since it was so warped that it was hard to shut.

She was too agitated to rake and went to the shed to check the lock. It looked like it might rain again. She picked up the rake and stood leaning on it. She had planned a speech based on a list she made in her painting notebook that morning. He was to rake on the other side of the house and bag leaves for both of them. She went over it again. It seemed like a foreign language she had to practice to be sure that she would not become too nervous and say the wrong thing.

She finished a foot of another row of leaves. Joey was still in the cellar. She went to the cellar stairs. The paint on the underside of the doors was chipping off in large green chunks. The edges closest to her were covered with green mold and toadstools. At the bottom of the steps she looked back at the blue sky and peered through the door until her eyes adjusted to the light. "Joey." She cleared her throat to call louder. "Joey." There was still no answer. She heard him snickering and then with a short sigh he caught his breath and became quiet.

"Joey, this is silly. What is going on?"

The bare lightbulb hanging from the twisted asbestos wrapped cords dangled in the doorway to the root cellar. It swung slightly. Through the clear glass of the bulb, she saw the filament flail.

"Joey, the rakes are not in there." She didn't expect him to answer. Her own voice calmed her. Something fell softly onto the ground in the root cellar and a few beetles scuttled across the door jam and scurried along the wall behind an old rug.

She was almost to the doorway. "Joey?"

"Yes," his voice was low. She looked down at his feet as he moved into the doorway and saw his pants around his ankles. Only the toes of his old athletic shoes were showing. He shook as he controlled his laughter. He had an erection and his face was covered with a rubber Halloween mask, the devil with horns and instead of a pitchfork in his hand, he had a rake. He arched his back so his erection stuck out.

"You like my Halloween costume." Now he laughed so loudly that Irene thought of trying to shut the cellar door.

"What do you think you're doing? I called you over to rake leaves."

"Let's go upstairs," he said.

"You haven't raked any leaves," she said.

"Let's go upstairs," he repeated and when he tried to move he tripped on his jeans and fell toward her. As she was trying to hold him up, he rubbed his erection against her side.

"Upstairs," he said and she moved towards the basement holding his elbow to lead him. The basement was a separate room and had been built without windows. A little light came from the bulb in the storm cellar, but when they turned toward the stairs, it was dark except for a small line of light that came under the kitchen door.

"You're going to have to pull your pants up to go up." She rubbed her open hands across his chest and down to his thighs. He pulled her in towards him and humped.

"The devil has goat feet and humps like a goat."

"Pull up your pants."

"Okay, but I'm keeping the mask on. Until it gets too hot." He broke into a fit of laughing.

"Don't laugh," she said like she were talking to a child.

"Huh?" he said and they moved cautiously up the stairs.

She imagined that they were on a balance and with each step they came closer to tipping the scales. She guided him with one hand, held the rail with the other. She listened to her foot slowly and deliberately move to the next step, then her other foot follow and come down like a methodic beat of music. Then Joey came up, exaggerating his clumsiness, pushing into her. Then she moved methodically again.

"You know I can't see shit in this mask." His hand grabbed one of her breasts hard and she gasped and grabbed his hand.

"Okay, I'm sorry."

"What's up," Joey asked.

Irene had stopped at the top step. She looked down at the light seeping under the door. She opened it slowly, half expecting to see Fern's face peeping in the small rectangular window in the door. The kitchen seemed so plain and real, aluminum and Formica.

"Can I take my pants down until we get to the next stairs?"

"No." She pulled him up the last step and into the kitchen. The mask was porous rubber and the paint had come off where Joey had folded it to get it into his jeans pocket. There were two little holes for the eyes and a slit for the mouth. He had beads of sweat on his chest. When they reached the stairs, he stopped and faced her. He had forced his tongue out the mouth slit and chuckled. He shook his head and then moved a hand to the mask to line up the holes with his eyes.

When they reached the bed, Irene undressed and Joey sat on the edge of the bed to take off his shoes and pants.

"Why don't you take that thing off?" She walked around the bed to the other side and pulled the covers back.

"Why? You want to fuck without a rubber?" He laughed at his own joke. "No mask. Bare."

She sat stiffly. Joey lay on his back and scooted over to her.

"You know I'm clean. You know it," Joey pleaded.

He rubbed her back, came up with both hands from her stomach to her breasts. "You know I won't come in you."

She imagined herself out of control, delirious with passion, begging him to put on a condom. The idea of being out of control excited her. She stretched out across the bed. "That's dangerous. Dangerous for both of us. Really dangerous."

"Hey, I'm clean." He caught the chin of the mask on her left nipple and pulled it off.

"How bad do you want it?," he asked and placed his knees inside hers. "Bad enough to do it without a condom?"

"No," she said and he pushed his knees apart and moved up.

"No?" he said and slid up into her. "No?" He smiled and then buried his head in her shoulder. "You know it's different. You know that, don't you?"

"Yes, I do," she said and had no idea what she was answering.

"I could pop it off right now," he said and rolled over on his back with her following him.

"No," she said and pulled herself off and lay down next to him and stared at the ceiling.

"Just this once. Come on. Just this once. You know you want to."

"Well," she said. She watched herself and thought of how this person was incapable of making decisions, like she was hanging from a thread, her outer skin and face were thread and her flesh was a bobbin that twirled as the thread unraveled and she became a white core.

"Come on. You know you want it. You know."

She thought she would resist for a while to heighten her sense of being lost, a fight for control to make her lack of control more sensual. Then she happened to see the devil mask on the floor like a collapsed head. The horns had crumbled paint on the dull pink rubber and the large nose was maroon.

When she turned back, he was ripping open the package of a rubber and nodding his head anxiously as he rolled it on. He moved his tongue from her knees up along her inner thighs.

She took a deep breath and closed her eyes. She saw lines of red clouds pouring over an embankment.

"You going to let me take the rubber off." He thrust harder. Her body received the assaults between her legs and at her hips, then they rippled through her body. She tightened against them.

"Oh yeah, oh yeah. You going to let me take the rubber off." This time he hissed in her ear.

"Yes. Go ahead. Go ahead. Yes. You shouldn't." She repeated words in no logical order. She turned her head to the side and folded the pillow over her face. She thought she could hear the roar of the red clouds now.

"Whew!" he said and jumped out of bed still hard. He threw the condom on the floor and walked to the blinds. For a moment Irene thought they might be open and sprung up to look, then fell back. He stuck two fingers between the slats and spread them to look out.

"It's almost dark already. I can't get anything done. You could help me out with the car again. And if you pay me for raking, I'll come back and do it. I know where everything is."

"You didn't really do any raking." She felt like she had been broken and was trying to pull the parts of her body together.

"I was busy. I'll do it." He laughed.

He didn't look at her when she got out of the bed to get the money. She smiled sardonically at the caricatures of Doris as she took the money out. Twenty-five for raking and the forty for the car, three twenties and a five. She stood for a while in the guest bedroom and folded the money up to half the size of a postage stamp. When she walked back in, he was pulling his pants on. She stood by the door and watched him lace up and tie his shoes. He hopped across the bed to pick up the mask. As he hurried by her, she pressed the folded bills into his hand.

She heard him stumble and swear when he ran down the basement stairs and a moment later he drove off roaring the engine of his Pontiac Firebird. She picked the used rubber up off the rag rug. It felt eerily warm and human, and she thought of the mask.

Journal October 26

I went to bed early, a couple of hours before Tom got home. I didn't want to listen to his questions about the yard; if Joey had come, if we got the work done. But I couldn't sleep. I feel like I am with a stranger when I am alone. Lying in bed, it seems to be worse. When I heard Tom's drunk snore, I got up to listen, sat cross legged on the floor outside his bedroom. I guess it has been decided that we don't sleep together anymore. If I say anything, I can just hear Tom tell me, "But wasn't that what WE wanted, isn't that what WE decided." And I won't argue because though I never decided anything, I have the feeling that it is inevitable.

It was good to sit there and listen to something outside myself, behind the door, mysterious. I imagined what Tom was dreaming, wondered if Joey in his mask flashed into his mind and had to be explained in a dream story. Is there any fluidity between minds on a level at which we are not conscious? Do we know everything in our dreams that is hidden from us when we are awake? I didn't want Tom to know anything. I wanted him to be that body that I heard behind the door, sadly encapsulated, comfortingly contained. I wanted the door to get thicker and thicker one moment, and then the next wished it was a thin sheet of ice that could shatter by tapping it with my finger. Then these metaphors seemed so pathetic in the complexity of our years together.

And maybe because it is so complex and I can't see any action without its disadvantages that I do nothing, or do nothing but wait for the walls to fall. How much of life is simply waiting until the boat stops at a dock and I can get off and get on another boat? I am on the Tom boat, and for six years I seemed to be satisfied with the view from the boat, but now I see that it is going in the wrong direction. María Elena and Jens jumped boat more easily.

I took the notebook downstairs to the kitchen to avoid the sound of Tom. When I am wandering around the house, getting antsy, I can wish for him to call and when I hear his voice on the phone, it is like I am lying down and someone put a heavy stone on my chest and I can't move my hands to push it off. When he's home we avoid each other, meet for meals where we ask questions and don't listen to the answers. We play social engagement. Yet it seems important to play that, to not admit that we mean nothing to each other or worse.

I've never gotten used to rooms and so much space. In the apartments Tom and I had in New York, closets counted as rooms. Now my consciousness is never concentrated. It is seeping into some other space. I see myself waiting in another room and when I walk in there, especially if it is picked up and clean in the way Tom wants, I am surprised to see the room so indifferent to me.

I put the journal in the kitchen drawer, dug through it to look at Joey's note and as quietly as possible opened the door to the basement, turned on the light. Why was I going down there? When we first moved in, Tom talked of finishing it: a small gym, a workshop, a game room with a billiard table. But the floors are still damp, the lighting dreamlike, never reaching the corners. For a few moments I listened for mice scurrying, beetles finding darkness again, spiders walking on their stilts to the edge of the web, as if any of this would make a sound. I shut the door slowly. My mind exaggerated the creaking. I imagined the Crawfords waking to listen, Tom bolting out of bed. When it closed, I stood on the top step feeling perverse and sexual. My footsteps going down must have sounded like my footsteps going up with Joey behind me and I stopped to imagine Joey dragging his feet, stumbling into me with his naked body, grabbing me and laughing under the mask. "Unheard sounds are sweetest."

I had this funny image of myself dressed in a loose toga, maybe open to the waist, entering a cave to worship Priapus. Then along the wall I saw the piles of old rugs that Mrs. Fliplak had left when she moved. They looked like mummies leaning against the wall that I might disturb, that knew everything about me. I closed my eyes and waited, opened my eyes up and played the part of the sensible woman, whispered, "I'm going to get rid of that junk," as if I came down to the basement at two in the morning to plan a cleanup.

But it didn't cross my mind to go back upstairs. I was trying out ways of seeing myself. The practical viewer who invented practical reasons for going to the basement. "That table would be great in the shed." "Mice poison. Get mice poison." The amused viewer. "What in the hell are you doing?" "Some kid scratches you between the legs and you flip out." The worried viewer. "What does this mean? Why can't I control myself? What got into me?" And the voices seemed to play off each other. So the practical voice said, "This place needs a few windows, like next to the furnace." The amused voice said, "Great, so you and Joey can fuck for the neighborhood." The worried voice said, "Why can't I just shut up?" The amused in second-person, the worried first-person, the practical third-person. I didn't plan that.

Just before the door to the old cellar the floor above creaked, or a tree branch did. I froze and thought that my heart had stopped. I began to sweat and shiver. I saw Tom standing above me, waiting for another sound, searching for me with big gray eyes. Then I imagined that Joey had come back and was waiting in the other room, giggled at the thought of my shock when I saw him. He had called me on a subconscious level and this was to be a part of my humiliation.

The furnace kicked in and under the cover of its hum, I stumbled on. It was pitch dark in the cellar, even with the door to the rest of the basement wide open, and I wandered with a hand out in front of me, thinking of beetles running away from my path, or confusedly towards me and expected at any moment to feel one run up my leg or over my hand as I felt my way to the root cellar light. The walls were damp and cold.

I was almost used to the light when I found the doorway to the root cellar and turned in. I put my hands out in front of me to look for the bulb, careful not to move my hands too fast, make the bulb swing. I pictured Joey in the room, thought my fingers might move across his face, that I would feel his hips arch out and his cock shove against me. I closed my eyes to turn on the light switch, could see the red light that filtered through the blood in my eyelids, opened them to the empty room, here and there potatoes on the floor, shriveled up and long white eyes forking from them. There was a condom. I crouched down on my haunches to inspect it--strawberry flavor--and read the expiration date. It might have fallen out of his pants when he pulled them down, or he might have thrown it there, knowing that I would come back.

It's impossible to tell how long I stayed there. I reached a place in myself that was solid, but no consolation. I remember sighing, like this is what there is. And sighing louder and louder until I became conscious of the sound I was making. I kicked the condom between some broken crock jars. Going up the stairs, I wished I had picked it up, thought I would later.

I stood for a long time by the door at the top of the steps before I opened it. "Tom is on the other side," I chanted and wondered how much of this I really believed and how much was a dramatization that I had created, a plot that had carried me down into the cellar and now back.

In the kitchen, I looked at the sink and the counters, got up from the table and opened cupboards and stared accusingly at plates, cans, boxes of toothpicks and matches. "This is all there really is. Everything else you invent." I am so tired, but afraid of falling asleep, as if I had just had a horrible dream. And this journal seems to create another stranger, one that will continue to pop up and always be a face I cannot quite place.

The third time she woke to the phone, she went downstairs to answer it. She tested her voice on the stairs to see if it sounded like she had just gotten up and glanced at the kitchen clock.

"Did you just get up," Tom asked.

"No, I didn't," she snapped. "I've been outside working."

"Didn't look like you got much done yesterday. Lucille says that Joey went over."

"Is Mrs. Benson sick again?" Irene carried the phone to the counter and filled the coffee maker with water.

"When was she sick? What are you talking about? You're always making things up."

"I thought you said Lucille came in when Mrs. Benson was sick. That's what I thought." Irene exhaled wearily into the receiver.

"She has doctor's appointments sometimes. But she's never sick."

"He got here late. Joey got here late. He said he would come back to finish." She waited for Tom to speak. "He didn't say when. I'll do some today."

She suspected that Tom was reading the newspaper while he talked to her, a belated breakfast ritual.

“I’m calling because I made an appointment to see the studio space. This afternoon. Is that all right?” She imagined that he sounded just like this when he spoke with clients.

“Fine. That would be fine. What time?”

“Two. Is two good for you?”

It was 11:15. “Great. Thanks, Tom.”

She heated up what was left of the curry and ate it with stale microwaved tortillas, changed clothes, and went down to the basement to get a rake. She walked into the root cellar and kicked at the broken crocks. She panicked for a second when she couldn’t find the condom, knelt down and carefully picked up the pieces, afraid that cockroaches or beetles might rush towards her. It was under the last piece of crockery. She stashed the condom in her jeans pocket.

The line of leaves she had left the day before was now spread out so it was six feet wide instead of two. In ten minutes she got the pile back to its former shape. She filled two bags loosely with leaves and left a small pile. When she brought a box of the garbage bags back to the shed, she went to check the chair, forgetting that she had removed it. When she saw it under the window, she remembered that she had put it next to the trash barrel. Paper was taped to the seat the way she had done herself.

She showered and changed clothes. Tom was going to pick her up in twenty minutes. She made a list of things she might need for the new studio, wandered out to the shed to look around. She flipped the light switch on several times because one of the lights seemed to be burned out, then left them off. She jumped up onto the bench, where she had displayed the last of the triptych “Stony Faces” and “The Carnival Shooting Gallery,” both still only crude splotches of color. She pulled a knee into her chest and rested her head on it, a cat-like pose for the window that she imagined to be a camera, the panes like squares on a sheet of proofs. A cloud passed in front of the sun and the shed became dark as if a light had been turned off. Irene lowered herself off the bench and stepped to the window to look out. She saw scratches in the glass she hadn't noticed before. Something was etched in the upper left hand pane and she went outside to read it.

FUKKERS.

Tom honked. She rushed to put the lock on the shed door. The second time he honked, she forced herself to take her time and when the lock finally caught, she walked, then ran to lock the kitchen door.

"When I honk, you come running, girl." Tom was in a good mood.

"I thought since you were taking me to town, I should put some shoes on." She pulled her linen blouse down over the seatbelt and smoothed out the front of it with the palms of her hands.

"Barefoot and pregnant, huh? Maybe we'll have hillbilly sex tonight."

"Maybe," she said and tried to sound disconnected from the conversation. She doubted whether Tom would come home before she was already asleep.

"It's cheap. The heating is horrible. You'll need to start using Mom's car every day. It has windows to the north, west and south and you can more or less do what you want to with the space."

They walked in the back entrance of the old bank building. A metal screen separated the stock room for Discount Buddies from the stairwell. Tom already had the key and Irene wondered if he had rented it without getting her reaction first.

"Claude Manners gave me the key, said it would be better

if we nosed around ourselves." Tom swung the door open. Irene assumed that Claude Manners was the real estate agent.

"What do you think?" Tom planted himself next to the door.

There were three rooms that were connected by a hallway. One of the rooms, the biggest one faced west with six large windows with wooden ledges two feet off the floor. It looked out on a parking lot and a root beer fast food that had closed five years earlier, and the parking lot for the Val's U-4-U supermarket. The two smaller rooms had been offices. One was missing a door and the other one had a name written on the glass which was partially scraped off.

"You still haven't seen the bathroom. It's that narrow door." Tom pointed a small janitor's closet where a toilet and wash basin had been installed. The water in the toilet was rusty and the side of the bowl was stained by the water.

"What do you think?" Tom repeated.

"About the toilet?" Irene said.

"Sure. Isn't that why you came up here, to look at the toilet." Tom moved to the other side of the doorway. Irene went through the rooms again before she stopped in front of the north window to look out on the roof of the small barbershop across the street.

"It has possibilities. Better than most I've had."

"And besides the toilet, what do you think about the rest." Tom moved to the stairs.

Irene walked dreamily in front of the doorway to the south window without looking at him.

He came back to the doorway and dangled the keys from his index finger. "Want them? Want the keys? What do I tell Claude?"

"You drive a hard bargain," she said.

"I have appointments." Tom moved back to the steps. "I can drop you off at Mom's so you can get her car. Start getting some of the junk out of the house. Any unopened boxes come here."

"That's the hidden cost," Irene said. With sudden movement she passed Tom on the stairs so she could walk down in front of him.

"So what do we call it, The Toilet? Oh, Irene is at the Toilet. Yeah, she's painting in the Toilet. We're putting all unopened boxes in the Toilet. My wife spends her days now in the Toilet." Irene's joke turned to a rant.

"Has a nice ring to it," Tom said.

Neither of them spoke until he parked his Jeep Cherokee in his mother's driveway. "If you don't want it, I can call up Claude and tell him. You can paint in the shed for all I care."

"You drove all the way over here like the decision was made." She was afraid that Tom in a fit would back into the street and drive off and she would lose the studio so she opened the car door. "We could have driven home and talked about it."

"I don't have time."

"Well." She opened the door wider and put her feet on the ground without getting out.

"Shut the door and I'll drive you home, if that's what you want." The car gave a slight chug.

"Just give me the keys, Tom. The keys. And I'll be out of your hair." She twisted towards him to reach for the keys.

"Not likely," he said handing them to her.

After he drove off, she stood before Doris's door to pull herself together.

"I was going to use the car, if you don't mind." Irene saw

herself as an orphan that went from house to house begging for bread.

"Tom drove off without coming in? Just like him." Doris patted her hair as if she were still in front of the mirror getting ready for company.

"He was busy. You know, he has so much to do."

"You got the studio? He was so excited about getting you that studio. He's so proud of your painting."

Irene held up the keys.

"Wonderful. I'm going to pay you some day to do my portrait."

She thought of the caricatures. "I'd love to."

As she turned the car into the driveway, she saw three children running away from the shed. She didn't get a good look at them as they dodged behind the row of lilac bushes, and it wasn't until they emerged from the Crawford's grape arbor that she was sure that they were two girls and a boy, and guessed that they were maybe between ten and twelve. After she went into the house to change clothes, she walked to the shed with the intention of loading some of the paintings into the car. It was clouding up.

FUKKERS had been scratched out and was written correctly underneath. In the next pane an erect penis was etched, the semblance of which Irene had seen scratched on student desks hundreds of times. In the bottom left there was a clitoris that looked like two concentric leaves. In the pane under it was what looked like a dog or goat on its hind legs tiptoeing toward the bottom right pane with its swollen cock pointing horizontally towards the right pane where a woman lay with her legs kicking in the air. The woman held a stick in one hand with a bundle of scratches on the end which Irene interpreted as a paintbrush. In the other hand was a square that Irene imagined was meant to be one of her paintings.

For a few minutes she analyzed the scratches on the glass. It was hard to tell whether the animal's head had ears or horns.

New York Journal

Chago asked me and María Elena to go with him to the Halloween parade in the Village next week. I asked María Elena if she thought he might be bisexual, though I haven't had any indication. She seems to know about us, said something catty like, "You would know." I said, "If he is, I only know half." It seems good that it's out.

I went to the Met to see the section with Macronesian and Micronesian art. Those towering fetishes with the penises half the size of the giant figures, stretching above their heads, their hands stretched out to hold them up. The arms are probably a practical structural consideration. In the huge lofty hall, almost cathedral-like, I felt that I was witness to an homage to male obsession. There was one where the penis spawned a multitude of male figures that clung to it, shooting off of it in other penises. A moment came when I had to get out of there.

I walked around the reservoir in Central Park behind a group of German tourists. Some men passed us, looking off into the bushes, cruising for sex. Jens once took me for a guided tour of gay sex in the park. I sat on a bench by the lake to think about him. I associate so many things in this city with him.

Friday she finished moving her canvases, paint and brushes over to the old bank building. One of the women at Discount Buddies helped her carry things up the stairs and showed her how to take the spring off the door so it didn't shut while she was lugging boxes and canvases through the doorway.

Carla showed up with a vacuum cleaner, a mop and glass cleaner.

"This place has great possibilities." Carla wandered through the rooms with her hands in the back pockets of her jeans. "You could have a little arts and crafts shop in the front, maybe give classes in one of the other rooms, and have a room left over for painting."

"Maybe in time," Irene said shuddering at Carla's suggestions.

"It's not in a mall or main drag, but art and crafts shops kind of belong in old places." Carla held a smile until Irene nodded.

Irene wiped down the walls and took a broom to the ceiling to get rid of cob webs and seaweed-like strands of dust. Carla finished vacuuming and began to mop.

"You know, the only thing I really don't like about this place is that Tom found it and rented it without asking me." Irene was cleaning a window in the west room and Carla mopped around her.

"Some of the dirt on these floors must be prehistoric." Carla moved closer to the window and Irene lifted up one of her legs so Carla could mop under it.

"I know it's stupid, but I feel like I am letting him make all my decisions, like I have no will left." She stepped to where Carla had just mopped and lifted up her other foot.

"Don't be so negative. It's a great place. And it's away from him. You can make it cozy. And private." Carla seemed embarrassed by her last comment and hurried off to rinse out the mop.

"Did you get a chance to read any of *Bridges*?" She hunched over the mop and worked a large brown stain near the doorway.

"Some," Irene said.

"Isn't it wonderful. I knew you would love it, being an artist and all." Carla let the mop rest on her hip and smiled at Irene.

"I haven't read that much. You know, with moving in here and all."

"I want to talk to you about it. Maybe we can do that weekend, go to Des Moines or Omaha or even Chicago. Get a couple other women and go. Wouldn't that be fun?" Carla spoke in grunts as she pressed the mop head against a dark spot of gum on the floor.

"Well, sure," Irene said. "When I get set up here."

"Neat," Carla said.

Irene worked quietly. Occasionally Carla grunted or swore. It was dark outside.

"Are you doing anything for Halloween?" Carla asked.

"Tom's at some party for high school students that the insurance companies organized. He didn't tell me much." Irene had begun to gather her towels and cleaner in a bucket and to put the newspapers she had used for wiping the windows into a trash bag.

"We might go to a party. I thought you might have gone, too. It's at Jane's."

"No, I'm staying home to hand out candy. Just in case. I don't think I'm too popular in the neighborhood and if no one is home, they'll probably soap all the windows."

“Harold worries every Halloween.” Carla put the mop down and looked out the window.

I’m calling it quits.” Irene put the bucket in the corner. Carla emptied the mop water into the toilet.

“Thanks, Carla.” Irene put a hand on her shoulder and Carla slipped a hand around Irene’s waist. She looked at Irene and then down at the floor.

Irene walked to the doorway and gave the room a quick inspection, “It’s getting there.” She opened the door and held it for Carla.

When Irene got home, she saw five boxes that Tom had set against the wall. On four of the boxes he had written, “For the Toilet” and on the last one “FLUSH THIS TOO.” She picked one up to see how heavy it was, then carried it out to the car. When she had all the boxes in the back seat of the Oldsmobile, she went back to the kitchen. Tom was standing at the bottom of the stairs.

“I’ve got the flu,” he said. He wore a reversible jersey with a large rip around the collar. “I have a headache and a fever. Could you go out and get me some Tylenol? I checked all the logical and illogical places. None.”

“Sure,” she snapped.

“I thought you were home. I saw the pumpkin on the front porch. Thought maybe you were doing a Halloween thing.”

“No, I don’t know where that came from. Maybe a practical joke.”

“Sorry about the boxes,” Tom said as she pulled the door open, “But when I got home with this fever, they started to bug me. I guess I freaked out. I counted them. There are still twenty more upstairs, but I almost fainted bringing the last one down.” He grabbed a chair from the kitchen table and pulled it out to the middle of the floor before sitting down.

Typical self-dramatization, she thought. "Oh, I understand," she said in a way that sounded like she didn't and had no interest in trying to.

"Thanks," he said. He stared at the floor and hugged himself as if he were freezing.

She dropped off the boxes at the studio, leaving them on the stairs, and went to Val's U-4-U to buy the Tylenol. She tried to imagine what else Tom might want--Seven-Up, tissues, canned chicken soup--so he wouldn't get up in the middle of the night and ask her to go out. She turned down the soup aisle with her hands clasped at her waist and the red plastic shopping basket hanging from her right arm and came face to face with Joey and Lucille, who stopped talking when they saw her.

Irene walked to the soup section and picked up two more cans of soup than she had planned. She looked back. Joey glared at the meat counter as Lucille hissed something at him. Lucille glanced her way and Irene moved to the next aisle.

As Irene stretched to reach the cheap tissues, she was sure she heard Lucille say, "I don't care if your car doesn't run. I am not giving you any more money, understand?"

She checked the front porch when she got home and found the pumpkin. It lay in a pile of straw with black and orange bows. When she turned it over, she saw a card. "There was a kind of mindless certainty humming blithely along beneath our ignorance that ensured we would come together." She thought she recognized the line from *Bridges*.

Tom was in bed again when she got back. He asked her to take his temperature and when it was only 100 degrees, he asked her to take it again. She brought him the soup an hour later and he sat up in bed to eat it.

“I saw Joey and Lucille Towner at the Val’s U-4-U.” Irene appeared more bored than concerned about Tom.

After two slow weak slurps from the soup spoon, Tom said, “Oh, what were they doing there.”

“Shopping I guess. Like everyone else.”

He stared at her somberly and then sneered, “It was only a ruse.”

“Yeah, probably,” she said ignoring his attempt at humor. “I overheard him whining about not having the money to fix his car.”

“What were you doing, following them around the store eavesdropping?” Tom put the bowl on the night stand.

“I’m so interested.” Irene gave Tom a droopy-eyed frown. “Do you want me to take that?” She nodded towards the soup.

“Leave it. I might have some later. Could you take my temperature again? Just to see.”

She went into the bathroom and rinsed off the thermometer. She shook it down and placed it under Tom’s tongue. He kept his hands folded on his chest. She waited leaning against the doorway to the bathroom. When she removed the thermometer, he grabbed her hand.

“Are you delirious?” she asked.

“No, just feverish.” He tried to put her hand under the covers.

She pulled away and held the thermometer up to the light sconce on the wall. “Still one hundred. It’s not going up.”

“Irene.” He had picked up the soup again and set it on his chest.

"What is it, Tom?"

"You don't love me anymore, do you?"

"What a stupid question." She stood for a moment to see if he dared to say anything else. As she went out, she grabbed the doorknob to slam the door shut, but instead left it ajar.

Downstairs she heard him weakly calling her name and didn't answer.

Painting Journal

My commercial stuff is going to be Iowa mysticism, a series of old white frame houses with Victorian trim and cornfields, sunflower fields, rivers and fences that come up to the edge of the porch, like a model train setting for a real train. Everything has the dimension and perspective of the imagination and not the eye so the house dominates the sky, land, fields. I've seen pictures of the old red brick high school in Crandall, later grade school, that they tore down (fire hazard), the only three story building in town. I'm going to do that as a montage with those old inspirational paintings, like "Farewell" where the son in his suit says farewell to the parents on the farm. My seditious version would be the daughter in the three-piece suit. But I want just enough sentimentality in all of these paintings to make them sell. Tom keeps saying do flowers. Georgia O'Keefe, she sells. Better Grant Wood on acid than Georgia O'Keefe on Precious Moments.

Sunday morning Tom was better. He stayed home from church and hinted it would be a good idea that she went. It was uncomfortable being in the house together, like something they needed a lot of practice doing before it would work, so after bringing up his breakfast to the bedroom, she left. She sat next to Carla, who was there by herself. Harold was on a Christian men's retreat at Spirit Lake.

When she got home, Tom was sitting in the kitchen.

"You must feel better." She ran upstairs to change to go to the studio before Tom answered.

"I'm going to the studio, better known to you as the Toilet. Anything you want flushed?"

"It can wait. It must have been a twenty-four hour thing."

Irene cleared the dishes off the table. "You changed your lipstick, Tom. Your mother was over, huh?"

"No, I still wear the same lipstick. That was Lucille's cup. I called her over to bring me some papers."

"Papers? I didn't know you were smoking again?" She packed and unpacked the canvas bag she was bringing to the studio.

"You were the pothead," he said when she crossed the kitchen to the refrigerator.

"What, what does that have to do with anything?" She ran upstairs again.

When she rushed into the kitchen with an old blanket that she put in the canvas bag next to the door, he said, "Smoking again? You don't remember your joke. Ha, ha."

"Pothead. I'm a pothead. You have always looked for those little labels to disregard me." She flew off upstairs again.

When she came downstairs, she whizzed back and forth across the kitchen, opening cupboards, wiping off the counter.

Tom looked up occasionally from the table where he sat with his elbows on the table and his head resting in his hands.

"Let's drop it, please," he said

She picked up the canvas bag, turned to see if he was looking at her, and left without answering him.

Journal October 30

I keep asking myself, "Why don't I just leave Tom?" And my answer is another question, "Where would I go?" I called my father last night. I never feel like talking to him until two hours after he is in bed, so forced myself to call him at around six. As usual, I was desperate to get off the phone after five minutes. The litany of complaints. The news about my brothers. The neighbors' health problems. News about people whose names only sound familiar. I hung up feeling like an orphan who imagines conversations with a dead parent.

I play back my conversations with Tom. Great biting and ironic lines come to me after our encounters and I am overwhelmed by regret that I didn't think of it during the heat of verbal battle. When I say something cruel, I feel guilty later.

Tom wants it all--my pity and his girlfriend. Both of us have been acting so long as if our relationship would continue, that even now that there is nothing left, we don't know how to stop. How do you end something so nebulous and encrusted in past expectations?

As soon as Tom leaves the house, I wander around trying to sense who he is from his dirty clothes, his neat row of shoes, the tie pins, thumb for the twentieth time through his yearbooks. I dredge up old abuses, the time he told María Elena I didn't want to see her anymore, when he didn't tell me that Jens had gone into Roosevelt Hospital until he had been there for three days. I open the closet and swear at his suits. Then I catch myself halfway down to the basement, imagining a real satyr-devil face, instead of Joey's cheap rubber mask, and going over lines to myself, "Come on, you know you want it," "You going to let me take the rubber off." It frightens me to think of how excited I am at being out of control, of danger. I think of my friends who no longer have the choice.

I got through the first sixty-seven pages of Bridges. *Lyle and Carla seem scarier. Watch out for any book that starts off telling you that you are too cynical if you don't like it or believe it. Every paragraph has sentences that float off the page and stick to Carla's dashboard. Or to suddenly pop up under a pumpkin, or on the back of a Lothario's business card. Or as a New Age come-on line. What do I tell Carla when she searchingly asks me what I think about the book? Will I eventually ooze over the book in the way she does? Will I become Lyle's Francesca, the suppressed Italian war bride waiting for a man to appear, screw her and give meaning to the remaining twenty years of her life? Or Carla's Robert Kincaid, the hippie macho-man loner with beautiful feelings and nothing to think about for the last twenty-five years of his life other than a four-day affair in Iowa? Or is it Lyle's Robert and Carla's Francesca? Soap opera questions. One hundred and sixty-four weeks (no, not one hundred and sixty-five) on the New York Times bestseller list. Does Lyle think he is really the cliché of the sensitive loner, Camel smoker, artist? Can someone who gives up the richness of Italian culture for four days of sex with the Marlboro man be any model? I guess he smokes Camels. Please, don't Francescasize me.*

The window in the shed was broken after the paintings were taken out. It was a relief. A clear break in a bad relationship. It seems incredible that I thought I would somehow become a nurturer, friendly acquaintance, neighborhood eccentric. Was there a current of communication that I didn't understand? Some hate I exuded that their small young minds reflected?

I haven't been able to get Fern Gregor out of my mind or Joey telling her I had chased him in the culvert. How have I gotten so mixed up in his mind? I saw some of the older kids luring him into the culvert. A few minutes later he came out hysterical, ran up the embankment and across the street without knowing where he was going. A car jammed on its brakes and screeched to a halt. I don't think he even noticed.

It had been dark now for a couple of hours. A few young mothers, whom she didn't know, came with pre-schoolers, who dug through the bowl of bite-size Snickers and Milky Ways until Irene would gently pull it away. Fern Gregor brought her three youngest. The knock on the door was definitely hers, but when Irene went to the door, Fern stood off to the side at the bottom of the steps with her arms folded. Irene peeked through the curtain when they left and saw Fern inspecting their bags, as if she were evaluating the candy.

Carla called to ask if she had a gypsy shawl. Irene offered a flowered tablecloth for a small square table she no longer had. She came over to look at it, but didn't take it, since as she said, her heart was set on something with tassels." She called just before ten to pick it up, unable to find anything else. Harold waited out in the car because he didn't want to get out. Carla insisted that Irene go to the car to see Harold's Chippendale dancer costume, a bikini bathing suit with five dollar bills stuffed around the waistband and a white Best Western bathrobe with Chippendale written across the back. Harold sprung out of the car, swirled around quickly chattering his teeth, and jumped back into the car.

"You must have gotten those tips a long time ago," Irene joked.

"I don't work the usual clientele," Harold said through the open crack in the window.

"Extraterrestrials." Carla shrugged her shoulders. "I tried to talk him out of it."

"And now you show him off," Irene said.

Four older children came. Two of them, she thought one girl and one boy, both had Monica Lewinsky masks. The tallest one wore a large *South Park* mask drawn on a round piece of posterboard. The last one, whom she recognized as the oldest Gregor boy, had painted his face white, with black eyebrows and blood dripping from his mouth. He was dressed in ordinary blue jeans, a flannel shirt and a jacket that was too short in the arms.

"You have to take your masks off to get any candy," Irene said and laughed nervously.

She turned to get the bowl and before she knew it the four of them had come into the kitchen. She could smell marijuana on their clothes. The boy with the Monica Lewinsky mask said, "What do we have to take off to get candy?" The others laughed.

"Just your masks."

The girl with the Lewinsky mask lifted it up to her nose, then looked around to the others. She took seven Milky Ways in her fist and dropped the mask again.

"Anyone else?" Irene pointed the bowl to the other three.

"Anyone else?" the boy in the Lewinsky mask said and the others began to chant Irene's words. She put the bowl down on the table and looked each of them over. The Gregor boy walked out onto the steps and the others followed.

"Be careful," she said.

The four broke into a wild run up to the sidewalk.

She held the door and listened to them laugh and scream to each other, "Take it off." "Be careful." "Anyone else." "Everyone else." "Take it off." "Everyone else take it off."

She made a tour of all the rooms in the house, opened the window in the book room a few inches to listen to the sounds outside, walked to the door of the basement and laughed at herself. Tom called to check in and she wondered why he did that. She opened *Bridges* to the chapter "Ancient Evenings, Distant Music".

. . . he reached into a knapsack and pulled out a camera, draping the strap over his shoulder."

"First a lousy title, then faulty use of thesaurus. How do you drape a camera strap? Unless there is no camera pulling it down. You think? A camera strap as a fashion accessory for that rugged Robert."

The knock at the door startled her because it seemed like an answer to her question. She dog-eared the page and left it on the table. She peered through the window over the sink to see who was at the door. Joey stood on the step in his devil mask and a black cape to his knees. Under the cape he wore blue jeans. She opened the door, but didn't unhook the screen door.

"Trick or treat," he sounded stoned.

"No more treats." She shook her head.

"What about this," he said and opened the cape. Two circles were cut out around his nipples and his chest was painted cherry red. "Hot. Real hot."

Joey laughed and staggered, then put a foot back on the next step down to steady himself. She heard someone else laughing, and the girl she had seen in Joey's car walked from up against the house where she had been hiding. She wore a large black witch's hat, a black skirt with a ragged-v hem.

He turned to the girl, "Elvira, Elvira."

“Show her,” she said. Her coat was open and she put her hands on her hips to show her cleavage. She stumbled towards Joey and he grabbed her arm before she fell over.

“Show her, god dammit.” She forced a laugh, then choked on it.

“Here it is.” Joey held the cape up over his head and turned around and bent over. The back of the jeans were missing and his butt was the same color as his chest.

The girl stopped choking. She dropped her mouth, “God, lady aren’t you going to say anything. Huh? My god! I mean, it’s his fucking ass.”

Bending over further, he bumped the screen door, lost his balance and flew forward. The girl ran to where he lay on the cement in front of the steps and stood over him laughing.

“Fuck you, Lorry.”

“Cover your butt. I’ve seen it before.” She exaggerated the slur in her voice.

He looked at his palms to see if they were bleeding. Irene closed the door and watched them from the window by the table. He moved the cape in front of him so he could put his hands on it as he lifted himself up. He glanced first at the door and then at the window. Irene backed up, standing on her tiptoes so she could follow them as they walked to Joey’s Firebird.

She listened to the motor of his car as it revved off. In the brown easy chair in the living room she thought she heard his car racing down the alley, then up Main Street, then out past the high school. As she was falling asleep, she heard it roar by the house, tried to get up to look out the window, but her body wouldn’t respond to her and she decided that she was already in a dream.

Journal November 9

Carla and Harold went to a convention in New Orleans. It annoys me when she is around, but I am so lonely here that I get anxious at the thought that she won't call or come over. I met with her, Jane, and a woman named Stella at Big Boy's for breakfast last week. One of those sausage, bacon, and ham orgies. Carla told them that I had just finished Bridges. *For them it seemed to be the secular equivalent of a religious experience. I felt like the lamb who had just been saved. I never had the heart to tell Carla that I'd never finished it. I guess I have to try again.*

Lyle finally went to Tom with his proposal for redoing the yard. He wants to put a gazebo in the corner of the lot, near the intersection. I told Tom that if Pendayhaz became a big city, we could turn it into a newspaper kiosk since it's at such a busy intersection. He asked me what I was planning on doing in the gazebo that I didn't want anyone to see. He may have a point. Why would you want to get away from people here when there aren't any? Lyle explained that if you have something nice, you want to share it with others. I asked Lyle if we would get a commission for advertising for him. He seems a little slow on the draw, didn't get what I was driving at. He wasn't offended, just had his wounded love-pup look. He muttered something about art, love, and money that sounded like Bridge-babble.

When Carla found out that Tom had contracted him, she almost called off her trip to New Orleans. If she only knew that without her manipulations, I wouldn't give him the time of day. And I still have some standards. Unfortunately I haven't seemed to pay much attention to them since I got here.

I noticed that some of the kids on their way to school cross the street instead of going by the house. It depressed me to think that who I am to them seems so out of my control, but once in a while I stand in the yard as they are going by and watch the power I have over them. They're afraid to look over here. Then I go to the studio and paint like I am possessed. Alienation as inspiration. It's like I am in a pool and reach the side and turn and push with my legs and push into myself and not the water, and my insides are fluid. I reach the outer crust of my consciousness to push off into myself.

My image has abandoned me and been overtaken by others.

I have not seen Joey since Halloween. The next Saturday I woke up and looked out and the leaves were raked and set in bags by the driveway, silently, mystically. Tom said he gave him some more money since he didn't think I had paid Joey enough. What was I to say?

I'm glad there is no reason to see him. Yesterday the electricity in the kitchen went off and I had to go down to the fuse box in the basement. I got a weird feeling that he was there, just for a second and then I laughed it off. But I started to think about when I would see him next and figured it would be snow shoveling after the first big snowfall. First the leaves fall from the sky and then the snow. I look heavenward for my downfall. There is still pleasure in meaningless irony.

When she woke up, Tom was still asleep in the guest room. A thick wet frost covered the windows halfway up the pane. The tree branches and grass blazed in a white sheen in the morning sun and the windless world seemed to have set into a wet glistening plaster. Though it was already eight, she tiptoed down the creaky stairs, jumping to avoid a step that usually made a loud crack. She took a red sweatshirt and a pair of jeans from the dryer in the basement so she wouldn't have to go back upstairs for clothes. She stood at the kitchen door with her coffee to watch the children walking to school.

At 9:30 Tillie Pearson from Discount Buddies rattled on the chain link between the stairwell and the stockroom. "Mrs. Marston, it's the phone. Your husband."

She came to the top of the stairs wearing her painting clothes. Tillie was slightly hard of hearing so she had to yell okay" four times. She painted for a half hour and then changed to her street clothes to walk around the block to the entrance of Discount Buddies. The display room had a mix of old wooden display tables, some with sales and closeout stickers that had not been successfully removed, and newer plastic and metal tables. A strip of cement ran across the wooden floors where the tellers' windows had stood. A line of display tables stood on the line of cement. The door to the bank vault was still visible behind a gauzy sheet that had been stapled to the wall. Tillie sat on a stool behind the checkout counter and another woman, Barb Lemmon, hung one hand from the counter and had the other on her hip. Both women smiled at her without a break in their conversation.

Lucille answered the phone.

"Is my husband there?" Irene asked.

"Hold on. He just went to the bathroom. He should be here in a second." Lucille pushed the hold button and Irene heard a spiel for fire and flood insurance interspersed with "All or Nothing at All" sung by Frank Sinatra. Barb had moved away from the counter and was folding polyester ruffled blouses at one of the counters. The large expanse below the ornate plaster ceiling seemed to weigh on her silver gray head.

As Irene was hearing of the horrible devastation of fire for the third time, Tom came on. "Yeah, what is it?"

"You called me," she said.

"Oh, that's right. Do you want to do lunch? At about one?"

Tillie got off the stool with an order list she had been working on and Irene lifted up the phone cord so she could pass.

"That's fine. Will you pick me up?"

"One of my clients will pick you up, Lyle Bucker, the guy doing the yard. I'll meet you at Cake 'n More out on the interstate."

"Tom, I don't know if I want to go to a business lunch."

"It's mostly about the yard. He insisted that you be there. Be ready at twelve-thirty."

She heard Lucille's voice as Tom hung up. Tillie came back to the counter and smiled at her as she passed. "Doesn't bother me at all when you get phone calls here. I used to babysit Tom when he was just born. He doesn't remember."

"Thanks," Irene said. It was pleasant walking in the sun on Main Street, but when she turned the corner, she was in the shade and the west wind blew so strongly that her eyes began to water. She wrapped her arms around herself and trotted to the back of the building. She sat down on the steps for a few moments to rest, inspected a few of the boxes, and carried one with old letters upstairs. It wasn't worth changing into her painting clothes again.

New York Journal

I just talked to my agent and she got me an individual show in Chelsea. She wants ten new paintings by next April so I have to keep myself focused. My agent's marketing me as part of a new female art movement, shape-color-space.

I went out with a law professor from N.Y.U. who collects art. Imagine talking to someone who knows your own language. When I described him to Jens, he said, "Get your gaydar out. A single law professor who likes art?" Does a woman have to settle for a Tom, jock-businessman-spreading-gut-anti-avant-garde-culture, to insure straightness? New York can also skew you about life's possibilities.

I've seen a few, maybe two, cockroaches in the new apartment, both dead.

María Elena was a little distant at the studio. I hope she's not jealous about me getting the individual show. I know she herself was hoping to get one.

She put the journal away in a filing cabinet. Her plan had been to watch for Lyle out the window over the desk and run down to meet him outside. He was at the top of the stairs before she got to the door and made his way in by staring at the upper walls and ceiling as if he were inspecting them, ignoring Irene who was attempting to block the door.

"Take a look around," she said trying for sarcasm.

"This is where you work. Smells like paint."

"I'm a painter," she said trying again for sarcasm.

"Interesting. Very interesting." He nodded his head as he inspected the fifteen paintings that leaned against the wall and the two set up for painting.

"And you're alone here all day?" Lyle twisted his finger in the silver chain around his neck. He wore khaki slacks, a work shirt that had the two top buttons undone, and Birkebinder sandals with heavy socks.

"The women from Discount Buddies run in and out. There's always a message for me or they come up just to chat. And they always know whether I'm here or not. There's only that chain link fence dividing the stairs and the stockroom."

"But then they close at six," Lyle stopped to look out the window and looked at her conspiratorially. "Great light," he said. "At six o'clock the light must be great here."

"By six o'clock it's dark now."

"I'm a great lover of light. I love it almost as much as plants. My favorite is bounce light." He turned his head towards her as she had seen cows do, slowly, expectantly.

She recognized the term from *Bridges* and suppressed her laughter. "Well, I prefer thump light. Thump is my favorite."

"Hm," Lyle pondered this without knowing what he was pondering. "Bounce is what I like."

"I'm usually gone by four." Irene went loudly down the steps.

"Aren't you going to lock up," Lyle called from one of the back rooms..

"No, Tillie is in and out all day." Irene worried about Tillie hearing this as soon as it was out of her mouth. She waited for Lyle at the bottom of the steps. As he came down, she first noticed the sandals.

"Isn't it a little cold for sandals?" she said as she held the door for him. Barb Lemmon came into the stockroom and Irene waved to her and Lyle turned to see who it was. She slammed the door and Lyle turned to stare at her. "I love slamming doors. Especially screen doors."

Lyle looked shocked. In the truck he leaned over her to grab the truck handle. "It's tricky. Lift and pull real hard. I'm sorry about slamming it."

She shrugged her shoulders.

"I'm not like other men. I'm probably more real than any man you've ever known."

"Well, I'll have to keep that in mind." Irene crossed her arms and stared out the side window.

"This isn't my good car, but this old pickup is really who I am. I call it Jessie. The disappearing cowboy."

"And not Harry? Like Robert Kincaid in *Bridges*?" Her voice was sardonic, but he was oblivious as he beamed at her.

"What was Don Quixote's horse's name, *Rocinante*?" She grimaced back at his smile.

"Sorry, I don't know that. Wasn't *Man of La Mancha* wonderful art, though. To dream the impossible dream."

"I didn't know you smoked, Lyle." Irene pointed to a pack of Camels on the dashboard.

"I don't. That's kind of a reminder of who I really am."

Irene peered out the side window even though the axle on the old pickup was bent and Lyle had to keep pulling it back to the left so that she began to feel car sick. She took a quick glance over at Lyle and saw that he had rolled up one of his sleeves and was flexing his muscles. He glanced from his arm to Irene just as she was trying to turn back to the window before he saw her. During a bump in the road where he had to work at righting the truck, she looked over at him again. His face was set in a tense-lipped grin.

The truck weaved as he turned off the service road into the Cake 'n More. As he put on the safety brake, he said nonchalantly, "Four days can change your life forever."

She pulled at the handle to open the door, set her shoulder to the glass to push. "It's kind of tricky." Lyle leaned across her lap, placing his elbow next to her knee. He pulled the handle out and turned until it clicked and the door opened. "Four days," he said again without moving. Irene straightened herself out, lifting Lyle's arm slightly.

"Ebola will eat your flesh in a matter of . . . " she didn't finish because she was already out of the truck and had slammed the door.

He loped across the parking lot so he could hold the door for her. "I always have brandy and I don't let screen doors slam," he said.

Irene whizzed through the second door before he could reach it and pushed it shut as she walked in. A waitress passed with a tray on her shoulder and asked Irene to wait. She looked over the restaurant and found Tom and Lucille seated in the middle of the left dining room, which was separated from the right one, the smoking section, by a partial wall and plastic philodendrons that in places had become unsnapped from the main branch. Lyle appeared behind her a little shaken. Irene walked to the table without acknowledging Lyle.

"I've seen you a few times and talked to you on the phone, but we haven't really met." Irene extended her hand and watched Tom to see how he was reacting. He smiled contentedly, more relaxed than when he was alone with her

"Tom talks about you all the time," Lucille said smiling and fidgeting with her glass of cola.

"I bet he does," Irene said and widened her eyes. Lyle and Lucille turned to look at Tom who had begun to laugh.

Painting Journal

It's all one. All my paintings are one painting where the connections will always be missing, but can be supplied by imagination and now that I have space and can see them next to each other, I begin to work on one painting as a correction or comment on another. I think of "Stony Faces" and see the last faceless woman as an accumulation of light that has erased everything and my own painting as an accumulation of light that will eventually become so complex that it erases me. Look at Rothko. His early work is replaced by the even more dreamlike lines and that minimalism repeated again and again eventually erases him in a more obvious way than with most artists.

I paint my absence into the canvas.

Reasons Why I Might Sleep with Lyle

1. It would be for free, I think.

2. I would be an object of desire.

3. It is like a plot option that was never explored, Dulcinea goes to bed with Don Quixote.

4. It might lead to contacts with lawn boys besides Joey, start a real market economy with a heavier supply side. It didn't work for Reagan, but hey, people spent money like they were rich.

5. It is the ultimate act of humiliation. I finally become merely a character in someone else's romance novel. I would feel so cheap and compromised. Now that is appealing.

6. I could lead Lyle on, act like I really feel that our affair, though impossible, has completely transformed my life and I will think about him as I lie dying.

7. It would be Carla's worst nightmare.

8. It might make me disgusted enough to get out of here. Or depressed enough to stay. Risky.

9. I could write the real story, *The Ditches of Madison County.*

Carla called when she and Harold got in from the airport in Des Moines. The next morning she showed up at the studio while Irene was in the coffee shop across from Tom's office. She had started going there to read the newspaper and listen to farmers at the other tables. Carla was waiting for her at the Discount Buddies and pounded on the window and then ran out to meet her.

"How was New Orleans?" Irene noticed that Carla's face was more freckled and her forehead and nose were red.

"Beautiful. Beautiful. I got kind of burned, huh? They had the most wonderful new casino. You as an artist would just love it. It was so artistic. You know, I kept thinking, 'Maybe this is what Irene needs to inspire her so she has a breakthrough.' Honest."

Irene walked silently beside Carla until they got to the door to the studio. "Would you like to go to the Sunshine for coffee? I could use another cup."

"I don't know," Carla wrinkled her forehead as if she were making an important decision. "The only people who go there are old farmers and kids after school. We could go out to Cake 'n More."

“No, I was there the other day.” Irene had moved back to the sidewalk.

“It’s that the old Formica and linoleum and those shiny vinyl chairs depress me. It’s like being a teenager all over. Then the farmers are such an embarrassment. Those men don’t change clothes to go there. Some of them wear their chore clothes. Not my favorite odor, right? And the kids. I get grossed out every time I think of how the bottoms of those tables are covered with old gum. Some from probably when I went there.”

“It’s handy and I don’t feel like getting in a car. I’m taking a break from a painting and getting in a car would distract me.”

“And coffee at the Sunshine with me wouldn’t?” Carla laughed like she was shocked, but crossed the street on the way to the Sunshine and Irene followed her.

“So who did you go to the Cake ‘n More with?” They waited for the only traffic light in town to change.

“Did you go to the French Quarter?” Irene winked at Carla.

“Once. But it was so filthy. Bourbon Street, I mean. I let Harold go by himself and I stayed in the room watching movies. He came back at two every night smelling of beer and smoke and slept like a baby.”

“I met Lucille officially. At Cake ‘n More. A business lunch with Tom, her and a client.”

Carla rolled her eyes. “Tongues are wagging now.” She peered through the tinted glass into the café. “I bet they even have flies in the windowsill. It’s that kind of place.”

“I think that trip changed you.” Irene walked to the table she had been sitting at earlier. Her cup was still on the table, but the newspaper she had been reading was gone.

"Really? How?" Carla seemed flattered.

"You're more cheerful. Less guarded."

A couple of the farmers had been talking and turned around to see who was with Irene. The owner, wiping his hands with a bar rag waddled up to the table. "You want a refill and another cup? Anything else?"

"Let's have pie," Carla said loud enough to make it a public decision. She reached across the table to push Irene's shoulder playfully. "So we have even more reason to walk this afternoon."

"Pecan or cherry?" the owner said.

"Pecan," Irene said. "And bring me a new cup."

"Same," Carla said.

The owner walked away without picking up the cup and returned with the pie and coffee.

"Harold met someone on this trip. He made a phone call at eleven-thirty last night. Has that dreamy look all the time." Carla had only a small corner of her pie left. Irene had stopped eating so she could decipher Carla's hushed words in between bites. "One night he didn't come back to the hotel until eight the next morning. And I had to hear about it. You know."

Carla stared down at the pecan pie on her fork and continued. "You know, how this is the one, how he's been waiting for this, how it, well, how it was bound to happen."

"Hm. How do you feel about that?" Irene put her fork down on the plate.

"I'm used to it. It's a relief. But it's harder for me. A lot harder. It's always harder for a woman. At least I don't have to hear about his complaints. Those will come later when it doesn't work out."

“Been through this lots of times before?” Irene pushed the half eaten pie to the center of the table.

“Lot’s of times. That’s why we’re together. It never works out for either of us. Don’t you want your pie?” Carla dropped her fork into the pie and looked up at Irene.

“No. It’s too sweet for me.”

“I thought I was happy with someone a couple times. I left town and went to Dubuque to go to business school. Computers and stuff. Merchandising. After the last one didn’t work out I saw Harold. He wanted to move back here. So we got married.”

Irene went to the counter to pay and then stood by the entrance glancing at a *Weekly Shopper* until Carla joined her.

“Carla, I don’t talk to anyone in town besides you.” The day had become cloudy and colder and Irene walked at a good clip.

“Yes, I’ve thought about that a lot.”

“It ends here,” Irene stopped by Carla’s car. The Stick-ems on the dashboard were purple.

“Okay.” Carla had lost her energy. “Maybe we could walk off the pie later.”

“Tomorrow,” Irene said. “Today I have to get my nails done.”

“You?” Carla rolled down the window. “Remember, tomorrow at three we’re walking.”

Irene nodded as Carla puttered off.

She drove home to make the call to Crandall since it was long distance. “Oh Louie, I’m glad I caught you at home. This is Irene Marston, Tom Marston’s wife. I was wondering if you could do my nails. Or trim my hair? I know you probably don’t do nails.”

She passed Toby's Green Fingers Nursery. Lyle's red Cadillac Seville was parked in front of the Manager's Parking sign. He walked out as she was going by and she had a feeling that he had seen her.

Louie's apartment was over a furniture store. He met her at the door in tight jeans and a black t-shirt. He was wearing several bracelets and had on small silver lizard earrings.

"I hoped you would call. I'm trying to build up a little business. Would you like something to drink, coffee? A soda maybe?"

Irene took off her coat and hung it and her purse on moose antlers that functioned as a coat rack. "Nice stuff," she said taking in the decor. "A Coke would be fine."

"Most of it's not mine. It belongs to my roommate Phil. He collects movie posters, Judy Garland stuff." He slammed an ice tray on the kitchen counter. "The sofas are mine." Louie pointed to two formal Victorian sofas. "They belonged to my lover."

"Break up?" Irene asked.

"Kind of, I guess," Louie shrugged his shoulders.

"Did you always live in Pendayhaz and Crandall?" Irene picked up a framed photograph of Joan Blondell.

"She was voted the most beautiful woman in the world. I forget who it is. It's signed and there is something on the back. I forget what. If Phil was here, he would show you."

"Oh," Irene said and put it down.

"I lived in Omaha for a while. That's where I met Chuck. The guy who had the sofas. He died and my mother got sick so I moved back here. She's better. Lives in Des Moines now. I tried to live in Pendayhaz, but it didn't work. I stayed with an English teacher I had. He was choir director of the Lutheran church. They chased him out of town. I guess they chased me out, too."

"I may be next." Irene smiled at Louie.

"It's not much better here. Phil used to be a music teacher. Now he has this antique business. I put his inventory on computer. I cut hair back here." Louie walked to a small storage room.

"That's right, you study computers." Irene sat in the chair.

"Two nights a week at the technical school." Louie straightened the combs and scissors on the pink counter. He swung a sheet out in a gesture hampered by the size of the storage room.

"That's the future, right?" she said remembering his earlier comment.

"Mm,"he said. He seemed less convinced today. "The sinks are from a shop that remodeled and I got them cheap. They went from all pink to all black. I like the pink. It's funky." Louie leaned Irene's head back into the sink and placed a towel under her neck.

"Phil's real handy. He put in the plumbing. It's probably illegal so I don't do a lot of business."

She hummed a few answers to show him that she was paying attention. The warm water massaged her scalp and her whole body relaxed. He rubbed in the shampoo and Irene slid a bit farther down into the chair. When he rinsed out the conditioner, she felt a drop slide down her neck and then her back. The spell was broken.

"You're from New York?" Louie rolled the towel from her neck up around her head and rubbed it dry.

"No, I was born in New Jersey. I lived in New York on and

off for ten years."

"New Jersey to New York," he said as if he had just explained most of her life.

"And a few other stops. Have you ever been to New York?" Irene kept her eyes closed.

"Chuck and I talked about it. He wanted to go everywhere when he got sick. But I couldn't take off work and he didn't want to go alone."

Irene squinted with one eye to keep the water from running into it. "For a while in New York, you knew how sick someone was by how much traveling they suddenly did."

"Oh, I didn't know that," Louie said.

"I had a cousin who died from "AIDS." Saying it seemed to take her breath away. Her stomach sank.

"A lot of people thought Chuck had "AIDS", but he had leukemia. Leukemia was bad enough."

"It must have been." Her voice faded off.

"Did Tom know your cousin?" Louie put his hand over her eyes and sprayed water on her hair and then dabbed her forehead dry with a towel.

"He didn't like him. I could never figure it out. He liked my other gay friends. Some of them. At least he said he did." She tried to open an eye to look at Louie.

"Well, if he said he liked them." Louie finished clipping and began to blow dry her hair. She no longer felt relaxed. The muscles in her neck tensed up.

"He did say that," Irene said aware of how meaningless their exchange had become.

"How do you keep yourself busy?" He talked as if the smallest part of his consciousness was involved in the conversation.

"Unpack. I unpack hoping I won't because that will mean we will, or I will stay."

"Hm," he said.

"Five months unpacking. That must be something like seventy-two hours per box." She thought of saying something completely outrageous to see if he were paying attention at all.

"Haven't found too much in Pendayhaz that's made you want to stay, huh?" He chuckled absentmindedly.

"And I paint. I have a studio in the old upstairs of the bank. Above Discount Buddies."

"Yeah, my aunt Barbara Lemmon works there." He sounded interested.

"Sure, I know her. She and Tillie let me use the phone. I'm sure Claude Manners, the owner, would raise my rent or dock their pay if he knew."

"Maybe," he said and seemed to disconnect again.

"Hello, Louie." Irene was surprised by the voice since she hadn't heard anyone come in.

"I'm back here, Phil." Louie said sticking his head out of the small storage room. The hair dryer blew towards the ceiling. Irene stared straight ahead at the mirror which had pictures from *Cosmopolitan* and *Interview* taped to the edges.

Irene turned as Phil appeared in the doorway. He was short and stocky with a flattop and wore clothes from Land's End or the Banana Republic. Irene estimated he was about fifty.

"Phil, who is that woman in the picture, the one that is signed."

Phil's face became serious and he wrinkled his forehead to show both his interest and lack of understanding.

"Isn't that Joan Blondell?" Irene turned to Phil and smiled.

"Oh, that. Wow, I'm surprised you would know."

"This is Tom Marston's wife, Irene. I told you about her." Louie looked up from giving Irene's hair the final touches to speak.

Phil wrinkled his forehead again, then as he remembered it went smooth. "Oh, sure. At Charlene's. That was funny. Nice to meet you." He disappeared from the doorway.

"We're not lovers. He's my best friend." Louie put the hair blower away, wrapping the cord around the handle. "Sometimes we laugh about being this little gay island in the middle of a straight ocean. Like Tahiti. Exotic."

"Or like Bikini," she said and chuckled.

"I didn't know that was an island." He threw the towel and the sheet into the hamper.

Irene nodded at him by way of the mirror.

"Exotic and sexy, too, then."

Irene decided against giving the history of Bikini.

"Maybe we could do the nails some other time." Irene stood in the living room and Phil stirred onions in a frying pan in the kitchen.

"I wanted to tell you. I really don't like doing nails. I do them for some old friends." Louie became busy straightening the pillows on the sofas.

"Come over anytime. Just call, we're usually home." Phil turned back to the frying pan.

"It's twenty dollars." Louie stood by the door.

"Here's five for a tip. Much nicer than Charlene's." She fumbled a little with her purse.

"Tell Tom hello. He was nice to me a couple of times in high school. He wouldn't remember. But say hi from me." Louie held the door for her.

It was only five o'clock, but already dark. She parked in front of Crandall Cards and Gifts which had a paperback book section. Her car was the only one on that side of main street.

"Do you have *Lolita*? You might have it. They just made a new movie with Jeremy Irons." She was conscious that her hair was too styled for her jeans and t-shirt.

The salesclerk was a high school student with braces and hair that looked like it was copied from Doris Day in the fifties.

"Oh, gee, let me see. Yeah, yeah, yeah. Over here." The girl was excited about the thought of having the book. She led Irene to a long rack of paperbacks facing fuzzy stuffed animals. "You wouldn't know the name. I mean, the author."

"Nabokov. It's by Nabokov."

The girl repeated the name, lisping the f. "Could it be this, guy? Nay-bah-cove."

"That's it. *Lolita*, right."

"The girl thumbed through it. "Lots of long paragraphs. Looks interesting." She turned to the cover and inspected the short skirt, long skinny legs and bobby socks and saddle shoes. "Is it about cheerleading?" the girl asked handing the book to Irene.

"Something like that," she said.

She waited for a Plymouth Voyager to pull out of the Blockbuster parking lot. She made one round without finding parking and had seen the Voyager's lights go on. She looked through the sections for Comedy, Drama and Foreign, even thought of Action since the old version had a long car scene. The clerk had a clumsy football lineman body.

"We should have three or four copies. That's what the computer says." He gazed at the screen, typed a few keys.

"I looked. I looked everywhere." She ran her hand through her hair.

He scrunched his mouth up to one side and rubbed a pimple on his cheek. "It looks like they've all been pulled."

"Why?"

He shrugged his shoulders. "Beats me. That's what it says."

She had just handed the clerk her Blockbuster card and *The Bridges of Madison County*, when she saw the red Seville pull up in front of the store. It occurred to her that in Crandall there might be more than one red Seville that looked like Lyle's. She tried to hide behind the bulk of the clerk, but when he turned to put the video on the other counter, Lyle was looking right at her.

He picked up the video and smiled in a restrained manly way. "Seeing it again? Not the book. The book is a masterpiece."

"Never seen it," Irene smiled back hoping that would end the encounter.

"Come and see me. If you don't mind my boldness, you look breathtaking. I mean run-around-the-barn-screaming-with-hurt breathtaking."

She remembered laughing out loud at that line in *Bridges*.

When she got home, she would look it up and find that Lyle had taken poetic liberty or maybe it was just bad memory, hers or his she couldn't decide. She took the video out of his hand. "Maybe," she said. "Maybe I will."

Painting Journal

I began the house paintings. Carla said it was the first thing of mine she really liked. Forgive me my success. The houses are painted in a slightly sinister light, early evening, though the surroundings are midday. There's a pull between the inside hidden behind the sickly yellow light emanating from the paper blinds and the green fecundity outside. One of the houses is an old gingerbread Victorian and as the fields become more distant, I have changed them to supermarket counters and shelves in waves. There is less that is sinister about this house than the other two. It is merely falling down. One house is boxy stucco with a fat-lip porch and Venetian blinds. The third, my favorite, has aluminum shingles, and the cement block foundation showing. On the front porch there is a doll missing its eyes, a twisted play rifle, packs of candy cigarettes. The yard beyond the porch suggests a sea of plants and fields that might drown whoever ventures off the porch. There appear to be grass and mud covered hands and feet, a few opened mouths on the surface. Carla hasn't seen the final touches.

I worked yesterday on the color-space painting. The foreground is umber, the right is rust with a vertical wave of brown. A grayish-blue archway moves out of the darker color with dark blue lines creating a sense that the eye is moving inward and twisting behind the rust on the right. At the top I want to paint a separate focal point that will suddenly change the feeling of a tunnel moving in to one moving out from the canvas. I wish my painting could move completely away from the word, into the sensual and indescribable, animal, not human.

Before Irene left for the studio, she played the messages on the machine. Lucille had called and asked Tom to call her about the Peters' case. Irene wondered if the Peters' case, or was it the peter's case, was a code. She and Tom had referred to his penis as Mrs. Flannery, an old woman who lived under them in Brooklyn and had a drunken boyfriend whom she could not get into bed herself when he passed out. About once a month she called them to help her. The bed that she and Tom had in that apartment creaked, and Tom would ask if she wanted to disturb Mrs. Flannery when he wanted sex. It amused her that his penis was female. She would grab him and ask, "Is Mrs. Flannery disturbed?" When he first started working for Chase, he was usually more tired than she was. And she would entice Mrs. Flannery. When she met old female friends of Tom, she asked him in front of them if they had ever met Mrs. Flannery.

Carla left a message reminding her of the walk. Her voice was between upset and commanding. Irene imagined that she had called someone to learn the gossip about her and Lucille's meeting and also found out about Lyle. Four callers had not left a message.

She skipped coffee at the Sunshine. It was wet and drizzling and looked like the rain might turn to ice. Maybe Carla would cancel. She spent most of the morning moving between work on paintings of the Victorian house and the stucco house and deciding what the perspective of the fields should be, what angles and waves of rows would create a sense of separation and make the landscape look liquid and treacherous. The fields should hazily change into flourescent-lit supermarket counters and this should only be an extension, in no way the point, like a Van Dyck painting of flowers where there were insects and drooping petals. She imagined the background as in another way like a Dutch flower painting since she wanted flowering apple trees, trees with apples, ripe corn and beginning shoots, the way Van Dyck put spring, summer and fall flowers together, or maybe it was Hals. It took her a while to think out the color to make the houses seem deader and on another plane than the Rousseau-like background.

After she ate her lunch, she began a new space and color painting, tried to create a sense of depth without using the lines and pulsing brush strokes, but only by placing blocks or pools of colors on the canvas. At two-thirty she didn't feel like stopping, so she called Carla to postpone the walk, but she couldn't reach her.

When she got home she saw Joey and Tom's cars parked in the driveway, and left her car in the street. She went into the house and yelled for Tom, but there was no answer. She walked from window to window. In the corner window in the living room, she saw Tom on a ladder and Joey handing storm windows up to him.

Joey seemed to feel her looking and smiled broadly even before he turned to look at her. She blushed and went upstairs to change. She took her clothes off and peered from the bedroom window through a slit in the blinds. Joey and Tom moved the ladder to another window. Joey went off with the two screen windows. Irene watched him until he went around the corner. When he came back with two storm windows, Tom handed him the screen window he had taken off and took a storm window. Joey squinted up into the high thin clouds. Irene jumped back.

She washed her hands, trying to get off the paint on her nails. She got to the stairs, then went back to put on lipstick. When she saw that Carla was not there yet, she walked around to the back of the house.

"Taking the day off, huh?" She ignored Joey.

"Doing this doesn't qualify as a day off. We should have done this a month ago. No more Indian summers." Tom climbed down the ladder. "You going out walking?"

"With Carla." Irene stood back as they moved the ladder.

"Yard work season over?" Irene said. Joey looked up at Tom as she talked.

"Oh, I got a few Florida customers. But around here it's over, yeah." Joey gave her his cross-toothed sneer and Tom laughed.

"What do they do? Fly you down? Star gardener." Irene was glad to hear Carla honk and waved as she ran off.

Carla gave her the silent treatment on the way out to the football field parking lot. Irene made no attempt to start conversation herself since she had other things on her mind. When she finally calmed down, she noticed that there was only a large white sheet of paper taped to the dashboard, instead of a Stick-em, and it read, "Know who you can trust." This didn't sound like *Bridges*.

Irene was holding her ankles to loosen her hamstrings when Carla took off. She stretched leisurely. When she got to the road, Carla was strutting away, but it wasn't long before she stopped and bent over like someone who had just finished a marathon. When Irene reached her, she was gasping for air.

"Wow! Don't overdo it. Are you okay?" Irene was annoyed that she had to focus so much attention on Carla.

"No, I'm not okay. Do I look okay?" She straightened up to glare at Irene, but it looked like she might be crying.

"Maybe you should sit down." Irene placed an arm on Carla's shoulder and Carla made a symbolic attempt to pull free.

A car rumbled towards them throwing a circling cloud of limestone and dirt dust behind it. Carla straightened slightly and walked bent over for a few yards until the car passed. Irene noticed tears in Carla's eyes.

"Where am I supposed to sit down, in the road? Maybe the ditch? You know it's been raining." Carla cried openly and stopped walking.

"Is it Harold?" Irene asked.

Carla shook her head.

"Let's walk back to the car. It's too cold to stand here." Irene shifted from foot to foot.

Carla sniffled and started sucking on her false tooth. She began to trudge back to the car.

"It's not Harold. I don't care about Harold. It's friends who don't keep their promises." Carla spoke as if all life had been sucked from her body.

"I didn't know that Lyle was coming to that lunch," Irene said.

Carla dragged her feet.

"Tom sells him insurance. He hired him without talking to me to do the landscaping. I'm a big girl, Carla. He does nothing for me." She tried to sound mildly annoyed.

"You lied to me. You walked into the Cake 'n More with him." Carla took short steps kicking stones in front of her.

"Because Tom told him to pick me up, even before I knew who it was."

Carla snorted.

"This is absurd." Irene strutted away from Carla and

thought of walking the rest of the way home, but remembered that Tom and Joey would probably still be in the yard.

Carla was more composed when she got to the car. "We have to get away together and talk. I'm going to see if Jane, you, and I could all go to the Megamall in Minneapolis to go shopping for Christmas. I was going to ask you yesterday."

"Maybe after Thanksgiving. I have to see how my painting is going. I need to get some things straight with Tom."

"What is going on?" Carla took a deep breath.

Irene had seen Lyle's car, too. She said nothing until they parked in front of the house. "Carla, he stopped because he saw Tom's car."

Carla glared at her.

"Carla, Carla, stop." Carla jammed on the brakes and skidded within a few inches of Joey's car. Irene grabbed the dashboard, inadvertently ripping off the note.

"Let me say hello to everyone." Carla was almost out of sight by the time Irene got out. She heard Carla's voice coming from the other side of the house.

The ladder was up in front of the sink window where she stood. She could see Tom on the ground talking to Carla who glanced over her shoulder as if she expected Irene to appear. Lyle and Joey were nowhere to be seen. Then the ladder began to shake and Irene saw Joey's feet appear in the window. When she saw his knees, she rushed to a living room window where she could still see Carla and Tom. In the other side of the yard, Lyle and one of his employees, a short fat man with a bulbous nose, were doing measurements for the gazebo. The man held a long string tied to a stick in the middle of the yard which he moved a few feet in an arc while Lyle measured the distance to the sidewalk or the porch and then scribbled the measurements in a pad.

When she turned back to Tom and Carla, Joey was sitting on the ground and Carla was untying his boot. Joey's face was screwed in pain and Tom was hovering over him. She jumped when she heard a knock on the window. Lyle grinned and then held up the tape measure to explain why he was there. She nodded.

She hurried out of the house and into the yard. Tom was helping Joey up and Carla stood with her hands against his back in case he fell again.

"Irene, help me put the ladder away. Carla's going to take Joey into the kitchen and put some ice on his ankle." Tom seemed annoyed at her. Irene walked to the ladder without answering him and waited. When they finished putting the ladder away, she picked up Joey's tennis shoe, sniffing it when Tom wasn't looking. She carried it into the house. Joey winked at her as she came in and she suspected that he had faked everything.

"Oh, it's really swelling. Come over here. Look at it swell, Irene." Carla said.

"Do you think it's swelling, Mrs. Marston?" Joey asked and the broad grin as he looked up at her didn't match the worry of his voice.

"Oh wow," Irene said as if she were about to fall asleep. She dropped the shoe so it made Carla jump. At the stairs she turned and looked back. Joey formed a slit with his index fingers and stuck his tongue through it. Carla was bent over his foot like one of the magi. Irene shook her head and walked upstairs.

She was lying on the bed when Tom came up. "What's the matter?"

"What do you mean?" Irene rolled over so she faced

the wall.

"Carla comes running around the house, starts asking me all these questions about our yard. You disappear." His voice sounded concerned, as if he thought she were crazy.

"Just because I don't follow Carla around doesn't mean I disappear." It was an uninterested correction. She was not part of an argument.

"You can't act this way. You have to be civil. Carla asked me what was wrong with you." Tom's concern finally made her angry.

"She did?" Irene was off the bed.

"Yes," Tom asserted.

Irene went down the stairs first with Tom following her like the parent who has finally controlled his unruly child.

"I had better say goodbye to Lyle," Irene said in the kitchen.

"The ice helped. It feels a hell of a lot better." Joey spoke to the room.

Carla kept her eyes glued to the foot like she was afraid it might escape her and rubbed the ice vigorously against the ankle.

"Watch it," Joey said.

She walked out slamming the door. It had cooled off since the sun had gone down and looked like rain again. Lyle was standing next to his work truck. She felt stupid and didn't know what to say to him. He moved towards her making some strange hand movements that she interpreted as attempts at Robert Kincaid grace.

"I'll be back on Tuesday. Might have to come alone for some more measurements. I'd love if you could be here." He grabbed her hand in his.

"I paint in the morning." Irene looked around him to the man sitting in the truck. She caught him glancing over at them and imagined the Crawford family was gathered at a window.

"I won't be here until one o'clock." He sounded like a doctor reassuring a patient.

"Sometime in the afternoon." She pulled her hand gently towards her without freeing it.

"One o'clock," he said in a voice hypnotically stern.

When she got back to the kitchen, Joey was on his feet, though his shoe was still off. Tom was giving him an arm and Carla stood next to the window by the breakfast nook.

"Do you want to help him with his shoe, Irene?" Tom helped Joey sit down.

She held his heel with one hand and put the toe of the shoe on his foot, then carefully pushed it on. After she tied it, she let his foot down and pinched him hard on the back of the calf.

"Shit," he screamed.

"Be careful with that foot. It's more tender than it looks," Tom said.

Journal November 13

If I took all my past experience and added it up, I would not get this moment. What parts would I have to forget or erase to arrive here at point X?

Experience is not the great teacher. Life is too complicated for experience to be more than a push in another direction or a chain reaction which closes a whole row of possibilities in its name. Like faith healers, experience is expert in covering its failure, since any wrong move guided (perhaps guided is the wrong word) by it is explained as insufficient experience, as faith healers blame lack of faith. Does remembering bad experiences free us from them, Freudian psychology, or only drain us by making us relive (relieve) the mental turmoil? Bad experience can be the jolt to make us move on. Maybe memories of bad experiences can give us the same jolt. What is our guide? What is the end purpose? Can our desire be clipped to fit our small souls?

And what does any of this have to do with Lyle Bucker? If I sleep with him, I have to let Carla know one way or another, since I would be doing it to punish her. Or is it to punish Tom? Or myself? Or that part of myself that thinks I should have a fulfilling life? This is what you really get. And what has experience with sleeping with men I don't like and am not especially attracted to taught me? Don't do it. The feeling of self-loathing, of a split self, of disgust for desire is a mix of power and powerlessness, exhilaration and despair. But then sleeping with someone without desire is a type of control, too. If I do it and don't want to do it or desire to do it, is that control?

I fight my tendency to elaborate conspiracy theories. When I saw Tom and Joey putting up the storm windows, I had this idea that Tom and Lucille had sent Joey to me in the first place, that the whole town knew about it. The window in the shed with those obscene drawings meant that even the kids knew and were part of it. And Halloween, the kids again. It all seems a coincidence one moment and the next I see the whole town as an animal that has swallowed me and what I try to convince myself are coincidences are really enzymes in the stomach that are digesting me.

I saw Joey's girlfriend yesterday when I went to the post office. She said, "Hey lady, it's his butt," loud enough that the people in the line turned to look at her and then she doubled over laughing and tripped out of the post office. People shook their heads and the post office clerk watched her until she crossed the street. I felt like

I had an internal avalanche, like the blood was rushing out of my head to my feet. I imagined her leaning across Joey's front seat and telling him about our encounter at the post office. I wanted to tell her, "I know, I've seen it lots of times before." No, I don't really want to tell her that.

Carla showed up at the studio yesterday as some kind of apology. She oozed over the house paintings, though she told me she really felt the houses were better than the backgrounds." She wants us to get together with Jane to plan our escape to Minneapolis, though she seems to be leaning towards something closer to home. I don't think I could handle the drive, at least if she did any of the driving.

Before in my life, it always seemed that there was someone that was an outward focus that kept me from the internal maze. At least since college. The string of boyfriends. María Elena and Jens between them. Then Tom. Now I keep turning back to myself and it seems like the world is more and more my invention and I have run out of any interesting ideas.

Tuesday she painted some flowers Doris had requested for her bathroom. She had also supplied Irene with weathered wood from an old barn that she wanted Irene to use to create an early American feel." She sent Irene a picture from a magazine of someone's bathroom with three small paintings on wood of daisies, peonies, and irises. For a long time she had resisted painting the bathroom," as she referred to paintings for Doris when talking to Tom, but today for some reason it seemed perfect. She did a quick wash of glowing creamy yellow and then dabbed color on, folding paper into the thick oils to give some depth to the flowers which she wanted to be more real and sinister than Doris would have expected. With the palette knife she also dug out some of the grain in the wood to create a counter movement to the paint.

She cleaned up the palette knives and brushes at eleven and went home. Tom's car was parked in the driveway. She walked around the yard, then went in the house. She found Tom upstairs lying on the bed in his room.

"Taking your siesta." Irene waited in the doorway for an answer.

"No, I came home to pack for a meeting." He rose on an elbow to look at her.

"Did you get worn out?" She could barely see him in the dark room.

"No. I looked at your journal." He seemed to collapse again on the bed.

She moved the door so it was open only a few inches, then walked to the window so the dull yellow light from the blinds was behind her. "Why were you digging through my things?" She kept her voice calm. Her forehead was hot and she felt nauseous.

"I wasn't digging through your things. I saw the journal on the desk, began to leaf through it and came to those comics about my mother. Do you really think they're funny? What do you have against her?"

"So it was my painting journal?" Irene pulled the blind up a little. Tom winced into the light as he looked up at her.

"Those were really vicious and cruel." He sat up on the edge of the bed and shook his head in disbelief.

"So you had to go to bed." Her voice seemed out of place in the darkness.

"Who was supposed to see those and laugh at my mother?"

"No one was. You certainly weren't." She opened the blinds so she stood in silhouette with the light behind her.

“I’m leaving for five days. I’ll be back Sunday night.” He rose from the bed fully dressed. She wondered whether he had first seen the caricatures a while ago.

“Where are you going?” Irene asked.

“I told you, a meeting.” His suitcase and garment bag were already packed. She hadn’t noticed them next to the door when she came in.

She was sitting in the book room when he left. She yelled goodbye” and got no answer. She had forgotten all about Lyle until she heard pounding on the kitchen door. It was impossible to determine how much time had elapsed between when Tom left and Lyle arrived. He smiled through the glass in the door as if he were from another world, like a character from a children’s program. His teeth seemed huge in comparison with the rest of his face.

“Glad you were home. I’ve been thinking about seeing you since, well since last. It was nice of you to invite me over today.” He had made his way into the kitchen as Irene stood awkwardly holding the door. “Nice place. I was hoping you would show me the house,” he said from the living room.

“It’s not in a state to show anyone. I’m still unpacking. Every week I get . . . .”

Lyle seemed not to have heard her, “Are these the stairs to the upstairs?”

“No, those are the stairs to the downstairs,” she said slamming the door, but Lyle was already on his way up. Sitting at the kitchen table, she listened to his boots click from room to room.

“Maybe you could come upstairs and show me around.”

She didn’t answer him.

“Irene, Irene, maybe you could come upstairs.” His voice had lost its calm assuredness.

She trudged up the stairs. “You know, I am trying to get this house in order and keep up with my painting. It’s not in any shape to show anyone. Weren’t we going to talk about the gazebo?”

The doors to all the rooms were open and she looked into the book room first and finally into her bedroom. He stood with his cowboy hat on, resting a hand on the bureau.

“What are you doing in here?” she said moving close enough to him so that he could touch her.

“I feel like I have dropped off a planet or the tail of a comet and come into your life at the end of the lane,” he said in an ethereal Boris Karloff voice.

She shook trying to control her laughing. Lyle embraced her.

“Strong emotions,” he said and waited for her to respond.

“You know,” he said, “I could get on a plane and go to Sumatra, or Tibet, or Shangorilla and be with the daughter of an ivory merchant and I could be deep in her now, almost her soul, but I would rather be here.”

On “Shangorilla” Irene snorted involuntarily and Lyle pressed her against him so that she lost her breath. Her cheek rubbed against his bony ribs and her nose was smashed against his sternum. She gasped for air, trying to control her laughing which Lyle had interpreted as sobbing.

“Strong emotions,” he said and shuffled towards the bed, pulling her with him. She could feel his cock on her stomach.

“Some rooms are always better without all the lights on.” He exaggerated his breathing. He sat down on the bed and opened his arms like the pope.

"Darkrooms, maybe," she said and was down the stairs again before he could answer. Her own line seemed funny to her and she sat at the kitchen table trying to look serious. She moved to the chair facing away from the doorway, but thought it would be harder to keep a straight face if she could laugh while he was coming towards her, so she sat facing the stairs again and lowered her head.

It took her a few seconds to figure out why he had his shirt hanging out in front. Viagra she thought. He stopped with one leg out further than the other and his hands folded like the naked Adam covering his crotch as he fled Eden.

"Like Robert Kincaid, I have a duty to protect you from scandal." He took off his cowboy hat and held it in front of his crotch and tucked his shirt in, performing a few movements to accommodate his erection better.

"What about the gazebo?" Irene controlled herself, but the result made her sound meek.

"I have a Dinah Washington tape in the car. Do you have a tape player?" He seemed as if he had practiced his speeches, but was in the wrong play.

"Nope," she said.

"We could dance," he said as if he hadn't heard her. "Here in the kitchen."

"No, I don't have a tape player."

"Do you want to see me again?" Lyle said.

She knew if she tried to answer now she would laugh.

"Under better circumstances. You could drive your car so no one would see us driving out of town together. It's important to me to protect your reputation. You have to live in this town." He stayed a few feet from her. "I mean you don't live on a farm like Francesca."

"Who?" she said suddenly seeming imposing and short-tempered, but when she saw his horror, she added, "Oh yes, the woman in *Bridges*."

She walked to the door and turned back to Lyle who adjusted the angle of the cowboy hat. "I want to paint during the day."

He used his most sonorous voice. "When I think of you and art, I think of the café life in Nipples." It took him a second to realize what he said. "Café life in Naples. Naples, Italy."

She rushed out of the house, down the steps and sat on the steps of the porch next to where the gazebo was to go. She hugged herself as she laughed and then took a deep breath. "I'm over here, Lyle." She imagined that he had taken a double dose of Viagra. He came around the corner holding his hat.

"I wrote the name of a place about twenty miles west of here. You name the time and place." He handed her a sheet from his notebook with a map he had sketched and the name of a café and motel, the Round-A-View. He gazed at her with his sincere sad-dog eyes.

"I think you named the place already." She avoided his gaze.

"Any time."

"Thursday at five," she dropped her head towards the ground.

"Would seven be okay? Seven rhymes with heaven. Silver apples of the moon, golden apples of the sun." Lyle tried to raise his hands in plea, but seemed to remember why he was holding the hat.

"Celtic twilight," she said remembering how much she hated the early Yeats quoted in *Bridges*.

"Is that a kind of light?" Lyle asked.

She gathered all of her control to look him seriously in the face. "Yes, it's that seven o'clock November light."

"All of these years and lifetimes we have been getting to the point of meeting," Lyle put his hat on. He seemed to have forgotten his erection in the passion of misquoted lines from Robert James Waller's novel.

When she looked up from the ground she saw Fern Gregor walking across the street towards them. "Have you seen Joey?" she shouted though only a few yards from them now.

Irene jumped up and ran in front of Lyle before he could turn to Fern. "Gee, no," she said keeping herself between Lyle and Fern. Without saying any more, Fern strode on up the street.

"I have to go," Irene said. In a flash she was in the kitchen. He tapped on the window of the door and Irene held the map he had drawn up to the window without showing her face.

"Seven," he said and then knocked seven times and left.

Ten minutes later she heard Fern calling Joey's name as she walked home.

Journal November 17

It has become a game to check Lyle's accuracy against Bridges. It wasn't the ivory merchant's, but "the silk merchant's daughter" in Bangkok whose screams Robert Kincaid listens to as he "turns her inside out at twilight." But he gives up exotic foreign sex for four days of Deepak Chopra sex with a war bride from Nipples.

Oh, the inevitability of plot. Personal insecurity plot. What happens when you cannot stand to only imagine what would have happened? Tom is off at a meeting. Mrs. Benson is minding the store. I called to find out. I will drive Doris's car, the one she drove before Ralph died, the one she has wanted me to take since I got here, to the assignation with Viagra Lyle.

I wish Jens or María Elena were here so I could tell them about yesterday, so the absurdity of my encounter with Lyle had some dimension. When an event remains unshared, only in my mind, when it is secret, it seems to lack reality. It doesn't exist until it is told. That clear line between something happening or not happening doesn't exist. If it happens and I tell ten people about it, it is not the same as if it happens and I tell no one. It's like a dream that you tell and in the telling, it becomes clear. And if it is never told, it is forgotten forever almost immediately.

After Lyle left I laughed to myself about Nipples, Celtic twilight and the little actor behind the hat. Finally in the middle of one of these fits of laughter, I wondered what I was really laughing about. I sat there trying to move myself back a few paces to where I had been when I started laughing, and there was a knock at the door. It was the older Gregor boy, he said his name was Chip and he wanted to know if I had seen Joey. "Your brother?" I said and felt myself blush. He didn't speak, but nodded like I was an idiot. A little later I looked up their number in the phone book and called. They had found him asleep behind a chair in the living room.

Carla called this morning and left a message that she couldn't go walking. We hadn't made any plan to. I think I saw her car go by Discount Buddies. Maybe she was making sure I wasn't home before she called. I'll call her later. She would never understand the Lyle thing. Or what I want to say is she would think I understood it or should.

Doris called to ask if I had heard from Tom. We have to go to Thanksgiving at her house. I had no excuse.

By five it was already becoming dark. She got up from the desk to turn on the light and heard the phone downstairs.

"Hello, is this Doris, I mean Irene Marston?"

She recognized Louie's voice. "Irene, not Doris. Listen, Louie, everyone makes mistakes. Good to hear from you. Anything up?"

"Well, I had an open evening tonight and wondered if you still wanted your nails done. I know it's late. It could be some other time." Irene didn't answer immediately and he went on, "You know, if you can."

"Sure, sure, I could do it tonight."

On the way she stopped for gas at a station surrounded by cornfields. After she paid, she stood looking up into the sky.

She once saw a book on star gazing that showed how the stars changed and what they looked like fifty thousand years ago and what they would look like fifty thousand years from now. The shapes in the sky would twist and collapse, move on to other shapes. At the time the thought had overwhelmed her, depressed her, and she had brought the book to Tom who had said, "What do I care? I'll be dead." He could always maintain his sense of separateness from everything else.

Tonight she felt both part of and separate from the universe. Her cosmic insignificance and the inevitability of change made her feel free. She got in the car, turned the heater up high and rolled the window down a few inches to hear the air rush into the car. When the car was up to sixty, she rolled the window up an inch.

She walked in the open door.

"I heard you on the steps," Louie said. "You don't mind if we watch the end of this show."

"No, no," she said and sat in a big boxy armchair with some large throw pillows. It had been weeks since she had watched television.

"If he gets this answer, he wins fifty thousand dollars," Louie explained.

Phil walked out of the room and returned with a magazine that he set on his lap and read during commercials.

When the program was over Louie left the set on as he went to get the tray and a small table he used for manicures. Irene uncomfortably inspected the room.

"Bought anything new lately?" she asked Phil who put down the magazine.

"The doily on the radio," Phil said pointing to an old wooden cased RCA.

"Pineapple pattern," she said.

"Not many people know that." He put his magazine down again.

"I used to have a roommate who dragged me to flea markets and Salvation Army stores in search of that stuff and stole my dresses. He finally got to be too much. He always stretched out my shoes." She laughed nervously.

"You haven't been sharing that story with too many people in Pendayhaz, I bet," he said.

"Don't even know if I told Tom about the shoes."

They both looked over at Louie when he brought in a chair for Irene.

"Louie told me you painted," Phil said. Louie seemed content to concentrate on Irene's nails and the television.

"I've started again. In New York I got burned out. I was working in a gallery when I met Tom. The idea was that I would be able to paint here. I have a studio. It's the best thing about living in Pendayhaz."

"And what's second best?" Phil asked.

"That I'm not living in a third world slum eating out of garbage cans."

Phil chuckled halfheartedly.

A commercial came on the television and Louie pushed the mute button on the remote.

"You know last week after you were here, I was telling Phil about what you said about us being a gay island in the middle of Crandall and I said it was like Tahiti and you said Bikini. He told me that they used to drop bombs on Bikini. Did you know that?" Louie talked without looking up from the nail on her thumb.

"Yes, I knew that."

When the commercials were over, Louie again divided his attention between the television and her nails.

"I have a friend in town who paints. Her husband is a doctor. She and some friends run a little co-op gallery about ten miles from here in Walnut Grove. She has some painting in it. There's a lot of wood working, needlepoint, refinished antiques. If you want to meet her I could call her up." Phil showed no enthusiasm.

"Well, maybe you're not interested." He lifted the magazine again.

"No, I'd love to meet her."

"I'll call her then."

New York Journal

I was nervous. The critics from the New Yorker, New York Magazine, *and the* Village Voice *were there and Marie, the owner of the gallery, knew how to work them. She was pretty sure I would get a blurb in "Goings On about Town" in the* New Yorker. *As far as my experience goes, nothing is sure. I feel like I have been possessed by these paintings and now that they are in the gallery, I feel that they have broken off from me and I and they are free. Of course, now I start worrying about whether they'll sell. Having the gallery show will look great on my snob list.*

María Elena came and seemed happy to see me. She said she felt inspired and was going to try to take time off from work to paint more. She told me, too, that she had been afraid that our friendship was going down the tubes when I was with Tom. I seemed to never have any time for anyone else. And she never felt that comfortable around him. And to think I thought she had screwed him. He always managed to make his denials seem like a confession.

Jens met some guy from Iowa named Chuck with his lover Louie. He asked me if Tom knew them. Was he joking?

There are days when I wish I hadn't broken it off with Chago. That old itch. But it's best to wait for what really matters, a relationship of equals, fellow nurturers with a little cynical bite. What was that line in the old bolero that María Elena sings, "Amor es la mentira más fácil decir." *Love is the easiest lie to tell. Or to take whatever I have learned or think I have and try it out in another relationship where there seems to be a future. But I see complications at every turn. I can settle for a career now.*

Phil's friend Sherry Torrence called to come over the next morning to look at the studio. Irene tried to picture what she looked like from the reedy twanged voice.

"With Chuck and I, Chuck's my husband, Doctor Chuck, it's always a problem to get things done." Irene noted two other times where Mrs. Torrence, "but you can call me Sherry," had used I where she should have used me. Louie had referred to her as elegant, very elegant," probably meaning she was a good customer. Irene had imagined her thin, waifish and tall with a Hermes scarf, Rolex watch and heavy perfume, maybe in her thirties or forties. The only hit was the heavy perfume.

She hadn't been able to keep her mind on painting. For one thing she kept telling herself that she wasn't going to see Lyle and each time she told herself, she realized that the possibility was growing. She couldn't concentrate on the color-space painting, so she put up Doris's three flower paintings. The peony worked well with the paper and globs of paint coming off the rough board and she thought Doris would be dismayed, but it might grow on her. The daisy painting, despite her efforts, seemed too cute, just what Doris would love, and she left the two thick white daisies with yellow centers in the middle and created pulsing white, yellow and blue out to the edge. She put the iris up and walked to the window to check the street. A long white Cadillac Eldorado swerved neatly to the curb and parked. A large woman in her late fifties got out of the car and looked up and down the street before she zeroed in on the second floor of the bank.

Irene picked up the empty plastic water bottles and the Styrofoam cups that littered the floor and threw a sheet over two chairs piled with magazines and rags stained with paint and dirt. She opened the door and peered down the steps that hadn't been swept since she moved in. It was good that she hadn't replaced the light bulb, though a yellowish light seeped through the grime on the stairwell window.

Sherry Torrence was at the door before Irene was down the stairs. Sherry flung the door open and Irene was met by perfume that filtered through Sherry's long down coat that made her look like a light-gray walking mattress. A belt around the waist created a division between hips and chest that wasn't there naturally.

"Sherry?"

"Irene?"

They both nodded. In the stairwell the perfume became overpowering and Irene opened a window slightly when they got upstairs. Sherry took off her coat to reveal a bright red, purple, and yellow print blouse down to her mid-calves. She wore teal green techno-fiber harem pants.

"A real studio with poor heating and paint everywhere. You know, I've seen *La Boheme* five times. Four on television and once at the Metropolitan in New York City. Chuck and I went there on our thirty-fifth wedding anniversary. Is this your stuff? Wow. A lot of risk taking."

Irene pulled "The Carnival Shooting Gallery", "Stony Faces", "The Fall of Icarus in Iowa," and "Le Tub" from one of the back rooms and displayed them along the wall.

"Really different stuff. I'll have to get the doctor to buy something. Not for his office, but for our house. You have to come out and see us."

Irene walked behind Sherry as she went from painting to painting, pointing out technique she recognized, comparing Irene's work to other painters.

"Well, a bunch of girls and a few men and I are interested in painting and art and sell a little at this old general store we've turned into a gallery. We take turns attending it, like a co-op. Chuck says we're communists. That riles up some of the group."

Sherry laughed and took hold of the front of her shirt and pulled it away from her body a few times to cool off.

"We're some real rabble rousers." She approached within a few inches of an arm on one of the men in "The Carnival Shooting Gallery." Irene wondered what she was looking at.

"Last month some of us went to Santa Fe to a painting workshop. Frank Boa was the artist in residence for the week. What an experience! You know Frank Boa, don't you?" Sherry turned her whole body around to Irene.

"No, I don't."

"Oh you should. He's been in all the art magazines. Next month we're going to Pensacola to learn how to do Audubon birds with Zella Frick. She was on the cover of *Art Thinking.*" Sherry's face set into a broad almost surprised grin that Irene thought would last until she said the magic word.

"Really?" Irene had no idea who this Frick was.

"Really," Sherry said and moved on to "The Fall of Icarus in Iowa".

"Well, we all paint at home, but when Phil told me that you had a studio, I thought wouldn't that be a great experience, you know, to have a New York art studio experience here in Crandall or Pendayhaz. So I called up some friends and we would like to pay you for lessons. And maybe you could join the group." Sherry had zeroed in on a foot sticking out from between the roots of a cottonwood tree.

"Lessons might be a good idea. One day a week we could paint together. We could figure the payment later," Irene said and moved to the window as Sherry continued to look at "The Fall of Icarus in Iowa".

"You just have to tell me how to do them," Sherry said

moving slowly back from the painting.

"Do what?" Irene asked.

"Toes. I never have been able to do toes and fingers. Marvelous toes in that painting."

"Sure," Irene said. She sneezed and wondered if she were allergic to Sherry's perfume.

"Oh, oh, oh, oh," Sherry raised her large arms into the air and Irene went into a sneezing fit.

"These I have to have. I have some old Monet haystack in my bathroom and I'm sick of that morning or evening light, whatever it is. Chuck says it's farm art. Monet's a genius, I know. These flowers would be perfect." Sherry paced in front of them, stopping occasionally at the right or left and looking intently as if she wanted to see what was behind the paintings.

"Those are for a commission." Irene felt dishonest not telling her they were for her mother-in-law. She cracked another window to get some fresh air.

"On wood no less. And how do you get the depth? Of course, I want lilies. You will do lilies for me, won't you. The bathroom is peach to match the haystacks, or maybe it was the other way around." She laughed and Irene wondered what she thought was funny.

Carla was at the bottom of the steps as Irene walked Sherry out.

"You're not the woman who bought the flowers?" Sherry asked glaring at Carla in mock anger.

Carla pursed her lips and shook her head gravely.

"No, no, she's not." Irene made the introductions and seconds later Sherry drove off in her Eldorado, honking and waving out the window with her arm that looked like a large gray log.

"Do you want to go to the Sunshine?" Irene could tell that Carla was upset.

"No, I do not want to go to the Sunshine and I never have. I hate that place."

"I'm sorry. What about going upstairs?"

Carla pushed on her false tooth with her tongue and sucked it back with a rhythmic furor that Irene had never experienced before. "Let's go for a ride. I need to drive."

"I was in the middle of painting."

Carla twisted her head around and glared at Irene who had not followed her. "Yeah, I can see. Sherry what's her name. Just for a few minutes," Carla commanded.

After the first step towards Carla, Irene seemed to lose the power of resistance.

Carla jerked away from the curb.

"Carla, maybe you shouldn't drive when you are upset."

"I'm not upset. Maybe you didn't notice, this is Harold's car. A clutch. I'm just not used to driving a clutch." The car made a loud grinding sound as Carla shifted into second.

"Oh," Irene said and felt trapped. She looked out at the marquee of the movie theater.

"Harold is such a fool! I always knew it. He thinks that he and this guy he met in New Orleans are going to get together. He's going to tell the world. How pathetic!" She hit the brake instead of the clutch and Irene clutched the dashboard.

"Guy. You didn't tell me it was a guy." Irene warily leaned

back in the seat again.

"Don't tell me you didn't know."

"Well, kind of. How is this going to affect you?" Irene asked. They were now barreling out of town a good twenty miles over the speed limit. Irene tried to sound calm and analytical.

"Don't you see, don't you see . . . ?" Carla broke off sobbing.

"Pull over, Carla, so we can talk. Carla." The pitch of Irene's voice shot up when she saw a truck coming towards them.

"I'm okay," Carla shouted and wiped her eyes with the back of her arm. "My husband leaves me for another man, tells the goddam world about it. What will people say about me? I've had enough talk in my life. Something you don't seem to worry about." She pounded the accelerator and Irene gasped. The car rocked as the truck sped past them in the other direction.

She slowed the car down, took a deep breath, and looked over at Irene with a much calmer face. "I wouldn't even mind people talking if there was some substance to it. Real substance."

"Why? Isn't Harold really leaving you for a man?" Irene didn't dare look Carla in the face.

"You know. You know. Don't pretend you don't. Don't." The car was going so slowly that it began to chug in fourth gear. Irene felt car sick.

"Let Jane tell you about reputations and my uncle. And she was lucky." Carla tried to downshift into first and the gears ground violently. "I hate his damn car!"

"What can I do for you?" Irene paused between each word.

"So much," Carla said, then looked over at Irene and repeated herself fervently. The weight of Carla's foot fell on the gas pedal as she relaxed and the car seemed to absorb her passion. Irene reached for the dashboard again and her right foot automatically pressed the floor.

"I'll try," Irene said. "Carla, my paint is drying, my brushes will be ruined. That means something to me, too."

Carla continued with her mantra, "So much, so much, so . . . "

They had driven around two sections and were coming in to town again on the road they usually walked.

"Carla, we're in town. The speed limit." Irene wished she could get off at her house as they drove by. She saw some kids on the roof of the shed where she used to paint, who crouched down as the car passed.

"I want you to think about everything I have said. I don't need an answer right away, but I need an answer. I need one." Carla had lost control again on the last sentence.

Irene remained silent, looked a few times over at Carla and smiled, which seemed to placate her.

"Not right away, but I need an answer." Carla smiled back and seemed unaware that her tires squeaked against the curb as she pulled up next to the back entrance of the Discount Buddies. A few people in Val's-U-4-U's parking lot turned in their direction. Irene opened the car door, but Carla grabbed her hand before she could get out.

"The whole town probably knows about Harold right now. Everyone. They're all looking at me right now. But you know what? I don't care." Carla blinked with both eyes at Irene. "I can wait for the answer."

When Irene got out of the car, she took a deep breath of the cold November air and looked up in the sky streaked with thin rows of high cirrus clouds. "Carla, I don't even know what the question is." She slammed the door and strode to the back door. Upstairs she peered out of the window and watched Carla's car jerk off in first gear and stall. The jerks became more violent and the car rolled through the intersection without stopping for the stop sign.

At 1:30 she called Mrs. Benson to see if Tom had checked in at the office, but she said he hadn't. Driving home she parked in front of the Prairie Star movie theater. She read the marquee to herself, "B idges of Mad   C unt starring Cli t." Perhaps no one had complained because they were so used to seeing it that they didn't notice that someone had knocked off more letters. Maybe it had been that way for months and she hadn't noticed either. "Someone was laughing," she thought. "Someone was always laughing."

A few cars drove by. Tillie Pearson came back from a late lunch and honked and waved. Irene drove slowly away from the curb. She felt like Doris's car was taking her home and would take her to the Round-A-View later without her being able to do anything about it.

She parked the car in the street and walked to the shed. She no longer carried the key to the padlock so she looked inside through the broken window. Along the side farthest from the house, cement blocks and four-by-four posts formed a step up to the corrugated tin roof. Four rope stirrups were nailed into the studs of the shed, hidden behind the vines of a sickly clematis. She forgot all about the neighbors until she was on top of the shed.

In the middle of the roof lay a gray utility blanket that was folded and held down by eight large bricks. She moved four of the bricks and peered under the blanket.

Four tattered *Hustler* magazines had holes punched in the upper left hand corner and were strung together with a plastic cord that was tied to a roofing nail which was sticking halfway out. Red plastic file tabs were stapled to pages and were marked with women's names. She set her haunches into the ruts of the aluminum as best she could and set her feet in front of her to keep from sliding. She opened to "Coleen." The tab must have come off since a bite was taken out of the page and the tab had been replaced with a pasted paper reinforcement to the binding. Coleen squatted naked over a leprechaun doll with its finger in the air as if it were telling a story.

There were two plastic boxes for six-eight note cards with plastic snap lids held shut with thick red rubber bands. She opened the heavier one first. Inside were five airline flasks of whiskey and rubbers in a variety of colors and some small packages of flavored lubricant. She put the rubber band back on and opened the lighter box. There was a small bag of marijuana, rolling paper, matches, and twenty dollars in singles.

She had slid down the roof a bit so she put her hands on the cold metal roof and pushed herself further up. It flashed in her mind that she was like a squirming bug and the square aluminum roof was like a slide for a microscope. She looked up into the sky. It had clouded up but there was a break in the clouds and light fell on the roof of the Crawford house. "Always the spy feels spied upon," she said to no one.

When she was pushing the boxes back under the blanket, she discovered a notebook in a gallon Ziplock bag. "Rules for the Knights and Knightesses of the Mask." Her fingers were red and her nose was running. She considered taking the notebook with her into the house to read, but when she leafed through it, she saw that it was only a few pages long with notes in another hand for an algebra class.

The most important rule is to get in. To get in you have to be voted for by everyone, including members who aren't here. Yunger kids are not alloud and if they ever mess with our stuff, they will get the treetment.

Rule number two is that everything, everything, everything is secret. This is a secret society so it has to be that way. Cuz it is secret, everyone must use their secret names when speaking of the secret stuff.

Gore and Havoc are the leaders because they have sceen the lady naked. No one else has seen her naked. If someone else wants to become a leader, they have to see the lady naked with Gore or Havoc. This is the only proof. Girls have to see her husband naked.

If you don't pay your dues, you are out. O-U-T means out. Money is best, but other club stuff can be okay. Chek 1st.

This is the offfice-SHALL rule book. Except no other.

Walking across the yard, she wondered if they would know that she had looked at their stuff. They must have been home from school during lunch hour when she saw them earlier.

In the bathtub she finally felt warm again and let the hot water dribble to keep the bath water warm. María Elena had known a couple and one of the women was extremely obese and only got a good night's sleep in the bathtub where the water would make her a hundred pounds lighter, but her lover had to get up in the middle of the night to add warm water. The water seemed to do the same thing to her mind. She was in thoughtless suspension until even with the dribble of hot water, she became chilled. She sat up and drained off some water, placing her foot on top of the drain to feel the sucking on her toes. Then she ran hot water until she could hardly stand it. She placed her toes on the edge of the tub and stared at them. The ends of her hair dangled in the water and pulled it straight when she finally got out.

In the door mirror she watched the steam roll from her body and thought of morning fog in New Jersey in the swampy area behind her parents' house. She stretched out and stared at the indent her spine made. "Landscape by Irene Langer," she said. She wrapped the towel around her waist, put a leg up on the side of the tub. "Not naked, just obscene."

It was dark out. The clouds had broken up enough for the moon to shine intermittently, but most of the light outside came from streetlights, front porches, and the windows of houses. Behind the bare branches of the maple tree, she made out three figures on the roof of the shed, huddled together to protect themselves from the wind. She flipped off the lights next to the medicine chest and stood in the dark. The three turned to the house and a few minutes later crawled down. Irene left the bathroom.

The phone rang and she picked it up wearily thinking it would be Carla.

"Irene, it's Tom. I've been trying to call Mrs. Benson, but the line is busy. I forgot to pay the house electric bill. I think it's due today. It's in my office desk on the right hand corner. Could you stop by and tell her." Tom's voice had that absent I'm-doing-something-else sound to it.

"Sure. How is the meeting going?"

"Well, you know how these things are. And you."

"Oh, nothing ever happens to me. Nothing." She hung up before he said goodbye.

New York Journal

I got my first canceled rent check back. I had a little party and invited María Elena, Doris and Carmen, my agent, and a few buyers who are interested in my work. Chaguito came later, wanted to spend the night, but I shooed him off with María Elena.

Tom called just as I was falling asleep. He said he called on a whim but he seems to call early Saturday morning or late at night when I might be with someone. Why do I even care if he is jealous?

She left early in case she got lost and arrived at six-thirty-five. The pink neon sign for the Round-A-View blinked like a bleating lamb, she thought. She got out of the car to walk around the parking lot, heard laughing and voices trying to talk over each other coming from the restaurant. A few lights were lit in motel rooms and four cars were parked in front of dark rooms. A car pulled in with its windows partially down and rap music blaring from them. From behind her car, she watched the two young men in the car pass a joint back and forth. When they drove off, she walked to the edge of the parking lot. There were harvested cornfields as far as she could see and to the north a line of shrub and trees, which, she assumed, marked the course of the creek she had passed over a quarter of a mile before the restaurant. What was the view, she wondered. She walked back to the car and sat in the driver's seat with her hands in her coat pockets. The coldness of the car keys in her right pocket seemed insistent. She took them out and dangled them before her eyes. "Just because you've come this far doesn't mean. . . " She put the keys back in her pocket.

"Doesn't mean," she repeated again.

The lamp in the window of one of the motel rooms fell over and the light moved erratically across the shade for a few moments. A child began to scream. A bumper sticker on the back of the rusting station wagon in front of the room said, "Lick

Bush. Elect Clinton."

The lights of Lyle's pickup came at her and she felt paralyzed. In a soft professional voice he said, "Irene, I have the keys already. I fixed the room up for us."

"Great," she said and got out of the car without looking at him.

The motel room was at the end of a row of twenty motel rooms. A solitary lamp post seemed to be afloat on a sea of flat dark land. The fence of a cornfield was only a few feet off and Irene stared at the seemingly endless lines of broken stalks and thin finger-like roots that were visible near the lamp.

A gust of wind sent empty fast food bags and ripped plastic bags blowing against the motel where they stuck until the wind seemed to exhale and then were pulled into the parking lot again. "Even a garbage bag dancing in the wind can be beautiful," Lyle said as his face washed in poetic glow.

Irene stared at the trash. He opened the door and the light from the room seemed sinisterly infused by the orange and white striped wallpaper.

"Most men wouldn't think of it. But I don't want to be like most men. Brandy and music." He strutted across the small room to a boom box, then tripped back and shut the door softly which she had left open.

"I just got this Dinah Washington for tonight. They used the songs in the movie of *The Bridges of Madison County*. I thought you would like it," Lyle explained and enveloped Irene in his arms. She thought she heard the child cry again.

Lyle moved slower than the music. She tried to pull away from him at the end of "You're Nobody 'Til Somebody Loves You," but he seemed oblivious to the music and continued to rock from foot to foot like a metronome through pauses between the songs and their shifting tempo. When they swayed by the light switch, he turned it off so the room was lit by the flourescent light that came through the open bathroom door. He began to slide her dress up as they moved back and forth across the room. She listened to the words of "You've Been a Good Old Wagon" and wondered if Lyle had taken his Viagra. He dropped one of his hands down the back of her underpants and pulled her into him. She moved her arms to her chest to keep him at a distance.

"There's brandy," he said letting her go. "Most men wouldn't think of that. These Iowa farmers wouldn't think of it." He poured brandy into a juice glass.

"Aren't you having any?" She took a sip. It took her breath away and she could feel it sting down her esophagus and into her stomach.

"It affects me, you know," Lyle said shaking his head. He crossed his hands across his crotch.

"You know, you can watch me out of the corner of your eye if you're nervous," he said.

He got up and shut the door to the bathroom. Dinah Washington began to sing "Me and My Gin." In outline she could see him step out of his pants that had dropped to the floor. He pulled down his underwear and stepped on them with one foot as he pulled the other foot out. He kicked the leg with the underwear and sent red bikini briefs flying across the room.

When he reached the bed, she had taken all her clothes off except for her underwear and lay straight on the bed. She thought of Carla and hated her.

"How do you want it?" Lyle asked rubbing up against her. His breath smelled of Tums.

She didn't answer. Even though it was dark, she could make out vague water stains on the ceiling.

"It's going to be mystical," he said and placed one of his calves between her cold feet and pulled her against his side. "We'll be inside of each other. Then we'll be part of a new person. A new person. A new person." He began rubbing his cock against her butt and seemed to have forgotten that his words had any meaning. He moved his lips next to her and pressed his tongue against her lips, then licked her face in long lapping strokes. She twisted her face away, but when he plunged his slobbering tongue into her ear, she jerked her head back to face him.

He kept one hand under her neck and turned to get a condom that he had left next to the bed earlier that afternoon. He ripped it open with his teeth and spit the paper on the floor like a chew of tobacco.

"From the back," Irene blurted out.

He took his hand away from her neck and put the condom on. She thought he hadn't understood her.

"From the back?" he asked.

"From the back," she repeated and made a pile of the two pillows sinking her head in them and grabbing the front of the bed.

Lyle moved over her, knelt for one painful second on one of her legs. She moved a hand back to help him. He tried to curl around her to reach her neck with his tongue, but she kept her head buried in the pillow and waited for him to finish. He sounded like he was choking and groaning. He gave three violent jerks and went limp. Irene worried that the Viagra had given him a heart attack. She lifted her head from the pillow and glanced behind her. Lyle straightened up, but remained stiff and silent. She saw him reach into his mouth and straighten his dentures and she buried her head in the pillow again.

When the light came on in the bathroom, she peeked from the pillow. The headboard and the chairs had overstuffed red velvet upholstery. Dinah Washington was playing for the second time "Fly Me to the Moon." He came back from the bathroom wearing the white motel towel which bulged in the front. She was sitting up in bed with her fists around the sheets and holding them up to her chin.

"I have this room for three days," he said and shook his head at his good luck. "Three days that we will never forget, not through eternity." His penis gave a throb that she noticed through the towel.

He lay down on the bed next to her and seemed to share the view of the ceiling with her. He turned his head towards her. "Isn't this what it's all about," he said.

Irene laughed until she thought she would wet the bed in the Round-A-View Number 21. She staggered to the bathroom almost doubled over and looked back at Lyle through the tears that streamed down her face. He lay stone still like an Etruscan Sarcophagi. She came back from the bathroom to get her clothes and returned to the bathroom.

She fell into another fit of laughter when she left the bathroom and noticed that the bulge in Lyle's towel was gone.

The cold wind blew dust into her face when she opened the door. She took a deep breath. "Lyle, thanks," she said breaking into laughter again. "Lyle, thanks for the brandy."

"Can you come tomorrow?" he asked as she slammed the door and ran to the Cutlass. She pulled the car into a closed gas station in the middle of nowhere. All the lights were off except for a sign for Marlboro in the window. She got out of the car and gazed up trying to concentrate on the black expanse between the stars. The moon glowed behind some clouds. The wind pierced through her and she jumped back into the car and drove off. Passing the Pendayhaz city limits, she yelled to herself, "Carla, I hate you. Carla, I hate you." It sounded so stupid the second time that she shook her head.

She tried to sleep as soon as she got home, but when she closed her eyes she saw the fields around the Round-A-View and kept thinking that she saw them through the eyes of someone standing in Room Number 21 who maybe wasn't really her. "This is what it's all about," she repeated to herself until she fell asleep. But it seemed less and less funny.

The next morning she woke up late. The phone rang as she was coming down the steps and she got it on the third ring. The person on the other end said nothing and she was about to hang up when Carla spoke. "Irene, this is Carla. I just wanted to tell you that Harold's thing is off. He came home last night."

"Yes," Irene said.

"So, forget what I told you. Just forget it, okay. He's angry about me telling you. I never said it." Carla's voice broke.

"You never said it." Irene wanted to get off the phone.

"I might stop by your studio later. I might bring Jane. You know, the trip."

"I have work to do, to catch up. I'm late now," Irene said and waited for Carla to speak.

"Then tomorrow. I'll stop by tomorrow. Just for a bit."

"Okay." Irene put down the receiver.

She took a shower instead of a bath, running the water so hot that her shoulders and face stiffened. She put on some old work pants and one of Tom's old flannel shirts over a sweatshirt, rolling the sleeves of the shirt up so they came to her elbows. Barb Lemmon was outside the front of Discount Buddies smoking a cigarette when she drove past. She came around to the back entrance when Irene stopped.

"You had two messages. Lyle Bucker called and said you should remember the meeting about the gazebo tonight at seven. And Doctor Torrence's wife wanted me to tell you that she's going to paint her bathroom and said she wants the background for the lilies baby blue. You can check with her if you have doubts." Barb dropped her cigarette on the ground and put it out with the toe of her tennis shoe.

Journal November 20

I see myself in a motel with VL, Viagra Lyle, and the person looking is not me, but an imaginary I in New York or San Francisco or Hong Kong looking at myself, shaking her head or laughing at the absurdity of it all. This outside I laughs or shrugs in disgust, but even as this other woman cringes or laughs, the specter lurks that it was really always her.

I can't see my life as having any unity. The women, who were with the other men, who were my drunken or bored embarrassments, were other people who only existed at some brief moment in time and then disappeared and I remember like I would a great aunt whom I heard about. What seems to connect me to that person from before are the moments when I said something unintentionally cruel, like when I told Ivonne from the gallery, as a joke, of course, that only a harelip could love her, and her boyfriend had a hair lip, or incredibly stupid, like the time I insisted to a friend of Jens that Van Gogh was French because at least in my mind I thought we were talking about Gaugin. Or letting Tom take up my life so I didn't see Jens when he was sick and still in New York. I remember those things and they seem to burn into me. Or the points in my life where I seemed to have missed opportunities: men whom I now think I could have loved, phone calls from friends I never returned, career connections that I let lapse, important meetings that I blew off. It's never the good moments that still seem connected to me. Regret holds me to my former attempts at being Irene, connects them to my present impersonation. Virginia Woolf said that the past seemed so wonderful because we remembered it without anxiety. I don't have the same memory gene she did.

Looking at myself through windows, telescopes, and canvases. The option may be to not look at all.

Lyle called Discount Buddies and asked Tillie to get Irene. Irene told Tillie to say that she had just left and to tell him she hadn't come back if he called again. When she turned the ringer back on, the phone rang immediately.

"Irene, I have been trying to talk to you all day." Lyle had a hyperventilating urgency.

"Oh, you have?" Irene wished she had left the ringer off.

"You didn't come tonight." He spoke and waited. Irene could hear him sighing.

"No, I didn't."

The phone was silent and Irene thought that maybe Lyle had hung up. "Lyle?"

"Yes."

"Do you have any thing else to say?" She gave an edge to her voice.

"When can I see you again?"

"Never, Lyle. You can never see me again. I want to have nothing to do with the garden. Put the gazebo where you and Tom want. Don't call again to ask me about the gazebo or anything else."

He stumbled for a while. "We, I mean we two, have been traveling for millenniums and our meeting has been, has been, well, it's been our destiny. Like comet tails and meteors."

Her voice put an abrupt end to his rambling. "Listen, I am not sure at all that we have destinies, but I do know, that if we did have destinies, you would not have a clue about mine. Understand?"

He didn't seem to have heard anything. "I was thinking I might be able to come tomorrow and we could talk about the gazebo. Maybe at six and then we could go some place afterwards. To talk. Maybe just to talk."

"You know that gazebo?" Irene worked hard to control her voice. There was no response. "Lyle, Lyle, you know that gazebo?"

He answered like a child who had been caught not paying attention. "Yes, I do. Of course, yes. The gazebo."

"Well Lyle, you can stick it up your ass. Or Tom can stick it up your ass. Or you can stick it up his ass. Or . . . " Her voice got louder and louder and on the last word she slammed the phone down.

Immediately it rang and she let the machine pick up. "Irene, this is Lyle Bucker. I want you to know that this has never happened to me before with any woman. Any woman." There was a long pause. "Irene, Irene, I think we got cut . . .off. Irene . . . ." The message tape ran out.

She went to bed early and slept until Saturday morning. She walked through the dark house, made coffee without turning on the lights in the kitchen and brought a cup up to bed, drank it as she watched the sunlight on the blinds, and closed her eyes again. At eleven she went to the studio, but parked her car a few blocks away so no one would know she was there. She found a message on the door from Carla and another one that she had stuck under the door.

Dearest friend,

Harold left again, says this one is different. What a joke! I need to talk to you. You are the only one I can talk to. I think he wants me to kick him out, to make it easy so he has to throw himself in this man's, BOY's arms. He already sent him a thousand dollars so he could put a down payment on an apartment. What a joke!

You don't know what you mean to me. We could have something beautiful. I am never wrong about these things. I want you to know this. It is only fair.

Your tortured friend forever,

Carla

Dear friend,

Please read this note first. There is another note stuck under the door. Tear up the other note without reading it. Things have changed so if you have read it, forget it. Harold is very depressed. He said he was going to kill himself, but it is only to get me to feel sorry for him, but I have to take it seriously. If he did, I would feel guilty. Later I will be really angry at him. He deserves it.

So please don't read the note inside. I am scared to leave this note outside, but it is important that you read it first so you can destroy the other one without reading it. I tried to call you, but you are not answering your phone. Trust me. Do what I say. Our future may be at stake. Think about it.

A very sad woman,

Carla

She crumpled both notes up and put them in her pocket. She sat in her coat until the main room heated up. Discount Buddies was only open until noon on Saturdays and the heat was off downstairs until Monday morning.

She set up a blank canvas and did some sketches in her notebook of an arched passageway and tunnel that met at what in the canvas seemed infinity. Lines and scratches filled the surrounding area with an energy that appeared to be able to collapse at any moment like the side of a volcanic mountain and funnel through the passageway or tunnel into infinity. And yet it seemed to be energy without movement, just possibility.

With wide brush strokes she created a rhythmic background of light and dark blue, and as she was about to start the browns and murky reds of the passageway, she went to the window to look over the false fronts of the buildings across the street to the yellowish brown of the harvested cornfields beyond. Carla pulled up in her car and parked where Irene usually parked. She carried a white note in her ungloved hand. The other hand held the unused glove. Irene listened carefully and heard Carla walk up the wooden steps to the back door, pause and then walk down them again. She noticed that the note was still in Carla's hand when she got back into the car and drove slowly away.

At four she looked out the window again. The street was deserted and a dust whirlwind sucked up a few of the bargain flyers from Discount Buddies. Five cars were parked in Val's U-4-U parking lot. She watched two of them drive off.

She painted until it got too dark, then put on her coat, threw the rags off one of the chairs so she could sit down, and covered herself to the neck with a sheet. When the sun set, she turned on the light in the bathroom. Around seven o'clock she heard a car pull up to the back. When she peeked through the window, she saw Carla with a large brown envelope. She stood at the top of the stairs and listened to Carla trying to push the envelope through the door. Then it was silent and she heard Carla walk down the steps again. She sat in the car for several minutes without driving off. The ripped brown envelope blew into loading dock area of Val's U-4-U. Carla drove off in the direction of Irene's Cutlass.

She found three sheets of paper with Carla's large shaky lettering. She grabbed them on the way out and stuffed them in her pocket with the other two notes. The icy wind blasted against her forehead and her sinuses began to sting. She walked between the rotten fruit and oily smashed boxes behind Val's. She heard pounding and tiptoed back until she could see Carla at the door of the studio. Suddenly Carla glanced around as if she could feel that she was being watched and Irene ran until she reached the car.

The lights were out at Doris's house when she got there. She parked the car and walked home. The light in the shed was on. The frame of the window had been smashed. She got the key and opened it, but couldn't decide if anything had been taken.

Journal November 21

I have this fantasy of finding the children on the roof for one of their meetings, knocking on the window to get their attention and lifting the blinds on my naked body. Perhaps I could paint myself devil red. Outdo their own perverted little minds. It's irrational. What have they done? Imagined me naked? Broken a window and smashed the frame? Created a myth about me? Isn't that what we all do to each other?

With all of Carla's flip flopping (I am, I'm not, Harold is, he's not) if one of those trendy psychologists got a hold of her, she would set some multiple personality record. Guinness Book. *And that last letter! Page One, "God must have meant for our marriages to fall apart at the same time." Page Two, "Harold and I could go on like this forever. But even if Harold and I stay together, what I do with you will be different." Page Three, "Jane says the Tuesday after Thanksgiving would be great. Please don't let me down. And don't misinterpret anything I have written. Not even in your own mind."*

Sherry Torrence's silly chatter starts to sound fascinating. And Louie's People's Magazine world. I could almost laugh thinking of how I used to see myself as making Tom into the East-Coast sophisticate, and is this his revenge? Carla, Doris, and Lyle. Irene's World.

The next morning she got dressed and walked to Doris's to pick up the car. She thought it would be better to meet Carla again on neutral ground, like church. Doris saw her from a kitchen window and motioned her in for coffee.

"Oh I'd love to go with you, but I'm packing for Pensacola."

"Hm," Irene said blowing on her coffee.

"And it takes me so long to get going and so long to get ready and after church I always feel like I should make a big Sunday dinner. Those things stick with you." She looked up at the ceiling and shook her head. "Heard from Tom?"

"He called a few days ago. There was something I was supposed to tell Mrs. Benson." Irene thought she saw Doris's expression change.

"Call Tuesday so we can plan Thanksgiving." Doris got up

to pour herself a cup of coffee and stood by the counter as if she were waiting for Irene to leave.

At church she sat in the same pew as Carla, who was wearing dark glasses. Carla nodded to her and looked ahead at the pulpit, though the minister hadn't come out yet. Irene could hear the wind blow and shook with the chill she had gotten from walking from her car to the church. In the dark cloudy November morning, the romantic figures of the wispy dreamy-eyed Christ, the lamb lover of the stained glass windows, had lost their glow. The heaters along the walls hummed monotonously and the advent candles hanging from the ceiling over the communion rail swung slightly.

During the service Carla was always a few seconds behind everyone else, and once she stood up as everyone was sitting down and didn't sit down for a few seconds. After the service, she pushed her way towards Irene.

"Carla, what's wrong with your eyes," Irene asked as they shuffled down the aisle to the entrance.

Carla sucked on her tooth, "Eye doctor. I went to the eye doctor. He gave me those drops and told me to wear dark glasses."

Mrs. Kraus, the woman who washed communion glasses, turned to them. "That never lasts more than a few hours. Those drops don't."

"He didn't tell me when to stop," Carla said shaking her head and hunching up her shoulders. Carla dawdled until several people had passed and put some distance between her and Mrs. Kraus.

"Did you get my notes?" Carla lowered the glasses on her nose and looked over them at Irene with bloodshot eyes.

"Notes. Oh, Mrs. Pearson said she had been in yesterday to look at stock and had picked up some messages. She said she couldn't tell who they were for." Irene squeezed the crumpled paper in her coat pocket.

Carla pushed the glasses up with her palm with a quick hard gesture that Irene thought must have hurt.

The people behind them began to mumble and clear their throats. Irene picked up the pace. Neither of them spoke.

Mrs. Kraus was waiting by the door. "Irene, the altar committee has missed you."

"I've been busy," Irene turned around to look for Carla, but she was gone.

"Not too busy for altar duty," Mrs. Kraus grabbed her elbow to give it a school-marm pinch.

When she got home, she called Carla, but she wasn't home. "Carla, I just called Mrs. Pearson and she said she had left the messages on the steps to my studio. Thought they were probably for me. I asked her who they were from to see if they were yours and she said she hadn't looked at them. Call me when you get home. I won't be going to the studio." She imagined Carla barreling down main street, swerving from lane to lane and old men returning from church clutching their Bibles at curb sides. An hour later she envisioned Carla's car under the jagged V of a telephone pole that had been cracked by her car.

From the book room she watched the children on the roof of the shed. The Crawford's car was gone. She imagined that was the reason they were there today. A girl, who was passing out sandwiches, and two boys sat around the blanket. She recognized one of them as a Gregor boy. After lunch she looked out again, but there were only two boys and they weren't the same ones from before. She pulled the blinds to the side to watch and when she let go, it flew up startling her. She jumped back, saw the boys fall on their stomachs on the roof, and peer at the window. For several minutes she stood motionless as the light streamed in through the window. It wasn't until the phone rang that she moved.

"Hello, Carla."

There was a long pause.

"Carla, is that you?" She was about to hang up.

"You know I love you. I understand that it can't last. But what we had we can treasure for the rest of our lives and no one will have to know until we are both dead and.. . ."

Irene slammed the receiver down so hard that her hand stung.

She called Carla.

"I was just going to call you. I got the message. Have you read the notes?" Carla's voice was higher pitched than usual.

"No," Irene said. "Where have you been?"

"The car ran out of gas. Harold never puts gas in it when he borrows it." Carla sounded exhausted.

"All afternoon? Wow."

"It took me a while to figure out what was wrong. I thought Harold had maybe ruined the car, too. Well, give them back to me, the messages. There is one I don't want you to read. It's a personal thing." Carla sighed a couple of times.

"You know, I was just thinking that I did see something on the stairs, some papers. I think I threw them away." Irene grew cold thinking about how Carla must know that she never picked up anything at the studio.

"Well, if you could get them for me, it's important. Please. I won't be able to sleep." Carla began to cry.

"I know where I threw them away, Carla. Don't worry. I know." She waited a minute for Carla to stop crying. "Tom is coming home soon. I have to go. Come by the studio tomorrow. You can take them out of the trash yourself."

"Okay," Carla sounded consoled.

Irene drove to Val's U-4-U to buy deboned chicken breasts, a can of asparagus, some frozen French bread, a small round of Gouda to make a cheese sauce, small potatoes, and the best wine they had.

She fried an onion in olive oil, added flour, some sherry, then the juice from the asparagus and made a white sauce. She added the cheese. Then she fried the chicken breasts, covered them with the asparagus and cheese sauce, put sliced French bread on top to soak up the cheese sauce, and then broiled it. She kept the water boiling for the potatoes, had to add water several times. She could reheat the chicken in the microwave.

At eight-thirty she turned off the water for the potatoes, cut herself a piece of lukewarm chicken and asparagus, and took it upstairs to eat while she watched television. At nine she heard Tom drive in and went down to the kitchen.

"Hey, it smells great," he said. He dropped his suitcases next to the door.

"You hungry?" she asked and turned on the water for the potatoes.

"No, I ate already."

"It'll be good tomorrow." She turned off the stove and wrapped the casserole in aluminum foil and put it in the refrigerator.

"I've got some wine, too. Would you like some wine?" She looked at him with her brow raised.

"Sure, why not?" He carried the suitcases upstairs to the guest room and came down again.

She handed him a glass of red wine. "How was your trip?"

"You know how those things are. How was your week?" He ran his hand through his hair like he was trying to stay awake.

"Nothing ever happens here. I worked at the studio. I had coffee with your mother." She remembered the discussion about the caricatures and wished she hadn't mentioned his mother.

"I'll take this upstairs," he said lifting his glass of wine up. "I have to do some things for tomorrow."

The next morning she woke up with Tom pounding on the bedroom door. "Irene, Irene."

"What is it? Tom, are you all right?" She stumbled to the door with her pajama bottoms hanging down on one hip.

"Did you tell Mrs. Benson to pay the electricity?" He flicked the light switch on and off several times.

"Well, I think I did." She felt her stomach twisting.

"What do you mean? You think you did? It's not something you do in a dream state, goddam it. I call you up and you make a fucking big deal about doing nothing, nothing to do, and I ask you to do one little thing. One little thing." He threw the towel in his hand on the floor and marched off.

"Irene! Irene!"

She put the pillow over her head, then got up and went to the door without opening it. "Yes, Tom." She tried to sound weary and penitent.

"I can't live like this. I just can't. I'm moving to my mother's until the electricity is back on."

She watched from the kitchen as he threw a suitcase into the back seat of his Cherokee and roared off. She went back to bed. Around ten she heard the radio go on in his room and a few seconds later the buzz from the refrigerator.

"Tom, the electricity is back on." She held the receiver waiting for an answer.

"Well, you should probably throw out everything in the refrigerator. I'm not going to take a chance eating that stuff. I don't understand you. What is your problem?" It sounded like he was spitting into the receiver.

"Tom, I don't have a problem. I forgot. Okay." She held her body stiff.

"Whatever you say," Tom said and hung up.

She called him again an hour later. Mrs. Benson answered. "I don't want to bother my husband, but would you just tell him that we're going to his mother's on Thursday and that she said she was leaving for Pensacola on Sunday. I told her we would take her to the airport."

"Let me see if I got everything." Mrs. Benson repeated the message back to her. "I make a habit of repeating messages back. That way I can always be sure I didn't make a mistake."

"Good idea," Irene said.

"Wasn't he at his mother's this morning?" Mrs. Benson asked.

"Yes, that's right." Irene hung up.

She sniffed at the chicken and asparagus. It seemed fine, but she dumped it into a black garbage bag, along with a jar of mayonnaise, some cold cuts, and cheese that had been a fuzzy blue for two months. On the way to the garbage can she noticed that two of the large limbs of the Maple tree next to the shed had been crudely sawed and broken, so a wide swath of bark had been ripped off for a foot under each branch. When she came back from the garbage can, she inspected the tree. Kristie Crawford yelled at her from an open window and she walked to the other side of the shed to hear her better.

"Have you seen what's on that roof?" Kristie asked.

"Yes, I have. I saw the other day. It's the kids." She felt like her voice sounded too despairing. "A club, I guess. We'll have to do something. They might get hurt climbing up there."

"Yes, you will have to do something. My kids can see it from the upstairs window. You better get rid of it before they come home from school." Kristie shut the window.

She noticed that the cinder blocks and the four-by-fours had disappeared. She felt horrible about the tree, wondered if it would have to be cut down.

She went upstairs and looked down on the roof. There was a clear view without the branches. A brush and open can of paint stood on the far side of the roof. The same penis as the one that had been scratched on the window was painted across the roof, but with black spurts coming out of the head. The lines were thick enough so that the corrugation didn't distort the image.

She got a step ladder out of the basement, but it wasn't tall enough since the rope footholds had been cut.

"I have a larger ladder if you need one." She hadn't known that Kristie was watching her.

"I didn't know what they had painted. I feel horrible. I only saw this blanket on the roof the other day." Irene shook her head in apology.

"It's something, isn't it. Kids. Well, what about the ladder?" Kristie wiped her hands on a dish towel.

"Thanks, but we have one," she said.

The paint brush was dry and hard and the paint that hadn't been used with the brush was poured into the rain gutter of the shed. When she came back from the hardware store, Carla was pounding on the door of the house.

"Are you avoiding me?" Carla asked.

"No, but I forgot to tell Mrs. Benson to pay the electricity. Tom is furious. I had to throw some things out that spoiled and then the neighbors told me that some kids had painted an obscenity on the shed roof. I have to paint over it." Irene set the can of paint down next to the car.

"Are you telling me to leave?" Carla twisted a finger in her hair and clicked on her false tooth.

"No, come watch me. We can talk." Irene carried the paint to the ladder and Carla followed her up, but didn't crawl on the roof.

"Oh, that is disgusting." Carla shook her head.

"Haven't you seen it a thousand times carved on some desk?" Irene squatted to open the car with a screwdriver.

"Not where I went to school." She seemed offended.

"I could turn it into a whale and the squirts could become birds. What do you think? Maybe a few waves. Something the Crawford kids might like to look at." Irene smiled at Carla.

"You could paint the whole thing black." Carla was not ready to be friendly.

"Nah, too much work. If it was up to me, I'd leave it. What bothers me is that they ruined that maple tree." Irene used a 4" paint brush to add a tail, mouth, and spray coming out of the back of the whale that incorporated some of the semen. With the edge of the brush she added wings, heads and beaks to the rest of the shooting semen. She painted large black waves across the bottom.

"So Tom is mad at you?" Carla asked.

"He'll get over it," Irene said as she outlined a few clouds. There was really no reason to go on painting.

"You know what? You are in serious denial." Carla's voice rose like she was suppressing anger.

"Denial of what?" Irene asked, acting as if most of her concentration was aimed at painting clouds.

"That your relationship with Tom, well, that he didn't just spend four days with this other woman." Carla looked towards the Crawford house.

Irene pounded the lid of the paint on with the palm of her hand. "Have you ever heard me deny that?"

"You don't understand." Carla was angry again. "Your denial is more serious. It could destroy your life because it's emotional denial. I am so tired of pointing this out to you. It's serious. You have to get in touch with your inner child." Carla was pleading now.

"Stop by the studio later, about five, and you can dig the messages out of the trash. Are you sure you don't want me to read them?" Irene kept her voice neutral.

"No, I've told you everything now in person. I'll be by the studio later."

Irene watched her as she got in her car. She expected Carla to roar into the street, but she put on her blinker, looked behind her, and slowly drove away.

"I don't know, Irene. I wish you would have painted the whole roof black. It still reminds me of the other." Kristie was standing next to the ladder.

"Wouldn't you think of it if it was all black, too? I mean this way there is an alternative image." Irene tried to be careful as she climbed down the ladder with the wet brush.

"Maybe," Kristie said with a frown.

Tom had called and left a message. "Call me at my mother's when you get home from the studio." Irene tried to read his voice.

She left the door unlocked at the studio. For the first hour she sat studying the painting she had begun on Saturday.

Painting Journal

This new painting, another of the space-color-movement. There are elements of buildings, passageways, walls, windows recognizable only by their rough structure, creating with the familiar an unconnected sense of space. As I sat looking at it, I felt that I should place rough fish-birds like the transformed semen of the roof, flying penguins, like cave etchings in the wall of paint, markings that we ourselves make that we can't explain, that like Kristie Crawford's mind may hold more violent or primal images in even drawings for children. Are we always masking something? Are we even capable of knowing what it is?

She put a Beny Moré tape in the cassette player. Cuba 1950 finally hits Pendayhaz, she thought. She hadn't heard Carla come in.

“You really think when you work.” Carla stood with her hands in her pockets.

“I guess so.” She turned off the tape player. “Oh Carla, I have the worst cramps today. Could you get me some Tylenol PM? I think Discount Buddies has them. I’m about to clean up.”

Carla trudged down the steps. Irene found her coat and straightened out the messages and then crumpled them up as if they had never been read.

“Oh, your messages are in the trash. I think it is that one.” Irene pointed to one of the almost empty trash cans.

They lay at the bottom and Carla had to bend way over to pick them up. “You didn’t read them, huh. I kind of wish you had.”

“Do you want me to read them now? I could read them now.” Irene was washing up the brushes.

“No, not now. I don’t want you to read them now.” She stuffed them into the pocket of her leather coat. “Remember about Tuesday. Jane is really excited about Tuesday.”

“Let me change and I’ll walk down with you.” When Irene came out of the back office, Carla was waiting midway down the stairs.

“I don’t want to go to Minneapolis to the Megamall. It’s too far. What about Des Moines or Dubuque?” Irene had trouble locking the back door because the light over the entrance had burned out.

“We would still stay over some place. That was always part of the plan.” Carla became an obstacle on the steps.

“Well, sure,” Irene said and Carla turned to walk to her car.

"Good," Carla said.

"But I'm driving. That's part of the deal. You always drive. Now it's my turn." Irene laughed.

Carla stared at her blankly.

"I'll even get the car cleaned. Inside and out."

She walked around the yard in the dark before going in the house. With a knife from the shed, she carefully cut the bark from the hanging branches so it wouldn't continue ripping the bark from the trunk.

There was nothing to eat in the refrigerator. She put two eggs in a saucepan to boil.

"Doris, is Tom there?"

Doris didn't answer but a second later Tom took the phone. "I'm staying here for a few days to help my mother get ready to leave."

"You know, you don't live miles away. It's a five minute drive in ice and sleet. You don't have to move to your mother's to help her out."

"No, but I am. I think you know that there is more to it." Tom gave his voice that I-am-at-my-last-straw weariness.

"If I know a goddam thing, it's not from you." She hung up. She started to walk to the stove but swung around and glared at the phone, "You're an asshole. You are an asshole." It was as if she had just discovered a well-kept secret. "An asshole. Now I see it." She kicked the table and the phone bounced across the floor, the receiver finally slamming against the door.

Journal November 25

For two days I've been in bed. Tom came over to see why I hadn't been answering the phone. He saw it on the floor cracked when he let himself in. He picked it up and plugged it in. He said he was taking the answering machine to his mother's. He got some clothes and left. Acted like he was surprised that I was in bed. Are you sick? Something wrong? I didn't answer him so he left.

Carla came over. She talked to Tom. I told her the cramps I thought I had were really a bad case of the flu. She said that Jane was excited about Tuesday, though she would rather take Carla's or her own car since mine is an older model, might break down. I'm beginning to wonder if Jane isn't like Peter's case or Mrs. Flannery. Oh Jane is excited. Jane does whatever her husband wants. Now I won't be able to listen to Carla mention Jane's name without that thought going through my mind.

I'm having Lyle thoughts again. Depression and humiliation. I think about it and then scream into the pillow, "Who are you? You idiot!"

I pulled myself together enough to tell Doris I'd make it tomorrow. "If you're sick, don't come." I thought it sounded less like letting me off the hook, than warning me not to spoil her Thanksgiving dinner. Overcooked turkey, gravy the color of brown shoe polish that congeals as it hits the instant mashed potatoes, some string bean casserole with a mix of instant soup loaded with MSG. I'm always tempted to use María Elena's aunt's famous line at dinner, "Everything was wonderful, but the best was the butter. Where did you buy it?"

Tom goes off with Lucille and comes back to make me feel guilty. Everything gets turned in; my frustration, anger. If I had gone to law school, medical school, business school, I would have something to sell--my money-making abilities. I could move to the other side of the country, either side, get a job, be surrounded by interesting people, museums, movie theaters, street life. I might hate my job, but like my life. What can I do? Wait tables? Minimum wage sales jobs? If I were a man I could live in a low-rent hovel. Do I crawl back to my father until I can get some money together and move? A divorce settlement? What are my years from 30 to 36 worth?

I found some codeine aspirin Jens gave me once. Didn't even remember I had them. I might take some to get through tomorrow. Numb out.

Irene sat at the kitchen table while Doris scooted between the stove and the microwave.

"I just have to do my own gravy. I guess I'm old-fashioned. Everything else can be from a box."

Tom had left as soon as she had arrived to buy some frozen pies and canned whip cream for dessert.

"I hope you feel better. Maybe you should have stayed in bed. You don't look good."

Irene didn't think that Doris had looked at her since she got there.

"You don't seem to be leaving. All these Thanksgiving decorations." She got up and wandered into the hallway where a banner of crepe paper turkeys hung from wall to wall.

"It's Thanksgiving," Doris said as if it were obvious.

Only after taking seven codeine aspirins an hour before, had she read the ingredients and discovered that they were also caffeinated. She folded her arms and walked into the dining room where each of the four plates was decorated with a plastic gourd.

She pinched her arm hard, but felt nothing. Her mind was racing on the caffeine.

"Would you like some wine?" Doris called from the kitchen.

"No, my stomach doesn't feel like it."

"Could you open it anyway and pour me a glass? It's on the bureau in there. The corkscrew is next to it."

She couldn't feel her feet touching the ground as she walked into the kitchen with the wine. Doris looked like she was in an eight-millimeter movie, jerky and with a strange wash of color and light.

Tom had picked up Doris's brother Richard on the way back from the supermarket. She helped Doris put the food on the table and they sat down. It seemed to her that she had been seated by herself and the other three were together.

"I'd just like salad to start. My stomach."

Tom and Richard continued to talk. Doris handed her a salad of lettuce, water chestnuts, sliced onions and peas with a thick layer of mayonnaise and sugar on the top. No one had taken any yet and it glistened with an oily sheen. The top was spread in a circular motion that Irene for a second thought was moving. She jabbed the serving spoon into it.

"If you like it, I can give you the recipe," Doris said turning seriously to Richard who was repeating something the mayor had said at a recent zoning meeting.

"Okay," Irene said louder than she meant to.

It seemed like the food took forever to chew and she thought a couple of times that she was chewing with her mouth open and had to think about it.

"Be careful, it's hot," Doris said passing her the gravy. "I just got fresh." The line sounded hysterical to Irene, but she managed to control herself. She took the gravy pitcher with great care, felt her actions were perhaps exaggerated, didn't feel any heat. She passed it on to Richard without taking any, who quickly set it down and daintily grabbed the handle to pour gravy over his turkey, potatoes and what was left of his salad.

"You guys can go watch that football game. Irene, you do the dishes since I cooked. We can all carry our own plates into the kitchen." Doris carried her paper napkin in one hand and her plate in another. Richard wiped his plate with a dinner roll, seemed to swallow it without chewing, and followed her with his plate. Irene stared down at her plate, then glanced up to look at Tom.

"It might have been better if you hadn't come." He had pushed out from the table and had his arms crossed over his small paunch.

"Here?" she asked and immediately knew that it was the wrong thing to say and felt overwhelmed by the question herself. "Maybe," she said.

"What was that you said, Irene?" Doris yelled from the kitchen.

"I'll be right there." Irene said. Tom walked in before her. She ran into Doris, then Richard, then Tom as they set their plates in the sink and turned around to face her. She sensed an almost rhythmic clack each time like that of the subway turnstile. Doris was putting away the leftovers.

"Just let them soak a minute or two and then put them in the dishwasher. It doesn't get them clean otherwise. If you need anything, yell. I'll be upstairs packing." Doris scanned the kitchen. Irene felt that she was staring at her, but when she turned around to look again, Doris was gone. She filled the dishwasher and walked into the living room where Richard and Tom sat. Tom was on the telephone.

"I'm going." Irene said and waved. "Doris, I'm going. Thanks," she yelled up the stairs.

It seemed like it took forever to get home. The sun was out and it was in the mid-sixties. She opened her coat and felt chilled. She was so warm with it closed that it made her nauseous. She dug her fingernails into her palms, but felt nothing.

"You didn't stay for coffee and dessert." She didn't know how the phone got into her hands. She tried hard to concentrate.

"No, I felt a little sick. Nothing really. I said goodbye. Guess you didn't hear." She was conscious that her voice tailspinned at the end. It seemed like she was making it do that.

"You should have stayed home if you didn't feel well. I told you," Doris said.

"You did, didn't you?" Irene said.

In bed her mind raced and a few times she hit herself hard in the head, but it was numb. Disembodied consciousness, she thought and could feel anger rise in her again. She smacked herself again in the head.

She heard Tom come home. She checked the clock next to the bed, but it was still blinking from the electric outage on Monday.

"Tom, Tom." She heard him come up the steps.

"You okay?" he asked.

"Yes," she said and he closed the door before she could ask him the time.

New York Journal

Marie at the gallery wants ten more paintings. It's wonderful to paint for someone who can appreciate my work and challenge me. I never know what I will do next for her. María Elena's Aunt Josefa died and left her some money so she's quit her day job and is painting full-time. Jens went to Denmark, but is coming back tomorrow. I feel so strong I don't think about Chago anymore. The old itch is gone. For now.

Friday and Saturday she caught up with the laundry and cleaned the house. She made two trips to the studio with unpacked boxes, and brought one with linen back. Saturday afternoon she cleaned up the studio, filling five black garbage bags with trash. Tom had brought the leftovers from Thanksgiving home, so they heated them up in the microwave and ate upstairs watching television. He slept in his own bedroom, which she was glad about. It seemed natural.

On Sunday he took his mother to the airport in Des Moines and she decided not to go with them. Until about three she painted at the studio and then went home to call Carla to walk. She saw Fern coming up the street as she went into the house and got some sheets she thought she might be able to use. They were too small for the beds in the house.

"Mrs. Gregor, I was going through my stuff and found these sheets. They don't fit our beds. I thought maybe you could use them." Irene was out of breath from running in and out.

"Why would I be able to use them?" Fern seemed amused.

"Well, they're perfectly good. In New York we had smaller beds and I thought they might fit one of the kids' beds. But if you don't want them, it's okay." Irene wanted to walk back in the house.

"It is, is it?" Fern had her hands in her pockets but her coat was unbuttoned.

Irene walked up the steps.

"Listen, you want to feel sorry for me, so you won't feel so miserable about your own life. But you don't have to feel sorry for me. Feel sorry for yourself. I have what I want. Feel sorry for yourself." Fern seemed to be just starting. Irene closed the door and saw Fern gazing from window to window of the house as if she were searching for her enemy.

Carla only wanted to walk a mile, so they parked at the football field and walked back and forth to the corner of the cornfield.

"I'm worried about Jane. She was out in the yard and got really hot working and then she got wet." Carla said. "That drizzle. But she's so susceptible. Especially to colds."

"Oh," Irene said.

"I hope she's in good shape for the trip. She would love it."

"Remember I'm driving," Irene said.

"Don't you think we should ask Jane what she thinks?" Carla snapped.

"I'll call her up when I get home." Irene stood waiting for Carla to open the car.

"No, I'll call her. I'm sure it's okay with her. But we have to ask her."

Irene wanted Carla to drive by the studio so she could pick up some tablecloths that she had designed and made for their apartment in Brooklyn that she wanted to put on the table in the dining room. They passed the movie theater on the way and someone was taking down the marquee.

"I wondered when they would notice that." Irene said.

"Notice what?" Carla asked.

"Well, what they did to the letters. Didn't you read it? *Bridges of Madison County* became the *Bidges of Mad Cunt.*"

"You're just making that up," Carla said. "A company that does motivational workshops bought it. That's why they're taking down the marquee. They want to make it part of a training center. Didn't Tom say anything? I heard he was one of the movers and shakers. His mother owns a share in the theater. It was her uncle's. Sometimes Irene I think you live on the moon. Get your feet on the ground." Carla was getting worked up and took the corner by Irene's house so fast that Irene grabbed the dash.

Journal December 3

Tom made some wisecrack about the house being clean. I told him it was a once-every-six-months thing and he said he was afraid that it was more like menopause, once a lifetime. I told him no, that could last for years.

Before she reached Carla's house, she had already told herself that Carla would inform her that Jane would not be able to come, that she got wet and couldn't come. Irene sneered to herself and said, "Carla, shouldn't it be that she got wet, but couldn't come?" So when Carla told her, Irene exaggerated her disappointment.

More than once on the drive to the City Steer Hotel, Irene butted in while Carla was talking to say, "Oh, you know, I was just thinking that Jane couldn't come."

Carla's responses became more and more hostile. "Well, maybe next time." "Yes, I know." "Don't you have anything else to talk about?"

The last time Irene said it, she thought of her private little joke and snorted into laughter. "I'm sorry, Carla, but I just thought of something Tom said." Irene swerved recklessly onto the entrance ramp to I-80. Carla was distracted for a second.

"Well, let me in on it, okay?" Carla checked her seatbelt.

"It was something really dumb." Irene smiled over at Carla, who seemed to sum her up in a steady gaze and then dismiss her as she snapped her head forward.

"Maybe I should drive." Carla mumbled under her breath.

"Or have driven." Carla seemed to be correcting herself as if Irene wasn't there.

"Maybe," Irene said and cut in front of a car to pass a semi.

"Maybe," she said again and switched lanes so quickly to avoid an abandoned muffler that Carla gasped.

"Aren't you repeating yourself a lot today?" Carla snarled.

"Maybe," Irene said and slowed down.

They drove silently for ten minutes. Irene fiddled with the radio dial. "The devil goes to church. Don't be fooled by the devil. . . ." She turned the knob, "Now if your daughter thought she could go off and have sex with this guy at sixteen, she made her decision and you shouldn't give her a nickel. Kick her out. Next time she might think before she lets some penniless Romeo stick his hands in her pants. Are you listening to me? Not a nickel . . ." Irene turned off the radio.

"I was listening to that," Carla said as if she had suffered a personal affront. "I'm glad we decided to come late and sleep at the hotel because I'm going to need to relax after this drive."

"I thought we left late because of Jane, because Jane couldn't get away." Irene leaned into the windshield and looked up into the sky. "Might snow," she said.

When Irene came back to their table from the restroom at the Chez Steer Restaurant, she looked around for Carla.

"I paid, Irene. Over here. Here." There was only a partial partition between the bar and the restaurant, but the bar had a distinct underwater murkiness, as if the deep maroon carpet, the fuzzy wallpaper and the black bar stools sucked up the light.

Irene followed the sound of Carla's voice to the corner. "Oh, here you are."

"I want you to meet Larry. I was just telling him about my beautiful friend the painter from New York. He really wants to meet you." Carla poked Larry in the ribs and he turned his head toward Irene without moving his shoulders.

"Larry bought us drinks," Carla said as she poured half of Irene's drink into her empty glass. "Singapore Slings."

"I wanted to get you two the thigh opener. They really got a drink called the thigh opener." Larry twisted his head towards them slightly and seemed to be checking Irene and Carla out with his squinty smiling eyes.

Carla laughed loudly like she was shocked. Irene took a sip of her drink and pushed it away. The heads of two men at the other end of the bar bobbed drunkenly. Larry leaned forward to order another round. He didn't sit up again, but remained hunched over the bar.

"Maybe you girls don't got to have thigh openers. Singapore

slings will do." He laughed to himself.

Carla winked at Irene and pushed the drink towards her. "I know how to get drinks out of these guys," she whispered into Irene's ear, keeping her head close for a few moments without speaking.

"Carla, I don't like these. They're too sweet." Irene turned again to the two men at the other end.

"I really really wish you would have told me," Carla said and took a big gulp. "Really really." She dragged the tip of the tiny paper parasol from the drink across Irene's forearm. Larry was still mumbling and giggling about thigh openers. Irene yanked her arm back.

"Sorry. Okay? Sorry." Carla finished her drink and took what was left of Irene's. "If I get too rowdy, you'll have to take me upstairs."

"You girls like to do some serious partying. I mean fucking serious partying. I mean fucking. . . " Larry drifted off in chuckling incoherence. His elbows slid slightly forward on the bar.

Carla turned toward Larry and howled. He laughed louder without seeming to know why.

"Wow, I am dizzy. Get me to my room." Carla tumbled toward Irene. "Catch me. Catch me." The two men at the other end of the bar focused for a second on Carla.

In the elevator Carla stood stiff, her eyes zeroing in on the digital floor indicator until they were the only ones left in the elevator. "Do you think those were really thigh openers?" Carla laughed. She let her legs buckle under her, draping her arms around Irene's shoulders.

"Carla, I have to get you to bed," Irene said breaking away to hit the fourth floor button again.

"You have to get me in bed?"

"To bed," Irene said and had the key card out and the door open.

Irene was closing the bathroom door by the time Carla reached the room.

"You can run, but you can't hide," Carla laughed, then slammed the door.

Irene put on a long flannel night shirt that she had bought for a trip to Vermont years before. She had had to dig through five boxes at the studio to find it.

When she came out of the bathroom, Carla was sitting on the bed with her head in her hands. "It's good you came out or I would have peed the bed and then we would have had to sleep together."

Irene turned the thermostat down to sixty-five, got into bed and pulled the covers up to her chin. She watched Carla stumbling out of the bathroom with a pitcher of water, slopping water on the floor and heading towards the other bed.

"Oh, shit. Oh, shit. Oh, shit. Look what I did." Carla lay halfway on the bed with the empty pitcher next to her head. "I can't sleep in this bed now," she whined.

"We can ask for another room," Irene said.

Carla was silent for a long time. She switched off the light and lay next to Irene. She propped herself up on one elbow and peered into Irene's face. "Harold doesn't love me and Tom doesn't love you. What are we to do?"

Irene closed her eyes. She kept her lips shut when Carla kissed her. Carla's hair was wet and Irene took a hand from under the covers and wiped the water off her cheeks. "Carla, I'm trying to sleep. I know you're drunk, but try to pull yourself together."

Carla took her clothes off in the dark and threw them in a pile. She sidled up to Irene. "I'm drunk," she said and pushed her hand through the covers and across Irene's stomach. Irene stiffened.

"I'm so unhappy. I feel like my body is ugly just because it has been so long since anyone put their hands on it. Anywhere." Carla burped quietly. "Sorry. Just being next to you is so wonderful. Maybe that is enough. Do you think that is enough?"

"Carla," Irene barked.

"Let's not say anything," Carla pulled a hand out of the covers and put it across Irene's lips. Then she moved the back of her hand softly across Irene's forehead, her lips again, and then down to her neck.

"Carla," Irene said and felt that she was talking to the dark room. They lay still for a long time and she thought that Carla had fallen asleep. Carla shifted in the bed and pulled her hand down to Irene's knee. Irene lay with her eyes open, listening to the traffic outside, voices in the hall, and their breathing.

Carla tossed and turned and her lips came to rest on Irene's neck. She seemed to be having a bad dream, jerked Irene's nightgown up to mid-thigh, sighed, and her hand dropped between Irene's legs. Her breathing became heavier.

A long semi rumbled past the hotel. Irene concentrated on the stillness, thought she heard laughter, listened carefully. Carla's hand felt hot and uncomfortable on her thigh, like a hand in August that rests on your shoulder and presses clothes against sweaty skin. She imagined the hand changing colors like a kaleidoscope, detaching from Carla's body and lodging in her own.

Carla took a deep breath and as she let it out, she rolled over on her side and her hand slid up until her arm tangled in the nightgown. The movement of Carla's hand took on a more insistent nature, rubbing, pinching lightly, straining up. Carla shifted her weight to move on top of Irene.

Later Irene wondered what would have happened, how far it would have gone, if Larry from the bar and some woman hadn't come out of the elevator at that moment and tried to open the door to Room 408.

"Fuck, I can't get the damn thing in." He sounded like he was almost whining.

"Larry, what can't you get in. I want you to get it in." The woman squealed with laughter and Irene heard the two of them crawling around on the floor looking for the card.

"It's not 408 dummy. It's 308." They stumbled against the door as they were getting up. Carla rose slightly and Irene scooted out of bed, swinging one knee onto the floor and then the other before she stood up and ran into the bathroom.

When she came out, she heard Carla whimpering into a pillow. She stood by the bathroom door.

"Are you coming back to bed? I'll leave you alone. I know I'm horrible when I have nightmares."

Irene didn't answer.

"Irene? Are you coming?" Carla sniffled and expelled a loud sigh.

"Now let's see if you can get it in?" the woman cackled from the floor below.

"I can't sleep with anyone," Irene apologized.

"I never have more than one nightmare a night. Never," Carla said pleading.

Irene was becoming cold, but didn't move.

"You gotta get it in and keep it in, Larry."

Carla snorted in disgust.

"I can't even sleep with Tom," Irene said as if it were an amazing phenomenon. She pulled the blankets back on the wet bed and placed towels and a pillow over the wettest part.

"Larry, wake up. Get off of me."

She lay a long time listening to Carla clicking her tooth, then to her wheezy snoring. Later she heard the night clerk knock on room 308 to tell Larry and the woman to be quiet, but she hadn't heard any noise from them for a long time when this happened.

Journal December 9

Readers, I didn't marry her.

It was good I drove. Jane didn't go, though little Jane seemed all too anxious to go. It must be hell for Carla. How can you be so much a part of a place and know that if they really knew who you were, you would be an outsider. But I am not the sacrificial lamb. Nor the sacrificial small feline.

The next morning she was cold and withdrawn. Every time I was about to buy something, she came up behind me to explain why I shouldn't buy it. Poor quality, not right for me, not right for Tom's wife. She was so angry and haughty, I gave up.

I told her about María Elena, that in a certain way we had been in love, but that when Tom came along things cooled. After I had gone on for a while, she looked at me as if I had just materialized in front of her and asked me, "Why are you telling me this?" I wonder if we had made love, if she would have been as distant. Maybe she didn't want to see me as having a previous life, parts of me that she will never know.

The ride back was interminable. She only gave yes and no answers and gave them like I was the biggest idiot in the world. Answers to wh-questions were all, "I don't know," or stony stares.

When I was lying there in bed next to her and could feel her breath on my neck, I wondered whether I would just have sex with her and get it over with. Maybe another moment in my life, even in that week, I might have. And I would have hated her afterwards for a week or two. Listening while she was crying, I thought maybe I should have had sex with her, steeled myself and just done it. What complications I'd be in now!

I thought I smelled perfume on Tom's sheets. Well, he slept at home, I thought. But he hasn't been lonesome. I have these flashes where I regret so much cleaning the house that I want to take the garbage cans and strew the stuff throughout the house. Filth goddess.

Phil called and told me that I was Sherry Torrence's artist of the month. What is he doing in Crandall? We laughed and then he said she was silly but nice and that I could trust her. He also told me her husband is a chiropractic doctor. Explains a lot.

Lyle hasn't called. I did see his car parked in front of Tom's office. Perhaps they're working out the details of the bride exchange. Fuck both of them.

It was so bright in the kitchen when she got home, that she thought that Tom maybe had put 200 watt bulbs in all the sockets. She realized that he had changed the two bulbs next to the sink which she had intentionally not replaced.

"I have some news for you." Tom inspected his nails as she imagined he did when telling customers they weren't covered for whatever disaster had just hit.

"You do?' Irene took a dry towel and unscrewed one of the bulbs.

"I've been thinking. I need some space. I've rented an apartment and am moving there. I thought of moving into Mom's house, but it wouldn't be fair to involve her in this."

"And I stay here?" Irene was in a daze.

"You can do what you like. But I'll pay the rent for a while, at least. And maybe I'll come back on weekends and we can try to build up a relationship again."

She walked behind him so he couldn't see her. "No, if you leave, you're not coming back." She felt like this was the beginning of a solution, then lost that thought to a surge of anger.

Tom looked gravely down at his folded hands. "Why don't you be reasonable for once?"

"No. I've put up with enough. You drag me to this desert. That's what it is, a desert. You destroy all my friendships. You make me feel stupid and incompetent every chance you get. I'm sick of seeing your fat gut and listening to you complain about the way I look, to you sneer at what I wear, the way I talk, of you telling me what to say." She paced behind him and he turned his head from side to side trying to follow her. She darted to the stairs.

"Irene, Irene."

"What is it? What do you want?" she said from the stairs.

"Aren't you forgetting something?" Tom spoke with annoying calm.

"I'm probably forgetting a million things. A million." She shook her head from side to side as if she was choosing the spot on her list to begin the enumeration again.

"Aren't you forgetting that I am the one who is leaving?" He shook his head and smiled.

"And?" She moved back into the kitchen with threatening speed.

"Your little speech about all of the things you are not going to put up with anymore, that's the speech of the person who leaves, not the one who is left."

"That's another thing I hate about you, you think you make all the rules."

At about ten the next morning she looked out on the street from the studio and noticed that it was snowing large wet flakes. She went home for lunch at one. No one had tread the snow on the sidewalks up to the house. It seemed almost as if she were going there for the first time. The first thing she noticed was that the kitchen clock was gone. He had taken the everyday dishes and left her the bone china his mother had picked out for the wedding gift. Upstairs his closets were empty. The sheets and blankets were off his bed. His desk was gone, though the yearbooks were left in a pile in the corner of the room. Nothing was touched in the book room. The VCR was gone, but not the television.

She found a note on her bed.

I'll be back to pick up things. I'll try to come when you are at the studio so we don't have to meet. I should be finished soon.

TOM

Carla called. "I heard that Tom left."

"News travels fast," she said.

"Do you want to talk?" Carla had a professional clip to her voice.

"No. There's nothing to talk about." Irene felt this was a lie.

"Talking is good." Carla insisted.

"For whom?" A wave of boredom came over her.

"Just good," Carla said mystified.

She made a pile of everything she had ever gotten from Tom or from his mother. The clunky turquoise cowboy jewelry from Doris, Tom's baseball trophies, the wedding china, the Easter bunny soup tureen, the corn cob knives and matching corn cob sweet corn holders, the towels with their initials, the silk negligee Tom gave her on their fifth anniversary, his business school textbooks, the hot dish cookbook, the lamp from Ralph's home office, a little side table in the living room Tom had made himself, a cashmere sweater, a tool chest, photos of them together, the Ralph picture after she had cut herself out of the few photos where she appeared.

She made rounds of the house looking for things that had come from him, had some common memory, had been presents from his parents. It all went in the pile in the kitchen. She made a trip to the studio to get the three flower paintings and carried them home to the pile in a large garbage bag.

"Hello, is my husband there?"

Lucille sounded confused. "Well, no, he isn't, I guess."

"Would you be a dear and tell him he forgot some things when he left this morning? I think it's important that he get them today. He may need them. In this lifetime." She regretted the last line, rubbed her fists against her forehead and shook her head.

Barb Lemmon came out to give her some messages as she was going into the studio. "Lyle Bucker called. Something about winter planting. I couldn't really figure it out so I wrote the message down. And your husband."

"If Tom calls again, tell him I haven't changed my mind." She shut the door feeling guilty about being abrupt with Barb.

On the way home she passed the theater.

Start a Love Affair with Money

Classes in Wealth Accumulation

at the International Midwest Money Training Center

Starting 2000 Info. Marston Insurance 488-6644

New York Journal

I'm leaving. I gave up the rent controlled apartment. The landlord almost peed his pants he was so happy. I guess if I come back to the city, I'll have to live like everyone else, in a closet. I said goodbye to María Elena and Jens. I don't think I'll see them again.

The phone was ringing when she walked in.

"I don't want to talk to you, Tom." She hung up.

The pile in the kitchen was gone. A half an hour later there was a knock at the door and she thought it was Tom, but when she peeked out the window, she saw it was Chip Gregor with a snow shovel.

"It's supposed to warm up tonight. The snow should be gone by tomorrow." Irene kept her arms crossed to stay warm.

"But you don't know. It could turn to ice." He looked down at the shovel.

"No, maybe another time."

"Joey Towner told me you might want your sidewalk shoveled." He held the shovel handle in both hands. A mittened hand moved clumsily to his crotch. "He said you might want it real bad." Chip's face turned red and he closed his eyes.

"No, it'll be gone tomorrow. Some other time maybe." She stared at him. He opened his eyes as if he were waking from a dream, then walked away with the shovel scraping the sidewalk as he drug it behind him.

At the street he turned back. "Is it my mother? Is it something you have against my mother?"

"Your mother I understand. You can't shovel without snow. It's too warm." Irene spoke earnestly.

"Oh, okay," he said as if he now understood.

Pendayhaz Journal

Sometimes I make the mistake of seeing my life as an unread book. There is a protagonist named Irene Langer who faces obstacles until the story is over. The chapters seem to float into each other, endings and beginnings are the same, or a chapter begins in the middle of the last chapter or several chapters begin at the same point.

Every story is a simplification. But how do you have aspirations without a plot?

Joey Towner finished high school and left for a technical school in Des Moines. His mother told me that he wants to be a cable repairman. I feel I should warn him about the world. Not every woman who needs her cable repaired is going to be interested in the deluxe service. Only lonely, depressed women (perhaps some men) will be willing to pay extra for that and some may get very upset about the price or even that there is a price. He came over to the house with his girlfriend one afternoon. They were cute together. She has a year left in school. He confessed everything to her about us. I assume that everyone else he told about it, probably a lot of people, were supposed to be impressed by his prowess. But she told me that had a long talk about why he did it. I haven't asked her for the details. She wants to come to the studio to paint and get some advice since she plans to attend art school next year and wants to develop a good portfolio before she applies. She tries to convince me to get my tongue and nose pierced, but I am resisting.

Kristie Crawford called to say that she asked her husband to paint over the roof of the shed. The kids were fine with it, but it bothered her every time she looked at it, she said. She saw "that thing" as she put it. She wondered why they painted it like that since it wasn't like that at all. I didn't tell her that a few I had seen were just like that. She will have to wait until spring to blot it out of her mind.

Fern Gregor has left her drunken husband, senile father-in-law and her kids and moved to Chicago to pursue a career as an inspirational speaker and personal life force trainer. The idea came to her from an article in Reader's Digest. Before she left, she asked me if I could let Chip move in since he needed a strong female hand.

Doris met a retired costume-rental tycoon in Pensacola. He used to supply costumes to the New York City Opera or some place like that. I can't wait to see her dressed in Nabuko's jewelry, Brunhilda's breastplate, or Dido's headdress. She must think she died and went to heaven. I called up Tom's machine when I heard about it and asked him how Doris felt sharing her throne with another queen. No comment so far.

Carla has finally come out. The final blow came when Harold told her he was divorcing her and going to marry another woman. Now she says she doesn't care who knows about her or Harold. Revenge. She jokes about getting me between the sheets in a weak moment in front of whoever the woman of the month is. No one seems to have told Carla that lesbians are supposed to be faithful and highly monogamous. She's taken every one of them to church. The pew usually empties out when they sit down, so I got Sherry, Phil, and Louie to go to church with me. They may rebel soon since they say that six people suffering instead of two doesn't add up. Sherry and Phil did communion duty with Mrs. Kraus and got her drunk. I thought maybe we could try the Pentecostal Church if boredom was their complaint.

It turned out that Joey was really Claude Manner's son and Lucille had been two timing Tom since they were in high school. She got fed up with him pretty fast as soon as he was around all the time and told him just like that. From what I've heard, Joey had always known and Lucille managed to get money out of both Claude and Tom. Carla, her newest girlfriend, and I went out for drinks with Lucille one night. She told me all the gory details about Ralph's affair with Mrs. Benson. Tom brought Mrs. Benson back to the office to keep his mother from stopping by the office all the time.

I asked Tom to change his address so he doesn't have to come here every day to pick up his mail. He usually comes when I'm home. "You left me," I tell him every time he tries to start a conversation of more than a practical nature. There seem to be more of those than necessary, too.

Kristie Crawford has lost her mind. I see her everywhere with Lyle Bucker. Supposedly he has very complicated finances, so she has been working on his tax returns since January day and night. She's started to speak with this funny Italian accent. Lyle always walks up to her house with his hat in his hands and it's on his head when he leaves. She hasn't mentioned a word about the shed roof. I've asked her if she would take over the supervising of the building of the gazebo. I told her that I thought Lyle could start working on it after mid-April.

Tom's business didn't work out very well. I got a little bit of exposure when "The Fall of Icarus in Iowa" was in at an art show in Iowa City, so Phil and I are renting the theater from Tom, taking out the seating and doing an art and antique show. Louie has put up a web page and says we have had a lot of response. Sherry is doing the organizing. We're putting the Doris caricatures on the invitations.

Chip told me that the girls in the secret club formed their own club and I am a role model goddess. They have taken up painting.

It's nice for my ego having Chip salivating over me. But I am older and wiser. For the moment older and wiser.

María Elena says she wants to come to Pendayhaz and paint with me in May and then we're going to take a long trip together to some place far from here.

Lately I've been talking a lot to Jens, like those conversations I had with him right after he died. Internal dialogues of guilt. Now we talk about old times and what I might do in the future and invent stories. It seems both sad and comforting that so much of my life is now in the past. Whatever happens now is a small fraction of the whole.

www.ingramcontent.com/pod-product-compliance
Lightning Source LLC
LaVergne TN
LVHW091031080826
845145LV00002B/444

* 9 7 8 0 9 8 4 9 4 4 7 8 1 *